© *2009 by Louis Berry*

www.louis-berry.com

All rights reserved.

ISBN 978-1441423078

Printed in the United States of America.

Acknowledgments

For My Muse: Your whispers have been in my psyche for nearly as long as I can remember drawing a breath. Your strength is something that I sometimes feel unworthy to behold. I can only promise that as long as there is life in my body I will be true to you and the love I have for the soul that has always been there for me.

For Carol Scott: Thank you for sharing your unbridled enthusiasm for my writing, that has been unwavering since the day we met.

For Lorraine Cobb: Your passionate response helped me to gain a great deal of confidence in the pursuit of publishing this novel.

For Leslei Street: You gave so much of yourself to help further this project along, and it all came about due to a chance meeting. For that, I am eternally grateful.

Posthumously:

For Taylor Scott: We both shared a passion for writing and your untimely passing helped me to understand the urgency of making one's dreams a reality.

For Wilbur James: My grandfather who provided me with the perfect example of what a man should be. I can only hope that you would be proud of what I have done with your words during Richard's conversation with you.

Most Importantly-For My Family*:*

For Mother: Thank you for instilling in me the fierce self-reliance and objectivity necessary to complete such a worthwhile undertaking.

For Owen: Upon your birth I began to understand what the world was really about; that it was something to relish and enjoy. You have given me the perspective that I desperately needed.

For Mora-Lilli: You have taught me that family extends well beyond DNA. Family truly is a state of mind, and I will be forever grateful that you are a part of mine.

For Holli: Being a man's confidante has to be the most difficult task imaginable. One must be both critic and advocate, while showing measured restraint with each quality. You have mastered that balance.

Erstwhile

A Novel By:
Louis Berry

Chapter One

The day spent on the beach matriculated into an evening together in the very same spot. Richard dug with a shovel in the soft white sand as his wife ferried the evening's fare from the house. She carried a red thermos in her left hand that contained Sangria, and a picnic basket in her right. In it were crackers and Brie with slivered almonds sprinkled on top that had been warmed in the oven. He continued to dig as Susan placed the thermos and basket onto the seat of one of the couple's two chairs; Adirondacks that her husband bought not long after inheriting the house. They were sturdy and held up well over the years.

Richard stopped digging when he felt the hole was the right depth and width, then threw the shovel hard, blade first, into the sand pile. It stuck firmly in the heap and came to rest with the handle pointing toward him. From the house he had brought some old oak logs for the fire. They were stacked neatly in a pyramid, six feet away. Immediately upon finishing, he walked around the dunes looking for driftwood or old, dry palm fronds to use as kindling.

The couple had taken time to shower away the glaze of lotion and sweat that accumulated during the day. Each was smartly dressed. Richard had on a green plaid polo shirt that accentuated his eyes, and tan, pleated Docker shorts that displayed his muscular legs. On his feet he wore a pair of black Teva sandals.

Susan wore a sleeveless blue denim polo shirt and white shorts. Her shoulders were a red from exposure. She removed the appetizers from the basket and placed the Brie on the flat left arm of her chair, and the crackers on the right one of his.

Richard continued to search the beach while carrying a bundle of palm fronds and other small sticks cradled in his left arm. The flat heel on his sandals sank into the sand and when he rolled onto the ball of his foot, the beach that accumulated on the back of his cruiser dusted the back of his calf. His thoughts were occupied with the search, so he did not realize what was happening. Occasionally, he brushed the back of his legs with his free hand to remove what he thought were sand gnats.

When Richard felt he had enough debris to start the fire, he turned and began to walk toward the pit. He looked at his wife and the figure she cast in the late afternoon sun. The glow around her enhanced her appearance to an angelic state. He flashed the impish smile that she loved. Whenever they were alone together she provided the emotional salve necessary to mollify his innate despair.

"Are you ready for a drink?" she asked, as he dropped everything he held into the fire-pit.

"Let me get the fire started and I'll be ready," he said.

"You look like the cat that ate the canary. What are you thinking about?"

Richard stopped what he was doing and walked over to his wife. Slowly, he raised his hands to her face and gently cradled her cheeks. Pulling her softly, but firmly toward him, he gently kissed her. Then he slowly dropped his hands away from her face and moved them toward her waist. Interlocking his fingers, he let his hands come to rest at the small of her back. He felt his love for her in every part of his body. He could only describe the feeling as celestial. To him, it bore no re-semblance to the tedious nature of life. It was uplifting. Or, it might have been the high produced from looking at his beautiful wife in a bikini all day. His love for her was not purely physical, but he *was* drawn to her in a primal way. Richard unlaced his fingers and wrapped his arms tightly around her. "I'm sorry to squeeze so hard. It's just that sometimes I'm so overcome with my love for you, I'd just like to melt into you."

"How did I get so lucky?" She asked gazing into her husband's eyes.

He loosened his embrace, kissed his wife and backed away from her. Reluctantly, he returned to the task of building the fire. The sun descended quickly toward the horizon. Its warmth waned, the winds calmed, and the waves subsided.

Richard crouched over the fire pit, then stopped working and turned to his wife. "I think I'm the lucky one. I'm not sure what I've done in my life to deserve someone as beautiful, intelligent and sexy as you. Maybe it was something I suffered in a past life that the cosmic energy is trying to make right."

"I *really* don't think you have to have some sort of justification or rationalization for our relationship. It *is* what *we* make it."

He returned to the task at hand, thinking about what his wife said. When he finished stacking the wood, he carefully examined the miniature bonfire. *Would the shape allow for enough oxygen to fuel the fire? Yes. Will the flames from the burning debris spread evenly over the oak limbs? It looks like they will.* Richard removed a wand-lighter from his back pocket, reached into the pit and began to click the trigger rapidly. After the third pull, a blue and white flame extended from its end. He lit the debris and moved quickly to the other side and repeated the task. The rubbish caught fire swiftly. Flames curved over the oak limbs and the wood began to pop and crack. Twigs quickly burned, curled and dropped off the branches into the bottom of the pit. The embers turned quickly from a bright orange glow to gray ash as they hit the sand.

Susan moved toward her husband and handed him a glass of Sangria. He took it from her without removing his stare from the fire.

"How's it going?" she asked.

"I think it'll be alright. We'll just have to wait and see."

Susan walked over to her chair and sat down, took a glass that she had poured at the same time she made his and placed it on the arm of the chair. After taking a sip she sat quietly and watched him brood over the fire. He watched it burn the protruding knobs on the bark as the flames lapped over the wood. They glowed orange, then changed to a glimmering white as the heat grew more intense when the wind gusted, and then back as it died down. He sipped from his drink, and licked the excess from his lip. The firewood shifted in on itself as the debris that supported the bonfire burned away. Richard examined it carefully to make sure that there was enough oxygen to sustain the fire. When he felt comfortable that it had developed a life of its own, he walked over and sat in his chair.

"Would you like some brie?" his wife asked, as she reached toward him holding a cracker with a wedge of cheese on top.

"Thanks," he said, as he took it from her and ate it in one bite. Without a word he then stood and handed

4

his glass to his wife. She took it and looked at him curiously. Facing the chair, he leaned over and picked it up by the arms. It was heavy and he had to use the muscles in his back. He felt the soreness associated with the strain of fighting a fish earlier that day. Placing the front of the chair against his shins, he slid his feet along the sand and moved toward the fire, turning slightly before dropping the chair next to it. After helping his wife stand, Richard placed her chair facing his. They sat down. He leaned over and in quick succession pulled apart all four of the Velcro straps on his sandals, removed them and placed them on the sand next to him, before lifting his feet and resting them in his wife's chair; one on each side. Not a word was spoken as he gently stroked her hips with his feet.

"You're getting sand on my white pants," Susan said, albeit hesitantly.

Buzz kill, he thought to himself as he smiled.

She placed her feet on the edge of his chair and they sat with their legs intertwined.

"We're gonna miss the sunset."

"The sunset can't compare to you, dear."

Susan smiled and took a sip of her drink. He traced the outline of her frame with his eyes, enjoying how her shirt fell open nicely, exposing her neck and chest. Richard imagined himself leaning over and gently touching his lips to her soft skin. Her shirt was unbuttoned to a point just below the bottom of her breasts, exposing a hint of cleavage. She wasn't sure what was going through her husband's mind, but she did know that she was on display for him and relished the attention. The silence between the two spoke volumes. Neither words nor actions were necessary to feel love from one another. His eyes moved from her cleavage to her legs. He appreciated how silky her thighs were, and how they came together at her buttocks. Her calves were equally shapely and desirable. Appreciating her sensuality gave him cause to remember times when he had given his wife a full-body massage. He recalled how his hands moved over her, applying enough pressure so that any tension she felt drifted away. The desire for his wife became difficult to resist.

Richard finished his drink and looked around. There were a few couples on the beach enjoying the sunset.

"Would you like some more Sangria?" Susan asked, as she leaned over the arm of her chair to pick up the thermos.

"Sure," he replied as he held out his glass. While she poured he looked at the dunes near the house. Would they provide adequate cover? They would have to wait until after dark. "Thank you," Richard said, as his wife finished filling his glass.

"You're welcome," she replied and placed the thermos back on the ground.

He stared at the horizon. The bottom half of the sun was hidden by its edge. Susan shifted her body in her chair to face the setting star. "Isn't it funny how when you look at the sun in the sky, you don't ever see it move, but when it reaches the horizon it appears as though it's falling off the edge of a table?" Susan asked.

"Yeah, it is amazing." Richard thought for a moment. "I guess the horizon gives us a point of reference to measure its movement. Do you think we'll know when the end is near with the accuracy we do at the end of each day?"

"The only thing that scares me about death is facing it without you."

They sat silently, staring at the glowing orb, watching as it disappeared. At the moment the last sliver of orange dropped over the horizon, Richard softly impersonated the canon used to celebrate every sunset in Key West. "Boom!"

The sky's color ranged from light blue to black as the couple enjoyed their Sangria by the fire. When they finished the first pitcher she walked up to the house for a refill while he tended the fire. Neither was in any hurry to leave the beach. The number of passers-by dwindled the later it became. Being so close for so long without touching increased their libidos, while the alcohol they consumed lowered their inhibitions. Richard reclined his body in the chair, slung his left leg over its arm and leaned toward his wife.

"Let me ask you something." Susan's words were not full. She forced them from her inebriated mind and through a mouth numbed by alcohol. He didn't notice; his head was thick for the same reason.

"What's that?" he asked, as he slung his head, heavy with wine, looking at her through his eyebrows. Her eyes sparkled in the light from the smoldering coals. The few flames that were left created shadows that danced across her face.

"At what point in our relationship did you become committed to me?"

"Day one," Richard answered, without hesitation.

"No," she said. "Forget all the romantic bullshit." The wine spoke freely for her. "There had to be something I did that gave you an indication that I was committed to you."

Richard thought, but only briefly. "Do you remember when I came to pick you up for our weekend trip to the Bahamas?"

"Yes."

"My mind was on all the things we had to accomplish before we left; making sure we had our luggage, the time it would take to get to the airport from your house, and God forbid, what if we forgot our tickets? As we got into the car, do you remember what you said to me?"

"No."

"You said, 'you can kiss the girl now.'"

Susan smiled at the recollection.

"I don't know if you recall, but that was before we had ever made love, and that statement was one that conveyed the sentiment that with all the distractions in the world, the most important consideration is *us*. Until then I never knew that a relationship should be free of outside influences."

Susan looked around the beach. It was black and difficult to see past the glare of the glowing coals. There was no one in sight. *It is Sunday night. Everyone must be at home,* she reasoned. The tingling began in the pit of her stomach and radiated through her extremities. Her lust took over. She stood and walked to the back of her chair, then grabbed it and pulled. Resting its weight on its back two legs she dragged it away from Richard's chair. She then walked back to where her chair had been and began to gently sway. Each undulation of her body began with her feet, twisting in the sand, and then worked its way up her thighs, through her stomach ending at her shoulders. Susan flipped her head forward. Her hair fell into her face as she gyrated and looked at her husband through the veil she had created and smiled in a manner that he had never seen before.

There were no flames dancing above the fire, only orange, glowing coals. Richard worried that someone may see his wife, but rationalized doing nothing to stop her by convincing himself that it was too dark for anyone to see. The man was aroused and curious. She continued to sway back-and-forth in the cool evening breeze.

Susan felt her husband's eyes all over her body. He watched intently. She continued to dance as she slowly began to unbutton her blouse, one-by-one. The anticipation was almost too much for him, but he resisted walking over to her and undressing her himself. The pleasure of watching her dance was one that had never been equaled. Her actions lifted their bond to a devout status.

When Susan freed the last button she held her shirt at the bottom and allowed it to drift open, then closed it by bringing the two front panels together; teasing her husband. After several playful repetitions, Richard thought, *finally*, as she let her shirt fall open and off her shoulders. She held her arms straight down behind her allowing it to slide away and onto the sand.

Susan continued to sway; worried that she would not be able to maintain the rhythm of her dance while trying to unfasten her bra. She felt awkward as she reached, with both hands, behind her back to unsnap the hook. When her bra fell open, she quickly brought her arms together and held them tightly to her chest using her forearms to hold it as she clasped her hands. Still looking at him through her hair, she shook her head denying him the pleasure. She maintained this position while continuing to rock gently. When she moved her arms away from her chest she kept her hands clasped. Her bra slid down her straightened arms. His view was still obstructed, but her husband's intense stare assured her that she was not inept.

He sat patiently, waiting for his wife to discard her bra. Eventually, she did by tossing it, next to her shirt. There was no noticeable disruption in the rhythm of her dance, maybe because there was no disruption in his palpable, primitive craving for her.

The confidence she felt grew. Her body continued to undulate in unison with the light caused by the flickering flames that occasionally rose from the hot orange coals having found adequate oxygen to reignite. Slowly, she made her way toward her husband. He reached out, taking her by the waist. She gently shook her head and backed away. The dance was not over. Richard became frustrated and returned his arms to the chair's rests. His fingers fell over the edges and he gripped them tightly and gritted his teeth as his passion raged. He knew his wife was expressing something to him that transcended the physical, and that he must allow her to complete her story.

Susan's body continued to sway as she leaned over him. She removed Richard's taut hands from the chair and interlaced her fingers in his. Slowly she stroked the palms of his hands with her thumbs. Relax. Susan leaned into her husband. The strength in his arms provided support as she was suspended above him. Their clasped hands moved slowly outside the frames of their bodies as she came closer. Richard admired his wife's body. A lump developed in his throat as he watched her breasts change shape as she came nearer. Her flat tummy folded at her waist and showed barely a wrinkle. His heart raced, but he kept telling himself that this was her show. Let her lead. She gave a kiss so deep that Richard felt it all the way down to his toes. Every part of his body was tense with desire. Her lips melted into his and their unity became soulful. She pushed against his hands. He offered the resistance she needed to stand, but maintained contact with her lips as long as he could by leaning toward her. Once again his eyes were drawn to her bosoms as they retained their naturally perky shape. Her areolas were drawn tightly together. He imagined himself stroking her hardened mammillae with his thumbs. Sensual sensations stimulated part of his body, all without the pleasure of touching her flesh. It amazed and scared him to know that he was so into his wife.

Susan backed away slowly, maintaining the rhythm of her dance as she caressed her body. When she moved her hands to the button on her shorts, she smiled at him, as she performed their mock removal.

Richard could no longer hold his tongue. "Come on! You're killing me over here."

Without a word she continued her dance. She turned her back toward him. He watched giddily as she slid her shorts and panties over her petite, round bottom; hardly able to contain himself.

When the last of her clothing fell onto the sandy beach, Susan stopped her dance, walked over to her chair and removed a towel that was neatly folded and laid across its back. She spread it on the ground and laid on it, on her side, in full view of Richard. The glow from the fire illuminated her perfectly formed physique. Tan-lines created by the sun accentuated the parts of her body that he desired to touch the most. He dare not move until she signaled him over with her finger, *come here!*

Richard stood and made his way to the towel. He removed his shirt along the way and lay down next to her, then kissed her gently and embraced her. Her body was soft and warm. Susan wriggled away from the embrace as she sat up. Eagerly, she removed his shorts and tossed them onto the pile of clothes, then laid down and pulled him toward her. The two held each other. Neither had ever felt so close to anyone. Their hearts beat together, they breathed in unison, and their souls no longer ached for the perfect mate. Richard kissed Susan. It was a deep, long kiss. He rolled over, allowing his straight, muscular arms to hold his body above hers. She rubbed them with her hands and enjoyed watching his eyes as they absorbed every inch of her body.

She felt warm, from her belly-button to her thighs, as his hands gently stroked all of her. He resisted the surging primal urge that raged within him. It was not a selfless act, but one borne of the desire to experience everything they could offer one other.

The warmth that Susan enjoyed grew unchecked. Her desire needed to be satiated. "I want you in me," she whispered.

Richard did not rush. Slowly he made his way to the joining. Gently, he made love to his wife. Passionately, he threw his head back and looked toward the house. Something inside caught his eye. In the kitchen window he saw a red, stained-glass heart that Susan's deceased father had given her on her fifteenth birthday. Richard thought about how much the man meant to her. A great sense of doubt overtook him when he realized he had no idea what it took to be the kind of man that would enable his wife to experience the life that she deserved as they grew old together.

Chapter Two

Everyone embraces a personal portrait in their soul that defines their character and how they approach life. It is painted stroke-by-stroke, experience-by-experience and determines the light and shade of every emotion and can excite, sadden, give hope or lead to despair. Teaching the art of self-awareness is a great responsibility. Learning to question that which has been taught creates the path to enlightenment.

The drive from Orlando to Erstwhile took Richard and Susan Styles six and a half hours to complete. It was one they made several times. About half way into the trip the orange groves and interstate highways gave way to two-lane roads and towering pines. The hectic urban life they left behind was in stark contrast to the slow paced one that lay ahead. Neither would have the friendships they relied upon for their sense of self. It was up to each of them to support the other.

The town of Erstwhile was founded in 1837. For the briefest of times it was the largest city in the territory of Florida boasting over six thousand inhabitants. It was also home to the largest natural harbor that could be found along the gulf coast, which was the catalyst behind the town's rapid growth. Only a year after its founding the town hosted the initial of four state Constitutional Conventions. Three years after that, a ship anchored in the harbor brought with it Yellow Fever. More than half the residents of this budding metropolis lost their lives, and the others fled in fear of the same fate. Adding insult to injury, Mother Nature destroyed the abandoned town as the storm surge from an unnamed hurricane washed away all signs of the once proud settlement. The affects of its inauspicious beginning had yet to be overcome. Only thirty six hundred people found the resources to make a living. A century and a half later the town and its people continued to struggle to find their identity in an ever-shrinking world. Richard and Susan made friends during their frequent trips and found the townspeople to be proud and resilient. They looked forward to becoming a part of that communal fabric and making a difference.

The quaintness of the people was a major reason the couple decided to make the move. They desired to lead less stressful lives, but more importantly they felt as though they could have a greater benevolent impact on a small town like Erstwhile. The couple felt very lucky to be where they were in their lives and wanted to do something to help others.

Richard and Susan had spent the majority of their adult lives chasing careers. Perfection was what he strived for. Anything less was considered a failure. She was the consummate pragmatist, who tried to take away a lesson from all of her experiences. It was hard for her to face unpleasant situations. The growing pains felt throughout the early part of their relationship were due mostly to each of them reacting to conflicts based on the ghosts of prior relationships. Living as husband and wife was difficult enough without having to live down the mistakes made unto, and of, others.

Richard never allowed any woman to get too close. He was determined to be his own man, and to rely on no one. Sometimes that meant he pushed people away before they got too close. It was as if he sabotaged relationships. He often wondered to himself if he avoided getting involved because of the unknown responsibility of having a family. Being a husband and father scared him. The example of being a well-rounded and productive man had never been properly exemplified during his formative years.

"Did you ever think that there was a chance you would never get married?" Susan asked as she looked at her husband from the driver's seat.

"There were times, yes."

"Don't you think it may have been fate that brought us together when we met?"

"What do you mean, 'when?'"

She hesitated. "Well, I don't know about you, but I'm not sure I was mature enough to be married until we met."

"Hmm," was all Richard could manage to say. He stared out of his window and watched the scenery pass. After a few miles he asked, "Are you sure that this move is okay with you?"

"I was meant to be wherever you are."

He appreciated her reassurance but somehow it had not cleansed his conscience of his guilt.

Richard had inherited a lovely little cottage at Erstwhile Beach, along with a mercantile store in the downtown district. They dreamed of a day when their kids and their friends would become fixtures in their lives. The inheritance was from a maternal great aunt. He questioned, as he did most things in his life, why he was the one to receive such a gracious gift. The only conclusion was that she knew he would take the responsibility very seriously, and he did.

Ever since the night they met, the dream of moving to Erstwhile was discussed openly. The decision was made final after an old boyfriend of Susan's began stalking her soon after she and Richard were married. The first time he saw Ralph was as the couple walked through Paris on their honeymoon. Not until they reached Florence did Richard question Susan about the familiar face he had seen in each city along their way. The sightings continued after they returned home. Once she admitted the truth he was furious. Susan told him that she had corresponded with her ex-lover; that was how he knew their itinerary. He allowed the reason to go unaddressed. A younger more impetuous Richard would have been quick to judge his new wife. Calmly, but not without angst, he resolved to make this relationship his last. He was determined to stand by the woman he had chosen as his wife until their dying day.

Susan drove the couple's dark green Chevy Tahoe down the two-lane highway. She had left the last section of four-lane highway in Perry. The road was desolate and remote. The only scenery that lay ahead consisted of rows of pine trees and small towns like Carrabelle and Lanark Village.

Richard sat partially reclined and stared outside at the trees as they quickly passed by his window. He thought of the challenges they would face when they got … home. It was odd thinking of Erstwhile as home, but he smiled at the thought, nonetheless. Little things concerned him. He worried that he would have to charge his customers too much. The residents of Erstwhile were hard working people who didn't have a lot.

The analytical nature of his mind gave way to the fantasy of his wife, and how glad he was that she was with him. He rolled his head over on the headrest and looked at her. Feeling his stare, she looked at him. Their eyes met and they smiled at one another. Her gaze quickly returned to the road ahead. He enjoyed looking at her. His eyes traced the outline of her body and how it fit ever so nicely in the leather captain's chair. Her arms were firm and exposed by the black tank-top she wore. They extended from her shoulders without so much as a wiggle as she reached toward the steering wheel. Richard recalled the night they met. It was for drinks at Katie O'Brien's in downtown Orlando. He arrived early, wanting to take no chances by being late. It didn't bother him that Susan was tardy. He knew *what* he was waiting for. The entire north wall of the bar faced Central Boulevard and was made of collapsible shutters, which were open. He sat and watched as people came and went through the various doorways. Cars drove by intermittently. There were four sections of shutters, which meant that Susan could have appeared in one of the two outer segments, depending on the direction from which she approached. His eyes nervously darted between those two doors. *Finally*, she appeared in the one to his left. When the two made eye contact, she stopped in the middle of the floor and threw her arms out to the side as if to say, *ta-da, here I am*.

Richard smiled at the memory, and thought to himself, *I remember how my stomach tingled when I saw her for the first time*. His smile widened. *I still get the same butterflies every time I see her. How can I be so lucky?*

He shook his head, smiling almost incredulously at his good fortune. The most basic of urges began to overcome him. He turned and looked through the window, hoping to take his mind off his wife's beauty. While staring at the rows of pine trees soaring past his window an occasional two-rut logging road would quickly come into and out of his view. Nothing he did seemed to take his mind off the desire he had for his wife. *I wonder if I could get Susan to pull off onto one of these old logging roads? It's Sunday. No one would be out here working. And, the trees provide a lot of cover.* He looked back at her and smiled. *Nah*, he thought; *She'd think I'm a pervert.* Richard returned his stare to the landscape outside. He still could not chase away the thought of making love to his wife. *What's wrong with being a pervert? That's my wife. I'm supposed to be turned on by her.* When he realized that there was an abundance of saliva in his mouth. He chuckled to himself. *My mouth is watering at the thought of being with my wife!*

"What are you laughing about?" Susan asked.

"Nothing. I was just thinking about how the police station in Carrabelle is a phone booth."

She smiled.

He worried about not being honest with his wife about his true feelings, but Richard was unsure of how to suddenly broach the subject of making love. It had always just happened for them. While he continued to think about her, he wondered to himself, *What word could I use to describe how I truly feel about Susan? Respect*, immediately came to mind. *No. That word has been over used, and besides that, every man who has ever tried to get laid has used that word as some sort of bait, or assurance that random sex was the right thing. No, I'm thinking of a word that has more of an eternal feel to it.* He removed his wedding ring and looked at the inscription Susan had engraved on the inner band, *One True Love Forever.*

"What's the inscription on the inside of your ring say?" he asked.

Susan took her left hand off the steering wheel and removed her engagement and wedding rings with her right as she steered with her knee. "Love, Unconditional and Eternal," She replied.

"I can't believe you had to take your ring off to know what was inscribed inside," he joked.

"I knew what it said. I just wanted to make sure I had the words exactly right." She placed the rings back on her finger while keeping the heel of her right hand on the steering wheel. Once she had finished, she returned both hands to the steering wheel at the ten-and-two position just as her father, Lester, had taught her. Richard began to think about the inscription on Susan's ring. *Love, Unconditional and Eternal. That pretty much sums up how I feel about her.* Once again, he thought of making love to his wife, but not in the piney woods. *What is it that makes it so special?* Richard began to visualize them nude and embracing. It wasn't any specific occasion he thought about, but it was real and tangible. *She feels so right in my arms, like she belongs there now and forever. Whenever I hold Susan it's as though I could just melt into her, as if we were one. Our physical beings never get in the way of a singular heartbeat; breathing in unison, or the passion we create together.*

Inevitably, the yen and yang of life caused him to think of the day when he and Susan would have to part. It was a day he dreaded, but one he knew could only be the result of death. He could never fathom wanting to leave her. Looking at the ring on his finger Richard asked himself, *would she really be willing to stay with me forever*?

Chapter Three

Their first full day in town brought with it great anxiety. The shops along Maine Street were zero lot line, sharing a common wall with the buildings immediately adjacent, except for those that bordered a side thoroughfare. Such was the good fortune of the one Richard owned. Most of those in town had been in the same family for generations. Their owners were cordial to one another, but ever since the mill closed the tension among all of the town's residents had grown. Their way of life was being threatened and the only manner of living was that which had been handed down. They clung mightily to it or the closest facsimile.

"There it is." Susan pointed through the windshield of their moving car to a store on the right side of the road. An aluminum awning cantilevered over the sidewalk creating shade for the front of the shop. Straight iron braces were attached to its outermost edge and extended to the top of the wall. There were four of them supporting the weight of the canopy. On the space above the awning were the words, 'Mercantile Store.' The paint had faded from years of neglect. Unless someone was looking directly at the sign it was hardly noticeable.

Richard maneuvered the car into an open parking space. He opened the car door and stepped onto the pavement. The couple met on the sidewalk and walked to the front of the store. There was a two-foot high brick wall that ran its width. Above that was a window that extended upward to the ceiling. Richard fumbled with the keys he had just removed from the ignition, searching for the one that would unlock their future. He inserted the key into the lock and opened the door. Susan walked inside followed by her husband. The couple stopped after taking only a few steps past the counter. Dust had accumulated over the ten years that the store had been unoccupied. It was thick and gave the store a gray, dingy feel. The monumental task of cleaning it awaited them. Along the walls were shelves that extended from floor to ceiling along both sides and the back. A small wooden louvered door that led to the back room was the only space without shelving. It was apparent from the workmanship that they were meant to last. There were two units on the floor that stood five feet high and were situated parallel to the side walls dividing the store into three distinct aisles.

"Do you want the front of the store or the back?" Richard asked.

"The front. There's no telling what's waiting back there for you." Susan chuckled, as she pointed to the door at the rear of the room.

Richard looked at his wife. Even in an old pair of jeans and a raggedy t-shirt, she was stunning. The tingling sensation he always got when he looked at her came over him and it was almost too much to resist. However, he knew there was a lot of work to do. Without acting on his impulse, he swallowed the excess saliva in his mouth, walked to the back of the store, and disappeared.

Susan stood motionless, watching him as he left the room. She admired his frame and how he carried himself. When she lost sight of him, she examined all the different levels of surfaces, trying to decide where to begin. The cleaning supplies were in the trunk. Susan thought about what she might need. Throwing her hands in the air, she exclaimed, "I may as well get a fire hose."

After an hour of whisking dust from the top shelf with a broom, Susan couldn't help but feel as though she had made no progress. She had thought it would be the best place to start because any debris would fall onto the floor, which would be cleaned last. But by doing so, she was unable to see any improvement in the condition of the store. Feeling frustrated she stopped. With her right foot she wrote her name in the dust on the floor one letter at a time. "S-U-S-A-N. There, I can see part of the floor!" she laughed.

"How's it going?" Richard yelled as he emerged from the rear of the store, startling his wife.

"Just fine," she replied. "I don't feel like I'm making any progress, though."

"You wouldn't believe the things I've found back here. Susanna kept meticulous records. I've found every income tax return she ever filed, and they're all in a box in chronological order," Richard exclaimed giddily and then disappeared through the doorway as quickly as he had emerged.

Susan shook her head and giggled to herself, appreciating his childlike enthusiasm, and then continued to scrub while the idea of a hose, any hose, became more appealing. She stopped working as she walked to the front door and opened it, then wedged a chock between its bottom edge and the sidewalk. Air born dust had begun to irritate her senses, and she needed fresh air. *Then again*, Susan thought to herself, *a nice breeze might blow some of it outside.* She began cleaning, again. After a few minutes she was, once again, startled by a man's voice.

"Hello," the greeting came from behind her.

She turned to see a man that she did not recognize. He wore a plaid Polo shirt and khaki pants; each ironed and pressed to a sharp crease. His face was round and red and appeared unhealthy. It seemed out of place on his fit body.

"My name is Michael Talquin," the man said, with a well-heeled southern accent. Susan recognized his surname as being the same as on the bridge that connected the town with the beach. The Talquins had been residents of Erstwhile for almost as long as Richard's family, but had been much more successful, financially.

Susan walked over to the man and extended her hand. "Hi, my name is Susan Styles."

Michael shook her hand politely. "My family owns the furniture store down the block."

"I know the store. When Richard and I build our new home I'm sure we'll visit." Susan overdid the friendliness, but it was done without malice. She only wanted him to feel welcome.

"I would appreciate that." Michael paused momentarily, and then continued, "My brother is Stephen Talquin."

Susan had already made the connection. In their absence, he had done work on the beach house for the couple; or at least headed up the projects. Stephen, they had learned, was not the most diligent worker. They found that he would hire whomever he needed to get the job done. Neither of them had an issue with how he represented himself. Whatever they asked him to do was done, and at a reasonable price. "Yes, I know Stephen. He's done a lot of work for us," Susan replied.

Without emotion Michael stated, flatly, "Stephen has a terrible cocaine problem. You might not want to," he paused, "continue to associate with him."

"*What*?" Susan exclaimed.

"He spends his days lying around my grandfather's house."

"I'm not sure what to say. My husband and I have invited him to Orlando on several occasions trying to repay the kindness he has shown us." She was aghast.

"Didn't he stay with you?"

"No. We asked him several times, but he never took us up on it."

Michael looked skeptically at Susan, not knowing whether to believe her. She felt the intensity of his stare and it made her uncomfortable. "He took a delivery of furniture to some old friends of the family in Orlando that ended up disappearing. It was worth several thousand dollars. He said he was staying with you when it went missing. We suspected the money was used to buy drugs."

The revelation flabbergasted Susan. She did not know how to reply.

In a curiously congenial tone Michael left by saying, "Ya'll come by the store some time and see me." He then turned and walked out of the store.

Susan stood silently watching as he left. She was not really sure what happened. When Michael first walked in she was excited about the opportunity to make a new friend, but there seemed to be a line drawn in the sand. There had been many friends in her past that succumbed to the enticing qualities of cocaine. None of whom chose to live in the truth. She brushed aside the incident, knowing that there was someone she could rely on only steps away.

Chapter Four

It was the third day Richard and Susan spent preparing the store for its Grand Re-Opening. Susan stopped cleaning and began setting up the lunch she made that morning. She spread a quilt on the floor in front of the counter and removed the items from a picnic basket and placed them neatly on the comforter; bread, turkey, lettuce, tomato, onion, mustard and mayonnaise. The accompaniment was potato salad. Doing this for her husband gave her joy and he appreciated the effort she made.

Richard was in the back room. Earlier he found rotten wood on the shelving and spent the morning at the hardware store. Just as he raised his hammer to strike the first blow onto the head of a nail, he heard his wife's voice.

"Richard, lunch is ready!" she called.

When he came into the store Susan saw that he was covered in dust from head to toe. He stopped and slapped his jeans, knocking away the debris. His wife motioned to remove the sawdust he couldn't see by waving her hand just above her head. He quickly ran his hands through his hair. Decades of dry residue created a cloud in front of his face. Richard made the mistake of inhaling through his mouth. "Yuck!" he exclaimed, spitting out the rubble.

Susan laughed as she waved her husband over to the blanket. Richard walked to the quilt and knelt down. While resting in the kneeling position, he allowed his body to fall flat onto the ground beneath him. Rolling onto his back he stared into space. "I'm beat."

"We've got a lot more work to do."

"I know," he responded, as he pulled himself up and rested on his elbow.

She picked up the plastic plate that contained his sandwich and potato salad and handed it to him. "So when do you think we'll be ready to open for business?" Susan asked.

He thought momentarily. "I think we've got another two days of work here. If we can finish by Friday, we can take the weekend off and open on Monday."

"I don't think so. We've got a lot of work to do around the house, too!"

"Slave-driver," Richard said, as he took a bite of his sandwich.

"We *could* take a break from the store tomorrow and spend the day working on the house."

"That's not a bad idea. There are a few deliveries due Friday. We could spend Saturday stocking the shelves." Richard paused. "I say we do it."

The couple sat silently eating their lunch. Susan looked around; trying to estimate how much work there was left to do. Richard stared through the plate glass window at the front of the store. He watched the occasional person walk past. Some made eye contact; others did not notice the couple picnicking on the floor.

Richard's gaze shifted to a store across the street. Above it was a sign that read, *Erstwhile Bar*. He thought about how nicely a bottle of wine would go with their picnic. The last time he had wine with lunch was on their honeymoon. He chuckled under his breath.

"What's so funny?" Susan asked.

"Do you remember the picnic we had at the *Sacre Coeur*?"

Susan smiled as she remembered sitting on the giant hillside just below the French war memorial in

Paris. The vantage-point offered a remarkable view of the city. The Eiffel Tower could barely be seen in the distance. Paris appeared to the naïve couple as a sea of buildings, the roof tops its undulating waves. It was vibrant and alive. No matter how large and overwhelming it seemed, nothing could make them feel less than on-top-of-the-world that day. "How could I forget?"

"Do you remember when the Gendarme came walking up the stairs, clearing everyone off the hillside?"

Susan laughed. "Of course! We were scared that he was going to arrest us for having an open bottle of wine."

"Yes!"

"There we were, filled with our Victorian ideals, feeling as though we were doing something wrong instead of embracing the culture of the city."

Richard did not respond to his wife's statement, but offered a memory of his own. "I remember standing at the foot of the Eiffel Tower and looking up at the massive structure and saying in amazement, 'Wow! It's hard to believe it's over one hundred and fifty years old.' And then when we got to the top, my legs began shaking as I said to myself, 'Oh my God, this thing is over one hundred and fifty years old!'"

Susan's laughter trailed away as she said in a serious tone. "Let's not forget about the most important thing we did while in Paris."

"What's that?" Richard asked dryly.

She smiled. "Getting married, silly."

"Oh yeah, that's right, we did get hitched in Paris, didn't we?"

They were married at the American Cathedral on Avenue de Georges. Several members of the congregation stayed after the Sunday service to witness the union.

"I'll never forget Madame Dorothy Vlocott, my Matron of Honor."

"Yes. What a wonderful woman! I remember the large hat she wore with big, bright flowers all over the brim."

"And she wanted to invite us back to her home for tea, but was self-conscious about living in an old-folks home."

Richard's mood became melancholy. "The offer, in itself, was a wonderful gesture."

Susan smiled. "Yes it was."

"Remember Tom, the ex-patriot from North Carolina? When we were in front of the church and he was taking our picture, several people came by on roller-blades and shouted, 'Vive La Marie!' and Tom told us that meant, *Long Live The Bride.*" He paused. "And then he took us back to our hotel in his tiny little car that looked like the Inspector's car from the Pink Panther."

Susan laughed, again. "That's right. We had taken the bus to the church because we forgot to ex-change our money into Francs. We didn't have enough for a taxi."

Richard shook his head and smiled. "I don't think anyone on that bus gave us a second look. I guess they truly have a *c'est la vie* attitude. Can you imagine the stares we would have gotten, you in your wedding dress and me in my suit, if we had gotten on a bus in Manhattan?"

"We probably would have gotten mugged."

The couple laughed together at the memories. Inevitably, Ralph's image became as vivid as the attendees at their wedding. Richard was never certain whether or not he was a member of the congregation that day. He could only hope that Susan would have shown some restraint. Suddenly, his mood sank as the power that her ex-lover wielded over his psyche triggered a bout with depression. Without saying a word to his wife he stood and walked into the back room. His preference for the sweet dryness of red wine had been replaced by the craving for the smoky taste of bourbon. It was a libation that had gotten him through a lot of uncomfortable situations in his life, but not without cost. He had nearly allowed it to take over. Susan's love was the only thing that had broken its spell. The night they met in a bar was the last time he drank the concoction that possessed the ability to peel away the lifetime of calluses that was his protective shield, allowing him to feel and attempt to decipher what his life truly meant. Susan was the only woman he allowed to breach that vault. He had grown by knowing her, and tried mightily to forgive her indiscretions. She was too special to lose.

Chapter Five

The paper mill filed for bankruptcy protection nearly four years prior to Richard and Susan's arrival. For decades it had been the singular catalyst for life in Erstwhile. Daily operations ceased abruptly. Without it the town and its residents merely existed, struggling to find the one intangible quality that would define their purpose. From the highway the mill appeared as it always had. For months barges ferried away pieces of it as it was dismantled and salvaged until nothing remained but the metal skeleton. A ton of T.N.T. charges had been set in order to reduce it to a measly pile of scrap that would be laid to rest at the bottom of the gulf as an artificial reef. It would once again be the giver of life, but not without the pain associated with change.

Curious onlookers gathered along the roadside to watch the destruction. The hillside of an overpass was transformed into a makeshift amphitheater. Richard and Susan were two of the spectators. He held a large insulated mug filled with hot coffee between his legs. Its warmth felt good on the chilly morning. Susan had a matching cup filled with tea. They both wore jackets and their hands were shoved deeply into the pockets away from the cold.

Richard watched people as they arrived. He was interested in how they interacted with one another, as though they were attending a reunion. Oddly, the occasion seemed more joyous than somber. Having never spent a day of work at the factory could not dampen his or Susan's enthusiasm for the history they would witness. To them, it represented an opportunity for growth.

31

Richard noticed a large, shiny black truck as it drove the length of the parking lot in front of the gathered crowd. There was a large rebel flag airbrushed across its tailgate. In the bed was a gleaming aluminum cage used for hauling hunting dogs. On top of the pen was the carcass of a deer. A gooey pink mixture of blood and saliva dripped from its mouth and pooled on the metal surface beneath its head. Richard counted the number of points on the animal's horns. He knew how to measure a quality kill. There were eight.

"Well, that *was* a beautiful animal," Richard said softly as he leaned toward his wife. She only nodded.

The driver of the truck maneuvered into a parking space midway along a row of vehicles. He stepped out, dressed in full camouflage. Just behind him, from the same door, emerged a young boy. The child appeared to be no more than four years old, and was dressed in the same manner as his father. A woman, presumably the wife and mother, exited the passenger's door.

"Looks like a family affair," he continued.

"Do they *have* to go out in the woods and kill a deer in order to survive?" Susan asked, disgustedly.

The hunter walked proudly up the side of the hill amongst several of the spectators, some of whom shook his hand and congratulated him on the morning's kill. He smiled and strutted ignoring his family.

"Look Richard. This guy is preening for the crowd. *How pathetic!*"

Richard did not answer. His attention had shifted from the family who hunted together, to the Confederate flag on the tailgate. He stared at it until he could no longer see it as he retreated into his thoughts. For him, there was very little distinction between the varying emotions he felt. It was difficult to discern whether the man's display of such a volatile symbol was done out of pride or hatred. His thoughts were interrupted when he noticed another man at the foot of the mound. The man was being very demonstrative and spoke to the hunter. Richard watched intently, as he thought the man might be chastising the hunter. Soon he turned to the crowd and began to address them. He waved his hand behind him pointing toward the soon to be demolished mill. Richard could barely make out what he was saying. It sounded like, "Thirty years. Thirty years of my life down the drain. Some of you worked at this mill a lot longer than I did. Some of you are second and third generation mill-workers. Me? I'm a *Johnny come lately*, compared to you fine folks."

A man seated a few feet from Richard exhaled a heavy puff of air as he exclaimed, "Fu… bullshit."

"Excuse me?" Richard asked.

"Sorry 'bout that, buddy."

"No worries."

"That fella there ain't doin' any good for anybody here." The man laughed "Don't you like how he placed himself beneath the people he's speaking to by being at the foot of this hill *and* by building them up, emotionally?"

"Yes, I did pick up on that." He paused briefly. "Who is he?"

"He's the *old, ex*-president of the union, Lucas Johnson."

"There you have it," Richard said, using a local colloquialism.

"The only person he is doing any good is himself. I'm sure he has his eyes on a city commission seat, or some such higher office."

Richard and his new friend watched in silence as the speech continued. "The company that owns this mill and its powers-that-be have pulled the rug right out from under all of our lives. Our way of life is in jeopardy. Future generations of *Erstwhilians* are in jeopardy. Our retirement is in jeopardy. *This toooowwn* is in jeopardy!"

"Fucking idiot!" the man exclaimed; then looked past Richard to where Susan sat. "Sorry ma'am."

"Not a problem," she said.

The man looked at Richard. "I'm sorry I get so upset about all this crap, but in my mind this guy's no better than a drug dealer. He'll keep feeding them a load of bullshit so that they'll become dependent on him and his rhetoric, rather than relying on themselves. Hell, since the mill closed there have been several success stories of people opening their own businesses and doing quite well. *And*, most of the time it's because they are putting to use a trade they learned while working at the mill. But, there are enough people who will listen to him, and spend the rest of their lives blaming someone else for their troubles." The man pointed toward the mill. "If these people can't see this as an opportunity to better their lives, the notion that others can control them will forever be engrained in their psyches." He paused and leaned toward Richard and whispered so Susan could not hear him, "Lucas has always been one to slap his dick on the table in order to draw attention to himself." The man laughed as he leaned back to his original position and spoke in a normal tone when offering his assessment of the speaker's intellect. "*Lucas Johnson* is only smart enough to outwit himself."

Richard nodded politely and resigned himself to listen without offering commentary. Feeling out of place, he took a sip of his coffee and began to innocently look around. He noticed something that he found troubling. Richard leaned toward his wife and whispered, "Do you think any black folks ever worked at the mill?"

"Of course," she replied assuredly. But just as quickly as she answered, she began to doubt herself. "Don't you think?"

"If they did, they certainly aren't as attached to their former workplace as any of these folks."

Susan looked around and saw the same thing her husband had seen. There were no people of color present to witness the closing of a chapter in their lives.

Suddenly, a siren blared from the mill. After a few moments of anticipation by the crowd, several large puffs of smoke burst into the air at various points along the mill's structure. Two seconds after the sights of the explosions were evident came a sound that reverberated over and through the crowd. The shockwave thumped Richard's chest and made him feel as though his heart would explode. Tons of steel fell as a cloud of dust grew and hid the destruction. It would no longer be there for the residents of Erstwhile to love or hate, resent or embrace.

Chapter Six

Richard and Susan's house was the epitome of an old Florida beach cottage; small yet so full of character anyone would have a hard time not falling in love with all it had to offer. The view of the gulf disappearing over the horizon gave those who enjoyed the sight a sense that they were witnessing their own eternity and embodied a never-ending tranquility. Richard's great-grandmother purchased the property in 1947. Of her three surviving children, Susanna Towson's two daughters lived in neighboring communities and the house was conveniently located between the two. At first, Great Sue, as she was called, bought two lots for two hundred and fifty dollars each. When the owner of the two adjacent lots asked if she would take them off her hands, Sue hesitantly agreed. She ended up with nearly a half an acre of gulf front property. It was considered worthless because crops wouldn't grow in the sugar-white sand. On many occasions Richard wished she were alive so that she could see what a wise investment she had made.

In the year that Richard owned the property, he and Susan tried to use and enjoy it as much as possible. Each time they came they made sure they had a project to complete, but each visit was short, making progress slow. The house required a lot of work to make it livable, but they did not mind. Stephen Talquin handled emergencies. All other jobs were done by the couple working elbow-to-elbow. The investment of their sweat equity gave them a great sense of togetherness.

Richard was outside. He held a garden hose with a bottle of Windex outdoor window cleaner attached to it. Susan was inside painting the concrete block walls white. For decades they had been sea-foam green. She laughed as she rolled white paint onto the wall only to have the green show through a shade lighter. It took several coats to finally cover the old color.

She wore a pair of old faded jeans and a sweatshirt that ballooned over her torso hiding her sleek build. Her hair was pulled into a ponytail and covered by a red bandana. Susan stopped painting when she decided on some noise to keep her company. She walked over to the television in the Florida room and turned it on, changing channels with the remote control. Something on the local access station piqued her curiosity. While focusing intently on the screen, she backed herself onto a futon sofa that was against a wall on the opposite side of the room. Furrowing her brow she asked aloud, "What are they doing?"

There was an outdoor view of a large gravel parking lot that appeared to be next to a two-lane highway. Cars and trucks intermittently passed into and out of view of the camera, some moving quickly and some slowing to see what was happening just off the road on which they traveled, apparently showing the same curiosity that dumbfounded Susan.

Outside, the windows of the house were being pounded by the water and cleaner mixture as Richard swept the spray back-and-forth. Susan stood and walked over to the glass that he cleaned. She knocked on the window and motioned for him to come inside. He could not see her through the sheet of water that cascaded down the panes. She moved to the next one and motioned again. He still did not see her. Finally, she walked over and opened the door that led outside. "Come in here, Richard!"

"Is everything okay?"

"Yes."

"Okay then, let me turn off the water." He disappeared around the side of the house dragging the hose behind him.

Susan moved back to the sofa and sat down again. She continued to watch, making sure to absorb every detail in order to accurately report it to her husband. The back door opened and she could tell that Richard had stopped to wipe his feet on the mat. His footsteps creaked across the old hardwood floors louder and louder until he appeared in the interior doorway of the Florida room. Richard found his wife sitting, her unwavering attention focused on the television.

Without looking at her husband, she waved him over to the sofa and patted her hand on the cushion next to her. "You've got to see this."

"What is it?" Richard asked as he sat next to her.

"I think that they're having a competition to see who can throw that cast net the best."

Richard raised his eyebrow, "*What*?" He paused. "What is considered the *best*?"

Susan smiled and nodded, confirming to herself the understanding that she had gleaned from watching the contest. "They measure the diameter of the net and whoever has the highest score wins … I think."

The couple sat silently, intrigued by not only the competition, but also the surroundings. Ringed around the parking lot were several large pickup trucks that were parked facing outward. Every tailgate was in the open position. Two or three people sat on each one. Spectators sat in folding chairs in the beds of the trucks and there were others sitting on top of the cabs.

Upon seeing the configuration, Richard remarked, "Redneck stadium seating!" He laughed at his own joke as he looked to his wife for approval. When she did not respond he shifted his gaze back to the television.

The man officiating the event and the cameraman were one and the same. The video jumped as he tried to talk and film at the same time. After each contestant completed his throw, he yelled in a high-pitched, scratchy, southern drawl, "Alright, who's next?" The camera panned the crowd searching for the next contestant. It came to rest on a shy young man who refused to look into the lens. "Jimmy, are you next?"

"I have *never* seen anything like this," Richard stated, flatly.

The couple continued to watch as someone they assumed to be Jimmy placed his bottle of beer on the tailgate of a truck, walked over to the contestant area and readied himself by slinging the giant, and what appeared to be very heavy, cast net over his shoulder. Four-ounce lead weights were attached to its outer rim at six-inch intervals, covering the entire circumference. The challenger concentrated intently on the task at hand and it showed in his face. He rocked back and forth trying to obtain the maximum momentum without losing his balance. The length of his sway became greater and greater until it appeared he was teetering on default, and only then did he let loose the net. It ballooned open and fell to the ground. When it landed, the momentum caused the net to slide; creating a cloud of dust that billowed into the air and then was quickly carried off screen by the wind.

The loud, high pitched voice from behind the camera yelled, "Oh my! Are you in the four hunerd club?"

Jimmy shrugged off the question without a word and walked bashfully over to the truck where he had been sitting, picked up his bottle of beer and sat down.

"What's the four hundred, I mean, *hunerd* club?" Richard asked.

Susan, still not removing her stare from the television screen, said, "The way I have it figured is that it's a forty foot net. So, if it were to be completely open and spread out on the ground it would cover four hundred and eighty inches."

"Ah! That makes sense."

Richard and Susan watched the competition, amused, yet concerned at the same time. When the camera panned the crowd Susan saw, attached to a very long CB antenna, a giant Confederate flag waving stiffly in the breeze.

Pointing at the flag she asked, "Does that bother you?"

He looked at it, processing his thoughts until it disappeared from the screen as the cameraman panned the crowd. "I don't think so. We can't say that just because someone is flying a Confederate flag they're racist. This is the south and people are proud of where they're from." The position Richard articulated was done out of hope. "Besides, it's not the Confederate flag you have to worry about; it's the racist bastards who drape themselves in it that cause harm." He became uncomfortable and did not want to continue the conversation. "I've got to get back to work on the outside of the house. This is the one day we've allowed ourselves to do so and there is a lot of work to do."

"You're right," replied Susan, as they both stood and walked out of the Florida room.

Richard walked outside without saying another word to his wife. He was too deep in thought to bother with pleasantries. What he witnessed was all too familiar to him. The people he saw entertaining themselves reminded him of several people he had counted as friends during his lifetime, as well as family members. He grabbed the end of the hose and slowly dragged it to the front of the house. Moving away from this area of the state over a decade ago had been one of the wisest decisions he ever made. It allowed him to grow beyond what his hometown had to offer, but had it also caused him to forget the truth? His affinity for simple people made the vision of himself as an old man who spent his entire life in this town clinging to outdated values an easy one to conjure.

Chapter Seven

Susan convinced Richard that they had earned a well-deserved day off before opening the store for business. She could tell that his mood had become melancholy and wanted to cheer him up. Living at the beach gave him the opportunity to hone his fishing skills. It was an activity that he envisioned doing with their kids one day. There was a cool breeze off the gulf that made the warm fall day tolerable. They loved to spend days like this on the beach. He fished while she read. <u>For Whom The Bell Tolls</u> lay open in his lap while his bait soaked in the warm salty waters of the gulf. Next to his chair sat a five-gallon bucket that was filled with tiny baitfish. He spent an hour that morning using a cast net along the shoreline to catch them.

While he waited for a bite, Richard picked up his book and began to read. Occasionally, his eyes darted to the sand near his feet. There he could see the shadow of the fishing pole. A sporadic jerking motion excited him until he realized that it was being caused by the heavy surf pulling on the line as each wave passed.

A drop of sweat trickled from Richard's armpit, down his flank and rolled just over his ever-so slight love handle where it was absorbed by the waistband of his bathing suit. When the sun warmed his skin to a level of discomfort he laid down his book and took a refreshing dip in the cool gulf water. Whenever Susan saw him do this she laid down her paper and followed him. They would hold each other under water without saying a word. Their heads were the only part of their bodies above the surface. They cherished the serous nature in which the gulf embraced them, and made them one.

As they sat quietly, people passed intermittently and if they happened to make eye contact, pleasantries were exchanged, but never long enough to be intrusive. Everyone seemed to enjoy their privacy on a public beach.

"Have you caught anything?" a voice came from behind the couple. It startled them both. Simultaneously, they turned to see a man standing near their cooler, where Richard planned to store his catch. The man held a long sturdy walking stick that was almost as tall as he was. At first glance it did not appear that the man had a handicap. He was older and resembled a snowman in that his face was round and set nicely atop his similarly shaped torso. His skin, however, was golden brown. It was obvious this man spent a lot of time outdoors.

"No," Richard said.

"What're ya' fishing for?"

"Redfish, I hope," Richard answered, unconvincingly.

"Never heard of it," the man replied as his gaze wandered down the beach.

"Oh, the meat is flaky, white and delicious. You can't get it in the restaurants around here," Susan said.

"Do you live here, or are you just visiting?" the man asked.

"We live here. In that house," Susan replied, as she pointed to the house set atop the dunes. Richard shuddered. He never would have told a stranger where they lived, but the man seemed nice enough.

"We just moved from Michigan. We retired about six months ago." The man looked at Susan. "You know, I can never get my wife to come down on the beach. I ask her, 'why did we move to the beach if you're not going to go *onto* the beach?'"

"What did you do in Michigan?" Richard asked.

"I worked for Chrysler. I was a shop steward for the union," the man replied, proudly.

"Wow! Big three automaker *and* involved in the union. I'm sure you've seen some significant events in your day. You're a part of American history." Even Richard felt his praise of the stranger was a bit over-done. But he could feel his emotional state sinking and *needed* to find something positive to grasp onto; if it meant living vicariously through someone he just met, so be it.

The man furrowed his brow. "I guess so. To be honest, I never thought of it that way. It was always just a job to me." The man pondered Richard's compliment. A smile grew on his face, as it appeared he took more satisfaction in his career than ever before. He grinned at Richard as he walked away, "You two have a *wonderful* day!"

"You too!" the couple responded in unison.

Richard's attention returned to his book and Susan's to her paper. She read it veraciously every morning, soaking in every bit of information she could glean from its pages. The heat generated by the sun warmed the earth's crust and caused the wind blowing off the gulf to pick up quite a bit. She folded her paper to an eighth its normal size and held it firmly in her lap.

Richard dug his feet farther and farther into the sand while he read. The cool sand below the surface felt refreshing.

Susan interrupted the silence. "I *cannot* believe what I am reading!"

44

"What is it?"

"Over twelve percent of Mississippi high school students can't pass the written portion of their standardized exams, so what does the State Board of Education do? They removed that portion of the exam. *And*, all the kids in the past five years who didn't graduate because they failed the written portion are being allowed to graduate." Susan shook her head incredulously. She was so angry that several different thoughts darted through her mind. "These kids have got to be held to a higher standard than that. The state is doing nothing but giving up on them. And they're not doing those kids any favors. My God, these kids are going to have to compete in a global community against kids who are better educated. They're being set up for failure." Richard listened quietly as his wife continued, verbalizing every thought that entered her mind. "The people on the Mississippi Board of Education should be shot. They have to get these kids help so that they can pass the exam. They can't just arbitrarily eliminate the hurdle, or lower the bar." Susan stood and threw the folded paper into her chair. "I need to go for a walk!" she announced to the air around Richard.

Calmly Richard replied to his wife's rant. "I guess that is why Mississippi is last among states in educating their residents, not to mention healthcare."

Susan looked back at him but did not respond to his comment. Just as she passed under the outstretched line a fish struck the baited hook. The tip of the pole bent violently, almost hitting her. The once slack and drifting line became taut. Richard jumped up and tossed his book backward into his chair. He ran over and grabbed the pole, removing it from the sand-spike that held it upright.

"Are you okay?" he asked his wife while trying to gain control of the rod-and-reel. Richard tried desperately to situate the pole in his hands so that he could efficiently land his catch.

Excitedly, Susan walked over to Richard and flitted around him like a fly, trying to be of help, but not sure what to do. "What can I do to help?"

Richard clutched the handle. "I'm not sure. Just stay close to me." He strained as he pulled back on the pole, bending backward at the waist with his feet planted firmly in the sand. When he touched the pole to his chest he swayed forward winding the reel as quickly as he could, removing the slack and bringing the fish closer to shore. Just as he pulled and reeled, the fish fought instinctively to head into open water. The high pitched grinding of the reel's drag-setting sounded every time the fish made headway in his battle with the unknown force that was pulling it toward certain death.

Richard's back began to ache as he repeated the process of pulling back on the pole and then vigorously reeling. The fight went on. He stopped pulling and reeling for a moment and stood erect, stretching his back muscles that were so tense they began to tighten and cramp. With his focus taken off the fish, he noticed a small crowd of people had gathered to watch him. They were curious to see what he had on the other end of the line. He became nervous as he worried about embarrassing himself. Then the thought of something that he was unprepared to handle crossed his mind. What if he landed a mature shark?

"Susan, there is one thing you can do for me," Richard said.

"What's that?"

"If I happen to land a shark I need you to push it back into the water. Sharks can't survive more than thirty seconds on land."

Susan did not respond. She dropped her head and looked at her husband over the top of her sunglasses.

He continued, "Oh, but first you have to cut the line. There's a knife in the tackle box. Try to cut it as closely to its mouth as you can. I'd hate for this shark to have to spend the rest of its life with a piece of monofilament tickling his side as he swims."

Susan cocked her head back, still not aware of her husband's dryly delivered joke, and said defiantly, "How about you do that and I'll hold the pole?"

Richard laughed. At the same time he realized that he had not heard the drag since taking a break. He pictured the fish lying on the sandy bottom of the gulf, motionless except for the undulation caused by the ebb and flow of the current. The two combatants waited for the other to make the next move. When Richard began to resume his quest the drag sang. The taut fishing line sliced through the water, back and forth, as the fish changed directions, desperately trying to shake whatever tried to control its movement.

His back began to ache again. The momentary rest had not been enough to avoid cramping. He knew that he would have to land the fish quickly, or give up. Failure was not a well-received option.

Occasionally, an onlooker would tire of waiting and walk away. But as one left another stopped to watch. Richard was aware of each person who came and went. His focus was no longer solely on landing the fish. Every instance throughout his life when he had embarrassed himself in front of many people occupied his mind.

Susan stared out over the water, watching as the line slashed back-and-forth through the waves. She realized how thirsty she was, so she walked over to the cooler, opened it, reached in and removed a bottle of water. The cold bottle felt good as she wiped it across her forehead. She moved back over to Richard and stood beside him. "I wish I could help you reel that thing in, but I'm afraid that fish would drag me out into the gulf and you'd never see me again," she joked.

"That's okay. One thing you could do for me is let me have a sip of that water."

Susan held out the bottle and waited for Richard to take it from her hand.

"My hands are occupied here, Sweetie. Do you think you could pour it into my mouth?"

"Oh! Okay." Susan held the bottle to his mouth and began to lift it slowly until the water flowed freely. He struggled mightily to control the pole. Suddenly, the fish darted toward the shallow water causing the pole to jerk toward him. It hit Susan's hand. She was able to hold onto the bottle, but not before water exploded from it and onto his bare chest. The extreme contrast of his sun-warmed skin and the ice cold water gave him a shock. "Whoa!" Richard jumped back, still hanging on to the pole. A couple of people in the crowd laughed. He laughed, too. "Man, that's cold water!"

Without missing a beat, he reeled vigorously to remove the slack that was caused by the fish's tactical error. Richard focused on the spot where the line entered the water in relation to where the waves were breaking. It was *almost* to the point where he could slide the fish onto the beach with one last pull. He felt a primal pleasure as he fought through the pain in his back and hands as he realized he was winning the battle.

Richard began walking toward the gulf. No longer pulling and reeling, he wound the loose line onto its spool. He stopped fifteen feet from the water's edge and continued to reel until the fish emerged from the water. Pulling on the pole one last time, his catch slid across the sand and came to rest at his feet. The onlookers gathered closely around him; all of whom admired his catch. There were several school-aged children among them.

One little girl with blonde curly hair asked, "What is it?"

Richard smiled. "It's a Redfish, or Red Drum."

"How can you tell?" she asked.

Richard pointed to a perfectly round, black spot near its tail. "You can tell by that spot."

One-by-one, the crowd dispersed. He stood admiring the fish until he noticed the movement of its gills slowing. With a sense of urgency Richard squatted down and removed a pair of needle-nose pliers from the pocket of his swim trunks. He lifted the fish by pulling on the line with his left hand. With his right he reached into its mouth and grabbed the hook with the pliers. It was set deeply into its flesh. Richard felt the barb ripping and pulling as he tugged on it. Each time he yanked without the hook releasing its grasp his desperation grew. He was not sure how much longer his worthy adversary could survive. Suddenly, an activity that he had enjoyed countless times with his grandfather seemed barbaric. Life had become valuable to him no matter what form it took. Richard caused scars that the fish would carry for the rest of its life, all for the pursuit of an activity meant to build esteem.

Chapter Eight

Richard lay in bed, staring at the ceiling. He rolled his head over on his pillow and looked at the alarm clock on the nightstand. It was fifteen minutes past five A.M. His head was still thick from the night he and his wife spent on the beach. He planned for the store hours to be from seven o'clock in the morning until six in the evening. It wouldn't take more than ten minutes to make the drive. He wanted to stay in bed, but knew that he needed to be there to open at seven, if not earlier. Susan was fast asleep. He leaned over and gently kissed her cheek. They both worked hard preparing for this day and he told her to sleep as late as she wanted.

Richard gently removed the comforter, slid his legs across the mattress and dropped his feet to the floor. Slowly he sat up so that he would not jostle her. Just as cautiously, he stood, trying to distribute his weight evenly onto his feet so that he would not cause the aged hardwood floors to creak, and walked at a snail's pace. When he was far enough away from his sleeping wife, he picked up speed, exited his bedroom and entered the kitchen. He went about his morning ritual of making coffee and a bagel with cream cheese. The water dripped through the filter while he waited patiently. He leaned with his hands on the counter and stared through the window at the white sandy beach behind the house. The gulf waters were perfectly calm. Richard watched as the smallest of waves surged against the shore and then ebbed. Sandpipers stood, searching for their morning fare. When one spotted a morsel it ran, its skinny black legs see-sawing back and forth before plunging its beak into the sand. Richard smiled. His eyes were drawn to his and Susan's chairs. Everything was left undisturbed from their bonfire. It had completely burned itself out, leaving the pure white sand with a coat of grey and black ash. When the coffee maker beeped, signaling that its job was complete, his gaze left the beach and he found himself face-to-face with Susan's stained glass heart. He walked back into the kitchen and opened the refrigerator, removed the creamer and poured it into a mug he had placed on the counter. After replacing it and closing the door, he began to pour. Without paying complete attention, he allowed it to breach the top of the mug and spill onto the counter. "Shit!" he whispered. He placed the coffee urn back onto the burner, walked over and picked up his bagel in one hand and the napkin underneath it in the other. Before cleaning his mess he placed the bagel onto the counter, and then picked up the coffee mug and wiped its bottom and the counter with the napkin. It became thoroughly soaked. Richard gently wadded it to keep from extracting any coffee onto the floor. With his coffee mug still in his hand, he spun his body and did a hook shot with the napkin across the kitchen, toward the trashcan. With a splat it stuck to the wall just above the canister and heavy drops of mocha colored liquid cascaded down the side of the wall. "Dumb-ass," he muttered to himself.

After cleaning both messes he walked back into the den and sat on the sofa, mug in hand. He picked up the remote control from the table and turned on the television. Richard tuned to the local station he watched every morning. A smile grew on his face when he saw John Carpenter reading the local fishing report. He and John had gone to high school together. Richard held his friend, along with his twin sister Valarie, in high regard. They were both good people. It felt good to him to have such warm feelings.

When he bit into his bagel Richard's eyes were drawn to a picture on a shelf in the entertainment center. He stood, walked over and removed it. It was a photograph of him and his mother. Richard had his arm around her shoulders. He was easily a foot taller than she was. A tinge of amazement came over him as he thought about how someone can grow, physically, so much larger than the one whom was the giver of life. "Whatever," Richard said to himself. He replaced the photograph and walked back to the couch and sat down.

He drank his coffee and watched the morning news, but his attention was continually drawn to the photograph. It was taken on his twenty-fifth birthday. He examined his face in the picture. It was so young and fresh; naïve to a great extent. Richard thought about where his life had taken him and took great comfort in knowing he had learned to live with his malady. He was exactly where he wanted to be and with whom he wanted to spend the rest of his life.

The story behind how this particular photograph found its way onto a shelf in his den came to mind. Susan brought it into the relationship. Richard's mother had given it to her five years before the couple met. Each of their mothers had tried, all that time, to get them together. Susan's mother had shown him a photo of her, but did not allow him to keep it. He laughed as he thought about how they both refused to allow their mothers to set them up. It was way too desperate a move to find a mate. They showed their appreciation by getting married on Mother's Day.

His heart filled with pride as he recalled Susan telling him that she had carried that photograph around in the glove compartment of her car all of that time. She had even transferred it from car-to-car when she bought a new one. He stood and walked to the door of their bedroom. Stopping there he peered inside. Susan slept soundly. Her face was as bright as the day they met. He looked at his watch. It was time for him to leave. Excitement and nervousness filled his soul as he worried about opening the store for the first time. He took one last glance at his wife and then walked through the living room, picked up his cup of coffee and continued through the kitchen to the back door. Next to it was a series of hooks mounted on the wall. Each one had a different set of keys. Instinctively, Richard reached for the keys to the Tahoe, but stopped and thought for a second. It was the newest vehicle the couple owned. Why not leave it for her? So, he took her keys, opened the door, walked out of the house and got into her car.

Richard placed the cup of coffee in a cup-holder in the console between the driver and passenger's seats. He backed the car out of the garage and onto the highway. When he felt comfortable doing so, he reached for the mug. He took his eyes off the road, momentarily. The left front tire hit a pothole and the cup shook in his hand, spilling coffee everywhere except on him. He would clean it up when he got to the store. Placing the mug securely between his legs, he continued down the highway. Suddenly, a car emerged from a driveway and into his path. He saw that there was no oncoming traffic and swerved into the opposite lane avoiding a collision. The sharp maneuvers caused the hot liquid to splatter onto Richard's thighs.

"Shit!" He quickly tugged his trousers away from his legs.

Remembering that whenever Susan went to a fast-food restaurant, she put the leftover napkins in the glove box; Richard reached over, still driving the car down the highway, and opened the compartment. The door fell open to reveal just what he expected. Without removing his eyes from the oncoming traffic he grabbed a handful and placed them on the console. He pressed the napkins vigorously onto the stains.

When he finished cleaning his pants he smelled a pleasantly familiar odor. It was Susan's perfume and it had a very distinct place in his heart. She wore the fragrance on the night they met. He looked into the glove compartment and saw an envelope, picked it up and sniffed deeply as he thought about holding her. She had obviously sprayed the contents. Eagerly, he removed the letter inside. It was three full pages written in his wife's meticulously flawless handwriting. His joy was quickly overtaken by despair when he saw that the message was not for him, but Ralph. The depression he struggled with all of his life once again grew and he sank into his seat as he recognized the date in the upper right corner of the first page as the day before their romp together on the beach. Anger radiated throughout his body and his hands shook the paper. Nervously, he sifted through the note, unable to focus on any coherent sequence of words. Through all of his confusion a single sentenced radiated from the communication. *I have never known anyone that filled me with desire the way you did.*

Chapter Nine

The afternoon was overcast. The climate was unseasonably cool and the merchants along Maine Street had the doors to their shops open, taking advantage of the weather. The mercantile shop was no different. Leaving the door open rendered the bell above it useless. Fear of not providing the utmost in customer service kept Richard near the front. After all, it was the first day the store was open for business and he knew he needed to be available to meet his customers.

An older woman shopped quietly near the rear of the store. Richard sat behind the counter going over a list of inventory for the purpose of ascertaining whether he had entered all of it into his computer. He had already asked her whether he could help with anything. She politely refused and went about her shopping. Every few minutes he looked at her to make sure she was not in need of assistance. He would not say anything to her for fear of becoming bothersome.

Desperately, he tried to shake the thought that Susan desired Ralph over him. It appeared that this would be just another failed relationship. Ever since he met her he had repressed thoughts of old relationships because he did not feel it would be fair to his wife; nothing less than emotional infidelity. His inability to learn from them and cope with losses left him psychologically crippled to deal with the situation he faced. Depression became a defensive cloak of armor. He allowed nothing to pierce it, or anything to escape and give away his weakness.

One ex-love in particular entered his mind for the first time in over a decade. When they met his confidence had been destroyed by a woman who claimed her intentions were unadulterated. The relationship proved caustic, and Richard questioned the viability of his life's blueprint. He was convinced that he suffered due to the bad karma he created as a ribald youth. Kathy was breathtakingly beautiful and captured his soul immediately. Her influence extended well beyond their physical connection. Self-respect was an attribute that he was never made to feel worthy, and she convinced him otherwise. It was the first time he experienced a completely emotional bond to a woman. Susan was the only other person who had brought out those intense ethereal feelings. Kathy rejected several offers of marriage. After their time together came to an end he finally understood the wisdom of her refusals. She knew that he was searching for an emotional nirvana; something she could not provide him. What he became aware of was that if she had left her husband the resulting devastation would have overtaken the intense energy they shared. He realized that Ralph was his penance for the unscrupulous manner in which he led his life.

Suddenly, Richard felt a presence in front of him. Waiting quietly at the counter was a man who appeared to be in his forties wearing a red flannel shirt with the sleeves torn away, and blue jeans. His pants were stained with something unrecognizable. "Hello, how are you?" Richard asked.

"Man, if I was any better they'd declare me a controlled substance," the man replied, as he extended his hand in a friendly manner. "My name is Jarvis Anderson."

He shook the man's hand. "I'm Richard Styles."

"You're Susanna James' grandson, right?"

"Great nephew."

A perplexed look came over Jarvis' face, then he shook it away and continued, "I own the bait and tackle shop across the street."

"You're just the man I need to see. I've always wanted to learn how to fish and I'm sure that you can teach me everything I need to know. I'd like to learn so my kids and I will have a hobby we can do together." Remembering his battle with the Redfish the day before, Richard felt obligated to say, "I'm strictly a catch-and-release kind of guy."

"You got kids?"

"No, but my wife and I are trying though … hoping." Richard smiled. "I've got a lot of time to work on it." The words he spoke sounded hollow, as if he were trapped in the deep shaft of a coalmine, shouting to rescuers at the surface that he was okay.

Jarvis said nothing. He stepped away from the counter and looked around the store, nodding his head as he took in every detail. He spoke, not looking at Richard, as if what he was about to say was said only to pass time. "What you got there?"

Richard held the clipboard containing the computer printout so that Jarvis could see it. "You mean this?"

He looked over his shoulder toward Richard. "Yeah."

"It's a computer print out of my inventory. I need to make sure that my entire inventory has been properly input into the program that tracks it. That way I won't forget to make an order as I run low on certain items."

Nonchalantly, the man walked back toward the counter. "Let me see that."

58

Richard handed the clipboard to him. He nodded his approval as he looked over the list. "You say this comes from a computer?"

"Yeah. I have an accounting program that keeps my inventory, accounts payable and accounts receivable. It's really a neat little program. It's amazing how technology has made life easier."

"Yep, my accountant's been after me to buy a computer program for my books. First, I had to get a computer." Jarvis smiled impishly, "talked this girl I was datin' into givin' me hers."

"Wow! That was generous of her," Richard said.

"I ain't datin' her anymore."

Richard furrowed his brow, knowing there had to be more to Jarvis' story, but not altogether certain he wanted to hear it.

Jarvis continued proudly, "I get *all* my stuff free. Hell, I remodeled my entire store for free. They were tearing down an old buildin' at the Pentecostal Church and I got all my materials from them. I did all the work myself," he boasted.

"That was nice of the church to let you have their scrap lumber. I guess you're helping to keep a part of the church alive." The innocence in his words became evident after Jarvis' response.

"They didn't let me have it. I went there in the middle of the night to liberate it." Jarvis replied proudly. "After the mill shut down … well … a man's gotta do what a man's gotta do."

The man's swank bothered Richard. "But what if they had a use for that material?"

"They was just gonna burn it."

"Are you sure?"

"Yep. They told us in church one day that they was gonna burn it all. I felt like that was a waste, so I saved them the trouble."

In the middle of the night? Richard questioned. He wanted the conversation to end. "That was a good thing you did."

An uncomfortable silence between the two men caused Richard to sense there was something Jarvis wanted, but he wasn't saying anything. Richard looked to the back of the store to see if the old woman needed help. The basket she carried appeared heavy. "Ma'am, can I help you with those groceries?" he called out.

Jarvis looked to the back of the store to see to whom he was speaking. Crucifyingly, he looked back at the shopkeeper, who was oblivious to Jarvis' disdain.

Minnie replied, "Naw sir. I can get it myse'f."

Richard smiled and watched closely as she walked from the back of the store to the counter, so he could be there to help if she needed it. She strained to lift the heavy basket and he rushed to her aid. "Here, let me get that for you."

"Thank you, thank you," Minnie said, smiling appreciatively. "I'm not a young woman any more, you know."

Minnie turned to Jarvis. "Hello, Mr. Anderson." The smile disappeared from her face.

"Hello Minnie," Jarvis replied, with a look just shy of a scowl.

Richard carefully removed each item from her basket and scanned the barcode into the register. Once he had completed scanning all of the items he pushed the total button. "That'll be twenty-three sixty-nine."

"Oh Lord! All I got is twenty dollars. I didn't bring enough money. Can I put some of this back and have you remove it from my bill?"

Richard smiled. "There's no need to do that. Next time you're in just bring me the difference."

Jarvis straightened his body in the same manner a Marine recruit would upon the command of his drill sergeant, except that it was no sign of respect. He turned away from the counter and stared through the window across Maine Street, focusing on nothing in particular, so that he would not be made to witness the compassion offered to Minnie.

"You are such a kind man. Thank you," she said as she handed her money to him.

"Here, let me help you to your car with these. I insist!" Richard said. He made his way from behind the counter and picked up the bag of groceries and politely followed the old woman to her car. When they made their way into Jarvis' field of vision, he turned away from the window and walked back to the counter.

Richard walked back into the store and could feel the tension. He was in no mood to deal with someone he perceived to be socially unrefined, so Richard asked sternly, "Is there anything else you need?"

Jarvis felt no compunction about asking for something he wanted. "Yeah. I was wondering if you might see your way clear to let a good Christian man borrow a copy of that accounting program of yours."

"You mean to install onto your computer?"

"Yeah."

"That's against the law."

Shaking his head in disgust, Jarvis replied, "Them people ain't gonna come to this little town looking for no law breakers."

"That doesn't make it any less illegal. It's called *software piracy*."

Jarvis paused before responding. "But they ask four hundred dollars for it in the store. Besides, I gotta get rid of those big green sheeted books so my accountant won't charge me so much to do my taxes."

"Ledger books."

"What?"

"The books with green paper in them are called ledgers." Richard was irritated and spoke in a condescending tone.

"So, does that mean you won't give it to me?"

"That's exactly what it means."

Jarvis turned and walked toward the door in a huff. When he got there he turned and said to Richard angrily, "You can't be molly coddling them people like you do; not in Erstwhile."

"*What*?"

"You start extending credit to them people and they'll steal you blind."

"Jarvis, you think because I extend Mrs. Johnson credit and I refuse to break the law for you that I am somehow playing favorites, right?" When he didn't reply Richard continued. "You have got one screwed up set of values, my friend."

Jarvis, insulted and disgusted, turned and walked through the front door and onto the sidewalk. When he disappeared from view Richard muttered, "Fucking hypocrite." He sat down heavily in his chair. The anger he had been taught to use when handling stressful situations welled within him, but it was only momentary. Conscience took over and replaced his initial reaction with disgust over his duplicity. How could he expect more from Susan than he did of himself?

Chapter Ten

The first day as a shopkeeper had been a long one, exacerbated by constant concern over his relationship with Susan. Richard walked out of the store and onto the street, removed the keys from his pocket; closed and locked the door behind him. He walked toward the car and pushed the unlock button on the fob. The lights flashed and the driver's door lock popped open. Before getting into the car he noticed a flickering neon sign. The letters were situated in a vertical fashion and read, *Merlin's*. Briefly, he thought about not going home. It bothered him because he could never remember a time when, given the opportunity, he wasn't excited about seeing his wife. She had not shown up at the store. It was better that she hadn't. He needed time to sort through his thoughts.

The boldness in his step was rooted in defiance. Richard looked both ways as he crossed the street, and then hopped onto the curb in front of Merlin's with a bounce.

The door was dark and made of solid wood. The handle was long, made of brass and mounted vertically. Wooden panels in the upper half of the door separated three narrow panes of yellow, rough, opaque glass. The glass allowed for no clear indication of the happenings on the other side. It was unlike any other on the street.

Richard grabbed the door handle, opened it and fearlessly walked inside. He stopped on the other side and sized up the room. Directly in front of him was the end of the bar. It ran the length of the wall to the left. There were two men seated there. The fact that they sat next to each other made it apparent that they were together, but they weren't talking; only drinking. He looked to his right and noticed a pool table. There were two cues lying on top of it. The handled ends rested inside the corner pockets. They were crossed near the middle of the table. A white cue ball stained with blue chalk rested inside the crux of the sticks. On the wall behind the pool table he noticed an oversized Confederate flag. Its right edge was tattered and threadbare. Only then did he realize that the felt on the table had the same design and the cues were set along the bars.

He approached, but didn't want to sit at the end with his back to the door, so he walked around the front and took a seat. He sat far enough away from the two men to avoid being viewed as intrusive. The bartender leaned with his butt against the counter behind the bar, and held a folded newspaper in his right hand with a pen in his left. Richard surmised that the man was doing a crossword puzzle, and he appeared to be purposefully ignoring him. Feeling shunned, he spun around on his stool, looking over the bar once again, acting as if it was no big deal that the server was not interested in waiting on him.

Once again, he turned and faced the man. "Are you Merlin?" he asked, in a friendly manner.

The bartender looked up from his paper and glared. He tossed it onto the counter behind him and walked to where Richard sat. Placing his hands on the edge of the bar, he leaned forward and asked. "What'll ya' have?"

Feeling a bit intimidated, Richard hesitated. "I don't know. Have you got any specialty drinks?"

The bartender looked disgustedly at him. "I'm a bartender, not a fucking menu. What you see in front of you is all we have." He walked back to the counter, picked up his paper and resumed the position he held prior to the unwanted interruption.

Removing the hunch in his back, Richard sat up straight. Firmly he asked, "Can I get a Maker's Mark and Diet Coke, please?" *Shit*, Richard thought to himself. *I shouldn't have said 'please.'*

Without a word, the bartender slammed the newspaper onto the counter, walked to the bar and removed a highball glass from a pyramid shaped stack. He placed it firmly onto the bar then plunged a silver metal scoop into the ice machine beneath the bar, stopping just short of throwing the ice into the glass. One piece slid down the bar, coming to rest in front of the two men seated there.

"I'm sorry Jake!" The bartender cowered.

The man returned a glare in response to the bartender's apology. He placed the heel of his hand on the bar in front of the cube, pulled his middle finger back with his thumb, and with as much tension as he could muster, released his digit, propelling it across the narrow walkway between the bar and the counter. It ricocheted between several whiskey bottles.

The bartender finished making Richard's drink without protest. His demeanor had changed from mean to meek. There was only one man he knew that could create such an oppressive pall over a group. The man slid the drink across the bar until it came to rest in front of him.

"Thank you," Richard said, enthusiastically and as friendly as he could. He wanted the bartender to know that he wished to be cordial, unlike Jake.

He said nothing, but somehow seemed more open to dialogue. When he returned to his crossword puzzle, the man flashed a slight smile toward his new customer before dropping his stare to the newspaper.

Richard sat silently, sipping his drink and taking in the atmosphere of Merlin's. The cleanliness of the bar was surprising. The brass was free of tarnish and shined brightly. There was no smell of stale beer, or cigarette smoke. It seemed odd in a bar that had apparently been around for decades.

Several framed pictures were neatly hung in rows along the rear wall of the room. Lifting his drink from the bar, he stood and walked over to the photographs. He was surprised to see that there were several people in the photos that he recognized. The bartender was in all of the pictures. Richard realized that he knew, or had come in contact with every person in the photos. Jarvis Anderson was in one. He recognized his much younger Great Aunt Susanna in another. She was standing next to the bartender at the beach. She looked to be in her forties. *What a beautiful woman,* Richard thought. He continued to scan the wall, seeing the bartender standing next to a lot of locals, all of whom Richard had met.

A surreal feeling came over him as he realized that there were also pictures of the bartender with celebrities, all of whom he had met, as well. There was Clint Eastwood, whom he bumped into outside a restaurant in Carmel, California one summer while on vacation. Mel Gibson was in another photograph. Richard met him when the first scene of the movie *Lethal Weapon II* was being filmed. The old Orlando City Hall was being imploded, and the director used the actual demolition as the opening for the film. A picture of Burt Reynolds caught Richard's eye. It was a picture of him

in his football uniform from *The Longest Yard*, with the
bartender standing next to him.

Eager to talk about the photographs, Richard
quickly walked over and sat in the same seat he had vacated minutes earlier. He placed his drink on the bar. "I
see you have a picture of my Great Aunt on the wall,"
Richard said.

The bartender finished scribbling a word, letter
by letter, into the boxes of his crossword. Only when he
was finished did he look up from his paper. "Who's
that?"

"Susanna … "

Before Richard could utter her last name, the
bartender replied, "Susanna's your aunt?"

"Yeah," Richard said, relieved that the bartender
reacted positively. "It looks like you knew each other
for a long time."

The bartender rolled his eyes upward toward the
ceiling and to his left as he thought about exactly when
he and Susanna had met. "I guess we met in nineteen
sixty-five."

"That was the year I was born," Richard said,
excitedly.

"There's an interesting coincidence for you."

Richard smiled as he drank the last of his drink.
"Can I have another, please?"

Without a word the bartender took his glass and
dumped the remaining ice into the sink behind the bar.
He placed the tumbler back onto the counter, but
stopped as he thought twice. The man then dropped it
into a sink to be washed. He removed a clean one from
the same pyramid he had before and made Richard a
fresh drink. It was mixed a bit stiffer than the first.

"So tell me, are you Merlin?" he asked, again, certain that the bartender was in a congenial mood.

The bartender laughed. "Yeah, that's me, but it's not my real name."

"How'd you acquire that name?"

Merlin laughed at the recollection. "It was about a month after I bought this place, which ironically also happened to be nineteen sixty-five. I realized that there were people in town who wouldn't acknowledge my existence in public. But as long as I was in here serving up the alcohol to them, I was their best friend. So, I gave myself the name of Merlin since I felt banished from the outside world."

"What is your real name?"

"Richard."

Richard shook his head at yet another coincidence. "How well did you know my aunt?"

"Your aunt was one of the most well-grounded people I have ever known. She was one person who was never hypocritical. She came in here on occasion and had her Gin and Tonic. Whenever we'd bump into each other outside, she always greeted me like she was happy to see me. I've never felt more respected by anyone. She accepted me in her store, on the street, wherever. You must have had a quality upbringing."

Ignoring Merlin's statement, he asked, "So, she liked to drink, huh?"

"Oh yeah. She could bend her elbow with the best of 'em." Merlin paused, and then asked, "What brings *you* in here?"

"I was in the mood for a drink. Why? What brings most people in here?"

"Misery not only loves company, my friend, it seeks it out."

Richard and Merlin spent what seemed like hours talking about everything from his aunt to how each had come to cross paths with the celebrities on the wall. No one else came or went during that time. For the both of them it was a pleasant discussion in a desolate environment. Jake and his friend kept to themselves the entire time.

When it was time for him to go home, he said goodbye to Merlin. He stepped onto the floor and his legs gave way. The alcohol had numbed his body more than he realized. He turned to Merlin while leaning against the bar for balance and dropped a couple of twenty-dollar bills on the counter. "Will that cover it?"

"Barely."

He scratched through the wad of bills still in his hand. Finding a ten dollar bill, he pulled it from the bunch and dropped it on top of the two twenties. He shook his head as he realized how inebriated he was. The urge to urinate ached in Richard's bladder. For a moment he considered waiting until he got home. He shoved the remaining bills into his pocket, gave a half-hearted wave to Merlin and walked toward the restroom.

He entered the men's room and sauntered up to the nearest urinal. Once he had unzipped his pants and made the necessary arrangements not to pee on himself, Richard stared at the wall above the urinal. The music playing seemed especially loud. The song playing was Good Times, Bad Times, by Led Zeppelin. It didn't matter that Richard never had music lessons; he found it odd that as he listened to the song that he heard every note, every strike of the drums, and every inflection in Robert Plant's voice. He felt the soulful feel of the song in every ounce of his being. The alcohol had exposed every sensation in his body. When the words, 'When my woman left home for a brown eyed man, well, I still don't seem to care,' were sung with feeling, Richard's heart sank. "But I *do* care!"

When he emerged from the bathroom Richard was astonished to see his brother, Jeff, sitting at the bar. He walked over and sat down beside him. "What in the world are you doing here?"

"I just came in for a little libation, younger brother." He had always referred to Richard in a way that placed him beneath the elder. When he was young it annoyed him, but as he grew to understand the kind of person his brother was, he took great pride in being different.

"What have you been up to, lately," the older brother asked.

"Working my ass of as usual."

Jeff laughed. "That's the problem with you. You always worked hard, whereas, I always work smart."

Richard felt the warmth of his rising blood pressure in his face. "If you're so damned smart why can't you hold a job?"

"Because the people I work with don't understand my genius," Jeff said as he sipped his beer.

"I suppose you've never done anything wrong, have you?"

Jeff only shook his head.

"What about that summer when I worked my ass off every day pushing a lawnmower for miles through our neighborhood, knocking on doors, asking if I could mow our neighbor's lawns?"

"What about it?"

"I saved hundreds of dollars and you *stole* it from me."

"You gave it to me. Don't you remember?"

"No, I gave it to you so that you wouldn't kick my ass."

Jeff smiled. "You see, you did all the hard work and I did the smart work."

Without responding, Richard stood and walked the length of the bar, through the door and onto the street. It was painfully clear that there would always be someone there to take from him what he worked hard to cultivate.

Chapter Eleven

Susan sat in her Adirondack chair staring out over the gulf. The morning was new and the sun had not yet eclipsed the tall pine trees behind her. The Gulf of Mexico looked black. Her mood was as dark as her surroundings. Tiny early morning waves broke quickly and without conviction, slapping against the shoreline. She held a small photo album in her lap. It contained pictures of her and Richard's honeymoon in Paris. On the train into Guard de Norde, she suggested that all of the photographs be taken in black and white. The effect gave anyone viewing them the sense that the couple had been together for an eternity. She did not hold the same perception of their time abroad as Richard. Her flirtations with Ralph were of no significance … then. The letter she penned, only days earlier, was meant to be therapeutic and never to be mailed. She turned the album's pages slowly. One picture was of her and Richard at the base of the Eiffel Tower. The next was taken from its top. It was of the spot on the River Seine, where the couple sat on its edge with their feet dangling down the sloped riverbank. They ate pistachios and drank wine while they talked about their dreams for the future. She could not look at a single photo without a vision of her being together with Ralph becoming superimposed onto her consciousness. Her secondary man was supposed to be someone she could lean on whenever the need arose. His presence was quickly becoming a necessity.

When she turned another page she saw a picture that Richard had taken of the street in front of the hotel where they stayed. He leaned far out of the window, dangling above the street with her holding his feet, in order to capture the scene. The fresh vegetable market where they bought produce daily could be seen just down the road. On the other side was the florist where Richard bought her bouquet for their wedding. The wine and cheese shop they frequented was also visible. Each morning they were awakened by the sounds of the man who operated the vegetable stand calling out which fresh produce he had for that day. The memory brought a smile to her face. Innocent memories were tainted by the image of Ralph lurking nearby.

She closed the album, slowly leaned her head against the chair back and stared out at the gulf. Confusion caused by maintaining genuine love for two men began to overwhelm her. A stout woman who walked along the beach came into her field of vision. Her presence did not register. Susan's thoughts were still occupied by the triumvirate of lovers. The woman saw a potential new friend in Susan as she looked from the water's edge and desperately tried to make eye contact. Hoping her movement would attract Susan's gaze the woman continued slowly along the shoreline. She stopped and bent over to pick up seashells numerous times, trying to stay within her future acquaintances sightline. Even though her progress was filled with hesitation, she eventually made her way out of Susan's sight. So, the woman turned and began to walk in the opposite direction, once again, inserting herself into Susan's line of sight. She repeated all of the same delay tactics, and covered the entire length of Susan's field of vision again without being given a second glance. Not discouraged, the woman stopped and sat on the sand at the point of the wave-break. Occasionally, she looked over her shoulder, longing for a glance from this woman she did not know, but knew if they met they could be fast-friends.

Intellectually Susan knew that there was no way she could continue to encourage Ralph about the viability of their relationship. Or, was it Richard that she should be brutally honest with? She had no desire to make her marriage a *first*, but she also knew she couldn't live outside the truth.

Finally, the stout woman at the shore gave up on the coy manner in which she attempted to get Susan's attention. She stood and walked directly toward her. Susan did not notice this strange, outsized woman until she had covered more than half the distance between them. She was not in the mood to talk. The lenses of her sunglasses acted as her defense shield giving her reason to appear as if she did not see the woman.

"Hi. My name is Emma Bale," the woman introduced herself eagerly while still a number of feet from Susan's chair.

"Hi Emma." She watched as the woman boldly stepped over her outstretched legs and plopped herself into Richard's chair.

Still hiding behind her sunglasses, Susan looked at the woman out of the corner of her eye. She found it appalling that a woman as large as Emma chose to wear a bikini. Normally, she would not be so judgmental, but her mindset was bent on seeking out the shortcomings of others. When the woman sat down and her belly met her thighs, the bottom half of her bathing suit was completely hidden.

"I'm sorry; I didn't catch your name," Emma insisted.

"Susan." She paused, then offered only half of an apology, "I guess I was too caught up in my thoughts. I did not mean to be rude." She lifted the photo album from her lap and placed it on the arm of the chair.

"I could tell that you had something on your mind," Emma said, smugly.

Susan did not respond. Her gaze returned to the gulf. The women sat silently for several minutes. Susan was completely still. Emma fidgeted nervously; seemingly unable to control the fact that she wanted to inquire about what bothered her new friend. Finally, the question burst forth. "So what's on your mind?" This woman wanted inside her psyche so badly decorum became a casualty from that moment forward.

Susan thought better about saying anything to a woman whom she had just met. But, the stranger appeared to be in her forties and had the aura of experience. She might be understanding and offer sage advice. However, bowing to her cautious nature, she answered her inquiry with a question. "Where are you from?"

That was all the permission Emma needed. She spoke rapidly so that Susan had no chance to speak. "I grew up in Atlanta. After high school I went to the University of Georgia, majoring in Early Childhood Education. After graduating from college I moved back to Atlanta where I started my career. So, you're probably asking yourself how I came to Erstwhile. Well, my father was diagnosed with A.L.S. You know, Lou Gehrig's disease. He died about six months ago. Now I'm living with my stepmother. She and my father were only married four years, but she really needs someone to help around the house. I really don't mind sacrificing for the woman my father loved." Emma paused briefly. "Now what about you, sweetie?"

Susan still wasn't quite comfortable with her new friend. She thought better about being too forthcoming. But this woman certainly appeared to have a great deal of compassion for others. In an effort to avoid any uncomfortable questions she tried to slide the photo album from the arm of the chair and wedge it between its side and her thigh. Her attempt at discretion did not work.

"What's that?" Emma asked.

Susan sighed. She was unwilling to talk about the fact that she was in love with a man other than her husband. Maybe if she did this woman would leave and she could sort through her problems alone. She grabbed the album, picked it up and placed it on her lap. "It's the photo album from our honeymoon in Paris."

"Paris! I would love to go to Paris. It has to be the most romantic city in the world." Emma spoke rapidly. "Was it nice?"

"It could not have been more perfect."

"Awe. Isn't that sweet? Your husband must be the most romantic man alive."

"He really is." Susan hesitated, wanting to say more, but she didn't.

Emma picked up on her friend's consternation. "I sense that there is something more to your story than meets the eye."

Susan nodded.

"I'm a good listener, if you'd like to talk about it."

Susan drew in a deep breath and then exhaled. Not until that moment did she realize that the only woman she ever confided in died of a drug overdose twenty years earlier. The opportunity Emma represented, and having someone to talk to become oddly, instantly welcomed. "I know that I married the most wonderful man that any woman could hope for, but I'm not sure he is the right man for me." It was cathartic to confess her reality to someone.

"What makes you question whether or not he is the right man for you?"

Susan shifted her gaze from Emma to the gulf. She could not bring herself to utter the words while looking her in the eye. "I think I may still be in love with a man I've known since I was a teenager."

Emma's, "Hmm," sounded very condescending. "*What*?"

"Well, obviously I could be completely wrong, but could you be holding onto a past relationship for reasons that may have made sense to a teenager?"

"How could that be? I'm a mature woman. Plus, I have known Ralph all these years and my feelings haven't changed."

Emma paused in order to compose her thoughts in a tactful manner. "Could nothing between you and Ralph have ever changed because neither of you have ever embraced a change?"

"But I married my husband!"

"But you haven't let go of Ralph." The reality of Emma's words stung Susan. There was no way that she would tell her she wanted Ralph to be near on her honeymoon.

Emma sensed that there would be no more confessions. "Would you be willing to give up your husband to spend the rest of your life with Ralph?" Susan shrugged her shoulders. "Do you find it telling that I know the name of your lifelong love and I don't your husband's?"

"Richard."

78

Emma kept the conversation moving. "Have you been in touch with Ralph? Does he know how you feel?"

The thought of lying to her new friend was not something that Susan felt good about. She avoided discussing Paris. "I have written him a letter in hopes of getting in touch with my true feelings. I put everything into that letter, but I never mailed it."

"Did it work?"

Susan shook her head.

"What'll you do now?"

"I will do my level best to resolve the situation with as little damage as possible."

Chapter Twelve

The week passed as it had begun. Richard spent his days in the store while Susan searched for a solution to her predicament on the beach. Sunday was the only day the store was closed. Neither one took advantage of having the other's undivided attention. The beach no longer provided a venue for them to be together. It was a dark overcast day. Each of them struggled to understand what they desired before deciding how to proceed.

It was after noon; late enough for Richard to justify having a drink. He stood from his favorite chair and walked across the room to an antique bar-cart. Susan cut her eyes away from the newspaper she was reading and watched him move toward the liquor. She looked at her watch. It was too early for him to be drinking, in her mind.

The bar-cart was made of mahogany and intricately designed. There was a ring of hand-carved, horse drawn chariots that encircled its edge. Mirrored glass laid snuggly on top and a thin brass rail ran through small pedestal brackets encircling the neatly arranged bottles. Richard habitually reached for the Maker's Mark. He poured the whiskey into a highball glass and then placed the bottle back in its spot. His mood called for a stiffer drink, so he repeated his actions until he felt there was an adequate amount of bourbon to start him on his journey to the altered state of mind he craved. He walked from the living room into the kitchen and Susan, once again, watched him. She could see the change in him, but never thought that it may be due to her continued emotional betrayal. Her focus was on

Ralph and how he could fill the chasm created by her husband's withdrawal. His actions were all the justification she needed.

Richard opened the freezer and removed a handful of ice from the bin. He dropped them into his glass, but one reluctant cube fell onto and slid across the floor, coming to rest underneath the sink. The ice in the glass cracked and popped as the room temperature bourbon drastically raised its temperature. He closed the freezer and opened the refrigerator, then removed an already open can of Diet Coke and emptied it into his drink. There was no fizz. Richard didn't mind. All he wanted was something to soften the bourbon. He placed his right index finger onto a piece of ice, applied pressure and stirred the drink by moving the cubes around inside the glass. The number of consecutive days he drank increased by one. Richard walked from the kitchen to where his odyssey for a libation began.

"Aren't you going to pick up that piece of ice?" Susan asked without looking up from her paper.

"Oh crap! I forgot," Richard said. "I guess my mind was somewhere else." He walked back into the kitchen, picked up the ice and dropped it into the sink.

Susan ignored his stare as he walked, once again, back to his chair. The fact that she scolded him was taken as an affront. How could someone so guilty be so judgmental of others? He did not, however, wish to pursue an argument. Something deep within him knew that there would be no victors in such an emotionally charged confrontation.

Just as he sat down there was a knock at the door. Richard placed his drink on the table next to his chair, stood and walked to the front entry.

From the front foyer Susan heard her husband's voice exclaim, "Oh my God!"

She stood and walked quickly toward him. An unfamiliar woman stood just inside the doorway with Richard. The woman was dressed in shorts, a tank top and running shoes. She had an Ipod strapped to her left arm and the wire connected to the ear buds was draped around her neck. Something about her made Susan feel that she was at least a decade older than she and Richard. It certainly wasn't her appearance. The woman was beautiful and obviously kept herself in great shape.

Susan, unsure of what happened, asked, "What's wrong?"

"I think she's been shot in the arm." He pointed to a wound. Blood had begun to trickle steadily and profusely enough that it settled between her fingers where it dried. Susan rushed over to the sink, turned on the faucet and soaked a dishtowel.

"What happened?" Susan asked the woman for more details.

"I was running down the road, and the next thing I know I have this excruciating pain in my right arm."

"Where did this happen?" Richard asked.

"Right in front of your house," the woman said.

It was apparent she was confused and a bit trau-matized. Susan continued to wash the blood from her arm. She wiped away the fresh blood and the dried, co-agulated blood left a hollow shape around the outer edge of its flow pattern. Once the wound was clean, Richard examined it. "I can't tell if there are any frag-ments left. The bullet seems to have punctured enough of your arm to allow for entry, but I don't see an exit wound." Richard stopped and looked at the woman, who had a questioned looked on her face as she tried to size up just who her involuntary caretaker might be. "Not that I'm a doctor."

"Well, a doctor is just what she needs. I'll drive you to the hospital," Susan said.

Richard followed his wife's offer with one of his own. "Can I call your husband and let him know where you are?"

"That would be nice." The woman gave Richard her number and husband's name.

After he finished writing her information on a pad next to the phone, Susan led her back outside toward the couple's car. The woman pressed the wet dishtowel against her wound, hoping to slow the bleeding.

Richard called the woman's husband. Not until the phone began to ring did he realize he did not know her name. After assuring the man on the other end of the line that his wife is going to be fine, and that he should meet the women at the hospital, he returned to his chair and began reading the book he kept nearby. He could not shake the thought that someone had been shot just outside his home. Who could have shot this woman? *Why* would someone shoot her? There had to be a reasonable explanation. He placed the book on the coffee table next to his chair, stood and walked to the door. Before he had a chance to close it behind him he noticed that dusk had begun to blanket the outside world. He walked back into the kitchen and opened the drawer to the right of the sink and removed a flashlight, then walked back out into the gray night. Richard turned the flashlight on as he closed the door behind him.

Cautiously, he walked down the street that intersected the one that ran in front of their house. It led him away from the gulf and toward several hundred acres of woods. He shined the flashlight from one shoulder of the road to the other in a sweeping manner. Richard had no idea who he was looking for. All of the homes in that area were built sixty to seventy years earlier and had little exterior lighting. Richard thought to himself, *If it was a gunshot it could have come from a number of places*. The many trees, bushes and vehicles parked in driveways offered perfect cover in the dimly lit neighborhood. Only once did he pause and question why he wasn't worried about searching for a *gunman*. Regardless of any lurking danger, his desire for answers trumped logic.

Richard made a couple of passes up and down the street without finding anything significant. On the third pass, he heard an intermittent clicking sound that grew heavier with each one. It was loud and offered him a good indication of where to search. He shined his flashlight in the direction of the noise. The light illuminated a young boy, who was no more than nine years old, sitting on his bike. He held what appeared to be a BB gun and was pumping air into the cylinder.

"Don't shoot!" Richard said, as he threw his hands in the air, joking to mask his concern. He walked down the driveway, toward the boy, who stopped pumping and steadied the gun on the handlebars of his bicycle. The boy took aim by slowly *drawing a bead*. Richard quickly stepped behind a truck that was parked in the driveway. His obvious skill as a marksman was frightening.

"Have you shot anybody with that gun?" Richard asked, from behind the truck.

"I didn't see no lady running by here," the boy answered, in a defiant tone.

84

"Is your mom or dad home?"

"Yep."

"Would you go inside and get them for me?" Richard asked, keeping the vehicle between himself and the boy.

The boy stood from his seated position, still holding his gun firmly and ran inside yelling, "Pa, there's a man what wants to see ya!"

Richard shook his head in disgust in reaction to the boy's appalling grammar. A few moments after he disappeared through the front door of the house, a man emerged. He was tall and wiry, wearing blue jeans, a red flannel shirt and no shoes. In his hand was a greasy biscuit. The man had the same insolent expression on his face as his son. He took a bite of his roll. "Can I hep ya?" His southern drawl pierced Richard's eardrums like fingernails across a chalkboard.

"Your son shot a woman jogging by your house with his BB gun."

"It's a pellet gun, mister," the man scoffed, as if a BB gun was too juvenile for his son.

Trying to stay calm, because he was unsure what rifles, shotguns, pistols or crossbows might be trained on him, Richard continued, "Regardless, he shot someone, and I thought you might want to know. My wife took her to the hospital."

"So what the hell you want me to do?" The man sounded increasingly defiant.

"Well, it might be a nice gesture to go to the hospital and," Richard paused nervously, "have your son apologize; maybe offer to pay the hospital bill."

"What for? My boy has the right to bear arms. It's in the Constitution."

Richard could not believe what he was hearing. As calmly as he could, and in a non-threatening tone, Richard said, "Yes, but he doesn't have the right to shoot just *anyone*."

"How do you know he shot that lady?"

"He all but admitted it. He knew there was a woman jogging by your house before I mentioned it."

Maintaining his insolence, the man responded, "So, what are ya' gonna do, sue me? I know you run that mercantile store in town and if you sue me, I'll ruin your business."

Finding it increasingly difficult to maintain a congenial tone, Richard suggested the proper course of action for the second time. "Maybe if you took your son to the hospital and had him apologize, it might make things better for everyone involved. I'm sure she will forgive him."

"Mister, my boy has every right to shoot his gun. One day that boy is going to be a man, and he is going to have to know how to handle a gun in order to feed his family."

The voice in Richard's head screamed, *He can't practice on his neighbors*! He took a deep breath and tried to maintain rationality. It became increasingly difficult to look the man in the face, so he looked down at the ground and rubbed his forehead between his thumb and forefinger, soothing the tension. "No one is allowed to discharge a firearm in a populated area."

In an increasingly condescending manner, and while shaking his head, the man replied, "Mister, we ain't in the city limits," and advised Richard, "You need to get with the program, boy, iffin you're gonna live in Erstwhile."

Richard did not know how to respond. Without saying anything he turned and walked away expecting to feel the pain of a pellet as it pierced his back. He made his way back to the house incredulous to the intergenerational passage of outdated concepts. It was obvious to him that his own father was placing the young boy at a great disadvantage. His disgust turned to sympathy as he found himself recalling his own childhood and how he felt many times that his family had ill-prepared him to survive in an increasingly complex world.

Chapter Thirteen

Weeks passed, as Richard and Susan grew farther apart. Their relationship seemed to have passed the point of no return that he had experienced so many times before. The shorter his future became the less enthusiasm he had for it. He felt more isolated and alone than at any other time during his life. When he left the store he did not hesitate to place his keys in his pocket after locking its door. He knew exactly where he was going and didn't bother to look both ways before crossing the street. Instead, he boldly moved toward the flickering neon sign that had drawn him into its dark confines.

He approached the door to Merlin's and felt giddy at the prospects that awaited him inside. His anticipation bordered on juvenile. Confidently, Richard grabbed the oversized door-handle, opened it and walked inside. Quickly he assessed the seating arrangements. There were not many people there. The two older gentlemen still occupied the booth near the back. Jake sat in the same seat as the last time Richard was there. Merlin leaned with his forearms on the bar scratching letters onto the crossword puzzle that he held in his hand. There was a young lady seated, alone, at the opposite end of the bar. She sat on the last stool where the bar dissolved into the wall. From her vantage point she saw everyone in the room.

Richard walked over to the bar and sat on a seat to the left of Jake, leaving one stool between them. He remained patient, looking at the bartender and waiting for him to look up from his paper. When he spied Richard, he gave him a quick smile, placed his puzzle on the bar and began to make his newest regular a drink without asking his preference. Richard did not mind. He spun around on his bar stool rather joyfully and stopped so that he faced the pool table. Leaning back against the bar, he stretched his arms across its edge. As he looked around he could feel Jake's stare against the side of his face. The man's overbearing dogma did not matter. The bar had become familiar and cozy.

Without a word, Merlin placed his drink on the counter. He heard the glass as it settled on the bar behind him, turned around, grabbed it, started and finished it without interruption. Before Merlin could return to his puzzle, Richard held his empty glass in the air. For days he had tried to sort out what his life had become and the alcohol seemed to help.

While he waited for his second drink he took notice of the young lady seated at the end of the bar. She was an attractive woman who appeared to be a contemporary. There was something very familiar about her, but he could not figure out what it was. Lying on the bar in front of her was a pack of cigarettes with a lighter placed on top. A flute filled with white wine was next to them. She had one hand on the glass and the other rested on the bar next to her smokes. Her fingers were wrapped around its stem and her thumb gently stroked away the condensation. Her nails were French manicured. The woman was dressed in jeans and a smartly pressed polo. Her shirt was unbuttoned to the point of revealing her very ample bosom. Richard noticed she had a tattoo on her left breast. It was a red heart with a long ribbon, delicately wrapped around it. Richard guessed that underneath were several names of men with whom this woman had known, for good or bad.

She continued to stroke the glass as she looked around the room. He noticed when their eyes met the movement of her thumb became slower; more sensual.

When he finished his second drink, Merlin made him another. The alcohol began to loosen his inhibitions. He was relaxed and numb as he sat with his left forearm resting along the edge of the bar and his right elbow on its top with his chin in his hand. Once again, Richard glanced over at the mysterious woman. She looked at him. They smiled at one another. He gazed at her as she removed a cigarette from the pack lying on the bar. When she lit it she took a deep, heavy drag. The tip glowed white hot, and then returned to a normal orange glow as she removed it from her supple lips. She maintained eye contact by looking at him down the bridge of her nose as she tilted her head back and blew smoke into the air. It was all so sensual that he could not help but think she was interested in him.

"I wouldn't do that if I were you, literally and figuratively speaking," Jake said.

Richard looked around rather innocently, and replied, "Are you speaking to me?"

"Goddamn right I am."

"Do what?"

"Mess with that girl."

"I hadn't planned on *messing* with her. Why? Is she yours?"

Jake laughed. "She's been everybody's. I'm just trying to save you a little heartache. I know how you get too attached to women."

Merlin looked up from his puzzle and spoke directly to Jake. "Let the man make his own mistakes."

Jake threw up his hands in surrender, acquiescing.

Richard could not resist a confrontation. "You have never once given me any advice, so why do you feel like now is the time to insert yourself into my life?"

The bar fell silent for several minutes. No one recalled anyone ever speaking to Jake in anger. The woman at the end of the bar snuffed out one cigarette and lit another, but said nothing. Jake looked at Merlin and shrugged his shoulders, not showing Richard the respect of acknowledging his question.

Richard became angrier. "I'm not a child. If you have something to say to me then say it. Otherwise, you can live out your days in this bar and grow to be an angry old man if that's what you want."

Jake turned to Richard. "Well, I ain't your daddy either. If you're looking for someone to hold your hand and love you, don't look to me. The best advice my pappy gave me was, 'looking for love is like searching for aliens. You'll waste your whole life doing it and you end up with nothing in the end.'"

"Sage advice," Richard said, sarcastically. "But no matter what experiences I've had in my life with the people I love, good or bad, I wouldn't change a thing."

"Not even the disappointments?"

Merlin shifted his gaze from Jake to Richard. The woman at the end of the bar leaned forward, resting her forearms on its edge. Smoke billowed in front of her face. Richard saw the glare of her eyes through it all. He turned to see the two old guys in the booth at the back of the bar. They both watched Richard, intently. He lifted his empty glass into the air. Merlin got down from the counter, made him a new drink and slid it in front of him. He took a sip and explained. "I've had three men in my life that I've considered best friends. Two of them have committed suicide and one won't talk to me because I led an intervention to try and get him to stop using drugs. There is no way to avoid disappointment because our expectations of those we love are greater than we expect from ourselves. That imbalance, left unchecked, will cause us to spin out of control."

Merlin said, "I'll buy you another drink for that bit of wisdom, and any others you've got like it."

"It sounds like you're making my point for me," Jake said.

"No. The difference is that I believe that disappointment, and the lessons we learn from it, will eventually garner enlightenment." He looked at the two old gentlemen at the back of the bar, then at the woman. Through the smoke he could see a sly smile as it grew on her face.

While everyone was busy applying Richard's logic to their own circumstances, loud coughing echoed just outside the front entrance. The bar's collective attention was drawn to the sound. When the door opened a slender young lady walked inside. She had brown hair that hung just past her shoulders and carried a Louis Vitton bag in her right hand, holding it by the straps down by her leg. She stopped and looked around. Noticing that the door was still open, Richard sat up straight and then stood on the rungs of his stool in order to see who was holding it open. A man's foot held it by the lower left corner. When he finally appeared in the doorway he took one last drag from a cigarette, removed it by placing it between his thumb and middle finger and then flipped it onto the sidewalk.

The man entered the bar as he placed his left hand on the small of his date's back and escorted her inside. He cleared his throat constantly as they made their way to the bar, taking two seats to the left of Richard. He noticed the pinky on the man's right hand appeared to have been broken and not set properly. It curved away from his other fingers.

"Gimme a gin and tonic and a house chardonnay for the lady," the man bellowed, obnoxiously.

Richard tried to ignore him. He thought about how to move away without being too obvious. Maybe it was time to talk to the woman at the end of the bar. Suddenly, the man turned to him and slapped him on the back. "How's it been going, man?" he asked.

Stunned, Richard looked at the man, searching for something familiar about him. There was nothing. He looked into his eyes: still nothing.

"Don't tell me you don't remember me." He saw the uncertainty in Richard's face.

He shrugged his shoulders. "I'm sorry. You have me at a loss."

"I'm Carl Rodgers. I fired your ass about fifteen years ago," he said, proudly.

Richard remembered being fired by Carl, but this man somehow just didn't seem to be the same guy. "Yeah, I remember you," he said, hesitantly.

"I just thought I'd come see how you were doing," Carl said.

"You came to see me?"

"I thought I'd pay you a visit, yes."

"Why?"

"Because I know that you have something you need to say to me."

The memories of working for Carl bubbled into Richard's consciousness. "Now that you mention it, yeah I'd like to get several things off my chest. First, you didn't fire me. You didn't have the guts. You had to hide behind that Napoleon wannabe to do your dirty work. Next, you were the worst boss I've ever had. You spent all your time using the firm as your personal dating service when you should have been acting as a mentor to your staff; me included."

Merlin placed the drinks that Carl ordered in front of him and his date. He drank, as did his lady friend; then threw his hands in the air. "Hey man, it wasn't all bad. Remember that time in Key West when we were at Rum Runner's?" He turned to talk to his date, including her in the story. "I had gone to the bathroom and this guy," pointing to Richard, "was at the bar waiting for me. Well some chap walked up to my seat, and I mean this guy was *huge*." When he took another sip of his drink, he took with it a couple pieces of ice. He annoyingly crushed it between his teeth as he continued his story. "The fat guy pushes my bar stool away from him and Richard here thinks he's trying to move it out of his way, so he reached over and pulled it farther away from the guy." Carl shook his head as he tried to contain his laughter. "The fat guy thought the stool was right behind him so he went to sit down and began to fall. Richard saw the guy falling and tried to catch him. I come back from the bathroom and see little ole Richard trying to hold up this three hundred fifty pound fat-ass with a red face and a cigar hanging from his mouth." Carl turned back to Richard. "You've got to admit that has to be the funniest thing that has ever happened to you. I know it was for me."

Richard smiled. "Yes it was. But it is also indicative of just what was wrong with how you carried on our relationship. You weren't looking for a senior staff member; you were looking for a party-pal. And I ob-

94

liged." He paused. His epiphany became clear. "I guess I am just as much at fault as you."

"Anything else?" Carl asked, still gnashing ice between his teeth.

"Yes," Richard replied as he leaned onto the bar to look around his old boss. Looking into the eyes of his date that he recognized was Julie. "Hey, Julie."

"Hello, Richard," she said with a polite smile that was also sweet and somewhat innocent.

"Everyone always liked you. I had a lot of respect for your abilities and the kind of person you were; or seemed to be. But, I do need to let you know that you aren't fooling anyone at the firm. Everyone knew the two of you were sleeping together."

"*They did?*" She was astonished and embarrassed as she folded her left hand under her right to cover her wedding ring.

"And, everyone always wanted to know when you two make love does he cough in your face like he does everyone else's?"

Julie dropped her head. "Yes." Everyone in the bar laughed, except the couple.

"I thought so," Richard said laughing. "Oh yeah! One more thing. There was this time that I set up your *boyfriend* on a blind date. I happen to mention that fact to another staff member. Well, he takes me into his office and reams me a new asshole for talking to people in the office about his personal life." Richard grinned widely. "Not until tonight did I realize that he didn't want you to know about it. That's why he was so pissed."

Julie turned to Carl and stomped her foot on the floor. "Is that true?"

When he couldn't answer, she turned and walked away briskly.

"Thanks, asshole," Carl said.

"Anytime, *buddy*."

Without another word Carl turned and followed Julie. Approaching the front door he placed his left hand in his shirt pocket, removed his cigarettes, shook them and pulled one from the pack with his lips. He had it lit before he stepped outside.

Richard turned to Merlin. "I think I deserve another drink."

"Don't you think you've had enough?"

"The night is still young." Richard pointed at the empty glass in front of him.

"Richard, this'll be your sixth, and I've been mixing them strong."

"That's alright. I'm not driving home tonight. I have a cot in the back of the store. All I have to do is stumble across the street." Richard looked at Jake and smiled, wryly. "I'm good for three or four more, my friend." His attention then turned to the woman at the end of the bar. Once again they made eye contact through the ever-present cloud of smoke. He spoke in a loud voice across the bar to her. "You're gonna end up with a smoker's cough as bad as the guy who just left here."

She didn't respond. Sarcastically, she exhaled smoke and smiled at him. It was time to respond to the overtures she had made all night. He finally had enough alcohol in him to act on his impulse. When he stood, he found his legs were weak and he struggled to lift himself by pressing against the edge of the bar. Feeling self-conscious, he motioned to Merlin that he'd be taking his drinks at the end of the bar. The bartender acknowledged with a nod.

Richard made his way around to her and the woman pivoted on her stool to face him. She exuded sexual energy. He could not help but drink in every inch of her body with his eyes. It had been too long since he had felt his wife's supple flesh. He extended his hand and said, "My name is Richard."

She nodded with short, quick bobs of her head. "I know," she said as smoke seeped from her mouth.

"*And you?*"

She took another deep drag, exaggerating the inhale because she sensed that Richard liked watching her chest heave. She wasn't wrong. "You know who I am," she replied.

Merlin placed Richard's drink on the bar in front of him. He laughed as he took it. "What is it about tonight?" Half of his drink was gone in one gulp.

"It's obviously all about you tonight, sweetie."

Richard gasped as he placed his drink on the bar. Merlin had made it even stronger than the others. "Can I have a hint?" He asked.

"You'll figure it out eventually."

He looked at her intently. There was nothing about her that he recognized, so he started with her tattoo. "The ribbon around your tattoo; I assume there are names of men underneath?"

"You got it, sailor."

"Any names I know?"

"You know every one of them."

In order to buy himself some time, Richard picked up his drink and finished it, then motioned to Merlin for another. He held his hand to his mouth and belched, holding in the foul air, then turned away from her to let it escape. "Do I have to get out the baby book of names and go through it one-by-one?" he replied, derisively.

She took another drag from her cigarette, and said nothing.

"Come on! You've gotta give me a hint … something … anything."

She still said nothing.

"*Please.*"

She grew tired and said, "Think about high school."

"High school? That was twenty-one years ago."

"Why didn't you go to your reunion?"

"I did."

"Your twentieth reunion?"

"No … I missed that one. I was talking about the ten year reunion."

"Why?"

Merlin placed Richard's drink on the bar in front of him. He picked it up, but this time he only took a sip. "Maybe I felt that I needed to give up on my past."

"You were missed."

"*Really?*"

"Not by anyone but me," she replied, as she took another drag from her cigarette and quickly exhaled. "Don't you want to know why?"

Frustrated, he replied, "Lady, I don't even know your name."

She smiled. "It's Sara."

It came to him! "Sara Johnson?" She was the only Sara she had ever known.

"Yes."

Richard didn't know what to say, and the words he chose were not the best. "You look so different. You don't have that sweet, clean, fresh face that I remember."

Jake shouted from across the bar. "Was that supposed to be a compliment?" Just before he took another sip of his beer he blurted out, "dumb-ass!"

Richard looked at Jake and then back at Sara. "He's right. I'm sorry."

"No apologies necessary. I know what I've become, and I have you to thank for it."

"*Me*?"

"Don't you remember how poorly you treated me while we were dating?"

Richard searched for some recollection, but the only thing distinctive about their relationship that he could remember was the amount of time they spent parked in the woods. "I remember discovering what the naked female body looked and felt like, at least yours."

"There you go again."

"What?" Richard said.

"You constantly separated me from everyone else on *Earth* with comments like the one you just made."

Richard truly did not understand the gravity of what she was saying. "Can you help me out a little, *please*? I'm a bit drunk, and obviously a little slow on the up-take."

"Don't you remember when Charlotte Pitts got pregnant our junior year and was sent away to have her baby?"

"Yeah, thank God it wasn't mine," he said.

"That's it! You made the same joke in high school. But to me what you said was, 'I slept with Charlotte, but that baby's not mine.'"

"I'm sorry," Richard said, rather insincerely.

"That's not all. Don't you remember saying things like Charlotte has nicer tits, and 'Charlotte likes it doggy-style.' Or, 'If Charlotte wasn't damaged goods, I'd kick you to the curb and date her.'"

Richard did remember saying all those things and hearing them come from Sara's mouth after all these years increased their significance. Richard uttered a slow, drunken, "Fuuucck!" He tried to speak soberly; sincerely. "Sara, I had no idea the things that I said to you would ever have that kind of affect on you. I'm truly sorry."

"Well they did. I haven't had any confidence in myself since. Life, for me, has been a series of failed relationships. Because of you I have always been attracted to men who treated me like shit."

"I … I'm sorry," he repeated. The gravity of perpetuating poor behavior became painfully apparent.

Sara did not respond to his apology. It was as if he never made it. She picked up her cigarettes, slid them into her bra, then grabbed her pocket book off the bar and walked out without a word.

Jake watched her disappear through the door. He turned to Richard. "I warned you about talking to her, didn't I?"

Richard did not wait for more conversation from Jake or anyone else. He walked into the bathroom and up to an available urinal, and began peeing. The words of The Doors echoed through his mind. *People are strange when you're a stranger. Faces look ugly when you're alone. Women seem wicked when you're unwanted. Streets are uneven when you're down.* Long after he had finished, Richard found himself standing and listening to every word of the song. The lyrics that stung the worst were, *No one remembers your name, when you're strange.* He understood that no one would ever confuse him for a saint, but how could his relationship with Susan be so ordinary? It was more special than any he had known. Regardless of Sara's feelings, he felt as though he had learned from his mistakes. Being a pariah was a role he had come to accept and sometimes relish, but not when it came to the one woman he loved more than life. He realized that his inability to recognize people from his past was because he was incapable of understanding that his experiences had woven the fabric of his being.

Chapter Fourteen

The afternoon was without customers and Richard worked outside in front of the shop cleaning the windows. He held several Windex soaked paper-towels in one hand and the bottle of cleaner in the other. The roll was on the sidewalk next to him. There was not a lot of activity on Maine Street. Most of the people who invaded downtown during their lunch hour had returned to work. That left the merchants to perform various housekeeping tasks. Normally, paperwork kept them inside, but the air outside was unseasonably dry, cool and irresistibly pleasant. They took pride in their stores and it showed.

Two doors away from Richard's shop, Clyde Wilson swept the sidewalk. The man was well into his sixties. His store was filled with some of the most interesting pieces of furniture that had been acquired while traveling all over the southeastern United States. His kids were grown, so Clyde and his wife had taken the opportunity to purchase a recreational vehicle to prolong the many buying trips they went on each year in order to spend time together. He and Richard exchanged a pleasant smile and nod as they went about their business.

Clyde stopped sweeping when he saw an old Ford pickup weaving its way down the street. He folded his hands across the top of the broom handle, not surprised by what he witnessed. He shook his head in disapproval. Richard looked over at him and watched briefly, but didn't have the same interest as his neighbor, and continued cleaning the window until he was startled by a metal-crunching crash. Quickly, he turned to see what happened. On the other side of the street was an old Ford F-150 pickup, speckled with rust spots, smashed against a telephone pole. The streetlight mounted atop the pole shook violently, as did the wires that were strung along the eastern side of the street.

Instinctively, Richard dropped the items in his hands and ran across the street, stopping briefly to look both ways before accelerating his pace to a full sprint. When he got to the truck he saw a young man, around thirty years old, slumped over the steering wheel. There was no one else in the cab of the truck. Richard struggled to open the driver's door. The vehicle's frame had bent as a result of the crash, pinching it shut. Once he was able get it open, the man inside fell onto the pavement. Richard attempted to catch him, but the man's weight was too much. A bottle of White Horse Scotch, with only a meager amount of alcohol inside, rolled off the floorboard and onto the pavement next to the man's arm. It shattered on the street. Glass shards flew into the man's face. He was oblivious to everything that happened. There was a nasty cut across the bridge of his nose, caused by his face being thrust into the steering wheel upon impact. Richard tried to help him to his feet. After a mighty effort, the man was able to stand and lean against the front seat of the truck. Not until the excitement waned did Richard become aware of the odor that surrounded him. It came, not only from the broken bottle that lay at their feet, but it also oozed from the man's pores. He reeked of alcohol and was so drunk that Richard had to hold his hand in the middle of the man's chest to keep him upright. The stench was so bad that he extended his arm as far as he could in an effort to find fresh air. Every few seconds he turned away and inhaled. Finally, he lifted the man onto the front seat so that he could sit. Once he was on the seat and Richard stopped supporting his weight, the man fell hopelessly backward.

Throughout the entire ordeal he had been so focused on helping the stranger that Richard did not realize that no one else had come to the man's aid. People emptied from the stores and gathered along both sides of the street to watch. It dumbfounded him to see the disgust on people's faces when someone was in obvious need. Richard walked back across the street, toward his shop, to call the paramedics.

"I've already called the police," Clyde called to him. The police station was just around the corner and Richard knew they'd be there quickly. He changed direction and moved toward the man.

When he stepped onto the curb in front of his neighbor, he asked, "Why is no one helping that young man?"

"It's happened several times before." Clyde's tone was filled with disappointment. He looked over Richard's shoulder at the wreckage.

He struggled to understand whether that was an appropriate response or not, and still questioned why no one tried to help the man. Instead he inquired about his identity. "Who is that, Clyde?"

"That's Jeff Cunningham."

"Is he un-liked for some reason?"

"Oh no! Quite the opposite. A lot of folks here placed a lot of faith in that boy."

"Faith?"

"Yeah. He was a brilliant young man. Throughout junior high and high school he traveled to math competitions all over the country. He got a full scholarship to M.I.T. That's in Massachusetts."

"Yes, I know."

Clyde continued. "In the middle of his sophomore year his dad died and he had to come back to take care of his mother and younger sister. He had to give up on his dream. To forget his troubles he crawled inside a whiskey bottle and has stayed in one ever since."

"That's really sad," Richard replied, sincerely.

"Yes it is. A lot of people felt like he would put Erstwhile on the map. 'Local boy done good' kind of thing, you know."

"That's a lot of pressure to put on one person."

"*What*? How can having a whole town behind you be pressure? I'd love to have this entire town support me."

It was obvious to Richard the amount of pressure that Jeff must have felt, having to come home and listen to well-meaning people talk about what *might* have been. He was stunned that everyone's opinion of this young man was based on their expectations of him without consideration of his own hopes. Jeff had nowhere to hide, nowhere to just be himself. Instead of pressing the issue, Richard decided to inquire about Clyde's feelings. "How is it that this town is not behind you?"

Clyde pursed his lips, shifted his mouth from side to side and thought about the question. "I guess it pisses me off when I hear people say that my products are inferior, and that they are not true antiques."

"So, you take that personally?"

"Hell yes!"

"Why should you?"

"Because I take a lot of pride in making sure that I have the best quality furniture. I shop all across the nation and get what I feel is the very best for my customers."

"Pride! That's it. You take pride in what you do and you're influenced by what other people think, right?"

"Yeah."

"Don't you think that Jeff had pride in what he accomplished in junior high and high school?"

"Sure!"

"So, when he was forced to come home from M.I.T. don't you think he felt as if he had let the people of Erstwhile down? He felt the same way you feel when someone questions the quality of your furniture. Right?"

Clyde nervously swept the sidewalk, covering the same spot again-and-again. He did not know how to respond. His mind raced. He turned away from Richard and continued to sweep. Richard watched and waited for him to respond. After a few moments he stopped sweeping, turned and faced Richard, "Jefferson Davis Cunningham had more opportunity than anyone who has ever lived here."

Jefferson Davis? Richard thought to himself. A chill ran down his spine as he thought about the implications of being named for the President of the Confederacy. He shook away the thought and tried one last time to convince Clyde of the danger that comes from expecting more from others than we do ourselves. It was a lesson that was fresh for him. "Exactly! His opportunity was taken away from him due to no fault of his own. I think that's the worst thing that can happen to a man, to take away something so dear, something that he has worked his entire life to achieve. Taking away something like that will kill a man's self-esteem. It's all about the expectations we have of ourselves, not those we have of others."

"Are you trying to blame his problems on the good people of Erstwhile?"

"Gosh no. In Jeff's case it was circumstances that took away his opportunity, unfortunate circumstances. But it stings none the less."

A customer walked into Clyde's store. Smiling and quite relieved that he wouldn't have to continue the conversation, he said, "I have a customer," then turned and walked toward his store repeatedly picking up his broom and placing it on the ground like one would a walking stick.

Richard turned toward the accident scene to see that the police had arrived and were loading Jeff, handcuffed, into a patrol car. He returned to the task of cleaning the window at the front of his store, wondering about the ultimate consequences of Jeff's actions. The passion in his words was real, but it did little to alleviate the pressure he felt from his wife who obviously expected him to be something he wasn't. A great deal of effort went into making her happy early in their relationship. Gifts were bestowed upon her regularly. His actions created unrealistic expectations, which minimized her immediate need for the things that set Ralph apart from him. When it was forced to stand on its own, their marriage faltered atop a foundation constructed of counterfeit passion.

Chapter Fifteen

There were many secrets that Susan held onto tightly. Stubborn jealously had been the default emotion whenever she shared details of past relationships with other boys. An explanation of her dependency on Ralph was in order, but she had no idea how to approach Richard. The experiences she held closely embarrassed her. Ralph was the only man who had known her during the most difficult times in her life and had not judged her for what she did. She was not sure that her husband would be so forgiving.

She sat, staring through the windows at the rear of their house. Sea oats whipped back-and-forth with every gust of wind. Blue sky had given way to clouds rolling in quickly from the west that completely covered the atmosphere. Without the benefit of sunlight the gulf water was dark and violent. Waves capped by white foam stretched all the way to the horizon. Sea-spray exploded into the air as they crashed together. The signs were strong that there was a bad storm coming.

Her past became present as recollections crept into the forefront of Susan's consciousness. Unique dates, unusual experiences and places she had been with other men once again became as fresh as the day they happened. The power of her mind took her far away from Erstwhile and her troubled existence. Memories that had been stained by infidelity, manipulation and indifference were somehow pleasant again.

Susan felt more morose than when she sat down. She stood and walked across the living room into the guest bedroom. It was the farthest enclave from the master suite that she shared with her husband. Against the far wall, unpacked boxes filled with household items were stacked head-high. She walked over to them and looked along the bottom row until she spied the one she wanted. The boxes directly on top of the one she desired were removed. When it was exposed, she slid it toward her and from between two that lay snuggly on either side. Unlike the others, this one was void of any markings, but Susan knew exactly what she was searching for; memories she had kept from her husband.

She picked the box up and set it down on the bed next to her. There was no tape holding its flaps closed. They had been closed by alternating their over-under position. Opening it, she leaned forward and peered inside. The first item removed was a garter from her high school prom, which she lay on the bed next to her. Then she reached in and pulled out a hospital iden-tification bracelet that adorned her wrist while in rehab-ilitation for her cocaine addiction. Susan recalled spending her twenty-first birthday there. Her mood sank as she conjured memories from almost two decades earlier. What she had come to understand was that her addiction must be confronted head-on, every day of her life. She placed the bracelet on the bed next to the garter. From deep within the box she plucked a framed picture of her and a young man. His name was Court-ney Brown. The two young, fresh-faced people were on top of a snow-capped mountain in Vale, Colorado. Her eyes were drawn away from the landscape and back to the handsome couple. The smiles on their faces were grand, fresh and exuded happiness. Each wore a ski-bib, boots and goggles that were propped up on their foreheads.

Susan turned the picture around. On the cardboard backing that held it flush against the glass was a piece of duct tape. She pulled it away and with it came a jagged layer of brown paper. Placing the photograph in her lap, she held the tape in her right hand and peeled away the casing placed there long ago to reveal a gold and diamond ring. It was not especially impressive in size, but it held a lot of sentiment in its thin gold band. The halo was given to a woman who did not know what to expect from a lover; by a man too young to know what it was he wanted out of life. The passion was no less intense.

Susan was transported emotionally from the mountaintop back to Erstwhile when she heard a rapping on the back door. She lifted the picture from her lap and put it on the nightstand next to the bed, as she put the ring in the coin pocket of her jeans. She walked out of the guest room and back across the living room to the rear of the house. Large intermittent raindrops pounded against the glass. Reaching the back porch, she saw Emma with a windbreaker pulled over her head to shield her from getting wet. She had her right hand placed along her brow with its back edge pressed against the glass to shield the glare. When she spied Susan walking onto the back porch she smiled and waved vigorously. Susan walked to the back door and opened it. Emma hopped out of the rain and into the house. Once inside, she took off her coat, shook it dry, and paid no attention to the fact that she was getting her friend's floor wet. Emma handed the jacket to Susan as she would a servant who was expected to dispose of it; which she dutifully hung on a hook mounted on the wall next to the door.

"Hey, sister," she said, as she walked into the house.

"Hello, Emma."

"Have you got anything to drink?" she said as she walked over to a bamboo sofa on the porch and sat down.

"We've got Coke, or water. I think I may have some apple juice, if you'd like that."

Emma laughed. "On a cold rainy day like today, I think I need something a little stiffer. Have you got any scotch?"

"Is Glenfiddich okay?" Susan asked as she walked toward the bar-cart.

"I guess so," Emma said. "I'll take it neat. I hate watered down scotch."

Without a word Susan made the drink and walked back to where her guest sat and handed her the drink.

After taking a sip she said, "Whew! Is this the best you've got?"

"Well, it is aged twelve years and it's a single malt scotch."

With her hand, Emma waved away all responsibility for her lack of decorum. "Anyway, I didn't come here to discuss the quality, or lack thereof, of your liquor cabinet." Before she could finish her thought she noticed that Susan had the same far-away look in her eye as the first day they met on the beach. "What's the matter, hun?"

Susan shook her head. "I can't help but wonder if I've made the best decisions in my life."

"Can't stop thinking about Ralph?"

"It's not just him, every decision I've ever made seems like it has been a misstep." Susan took comfort in knowing that someone was *truly* interested in her well being and found herself clinging to the tenuously fresh alliance. She rubbed the outside of her jeans with her thumb, feeling the ring in her pocket. For her it symbolized a never-ending succession of choices resulting in pain. "Richard called a little earlier and asked if he could take me to dinner."

"Dinner, huh?"

"He said he had something he needed to talk to me about."

"Needed or wanted?"

"What?"

"Did he say he *needed* to talk to you, or that he *wanted* to talk to you?"

"I'm not sure. I think I heard 'needed.'"

"It's always been my experience that words are carefully chosen, but whenever they are employed haphazardly is when people get hurt. If he 'needs' to talk to you then there is something pressing he has to talk with you about. If he 'wants' to talk to you, then it's something less critical; like buying a car."

Susan stood and walked to the bar. Emma's words began to sink in and they reflected the reality of the dilemma she created for herself. Her mind raced with possibilities. Standing over the counter she looked at the various bottles of liquor and considered having a drink. She felt like less of a married woman and more like the young woman who painfully discovered just how cruel the world can be. Her stare moved from the bottles to the mirrored glass on top of the bar, examining her likeness. The longer she looked the younger she became. The telltale lines on her face, the signs of an experienced woman, slowly disappeared. The single manifestation became that of two as she imagined

Courtney standing behind her, peering over her shoulder at her reflection in the glass. He smiled at her and she returned the gesture.

He reached down and carefully slid the bottles away from the center and against the sides of the bar-cart, leaving an empty space in the middle.

Susan looked at Emma worried that she could see the apparition she clung to for hope. Emma smiled, oblivious to the inner workings of her friend's mind. Her gaze returned to the mirror where she saw a white, powdery residue. She recognized it from the many nights spent as a young person trying to alter her reality. A tightly rolled one hundred dollar bill, wrapped inside a small rubber band, fell onto the glass; tossed there by Courtney. He was unable to focus on her image. His eyes were glazed and there was a satisfied smile on his face. He pinched his nose and rubbed it vigorously to take away the sting.

Susan looked again at the cocaine dregs on the glass. She reached down and ran the tip of her finger through it, then placed that finger in her mouth and rubbed it along her gums. The mere suggestion of the happiness she once knew was enough to make her mouth tingle and go numb. Suddenly, she grabbed her wrist and remembered the hospital band she had re-moved from her box of memories. She shook away the illusion and walked over to where her friend was seated and sat down.

Emma looked at Susan, eyebrows raised. "I have a great idea."

"What's that?" she asked, still dazed and sug-gestively high.

"Why don't I show up at the restaurant tonight? I could be a friend from way back when. That way, I could provide you the strength you need to get through it. I know how much you need me."

"That would be nice." Susan did not realize that there was no reason for her to require the support of anyone. She reacted as she had been conditioned; to rely on others fully and without question. That need caused her to continually search beyond good circumstances for unattainable ones. In choosing Emma as a friend, she strengthened her resolve to alter the circumstances of her life.

Chapter Sixteen

The rain that drenched the beach had done the same to downtown Erstwhile as the storm moved through one area of town to the other. The crown of the road that ran down the middle of Maine Street had begun to dry with help from the newly emergent sun. Dark wet asphalt ran along the sides. In the curbs, small streams of water trickled into the storm drains. Precipitation that moments earlier had gushed from the gutterspouts only dripped onto the sidewalk. Richard stared through the front window of the store. The glare created by the sun's rays reflecting off numerous pools of water mesmerized him. Days like this were not uncommon to him. Steam rose from the street and disappeared. Heat created the storm and then reclaimed its offspring. Customers were few after such a circumstance. He decided a walk might help his apathy.

Richard opened the door and the bell atop the frame rang. The warm sun on his face felt refreshing. He walked north wearing a hollow smile. His thoughts were of the date later that night with Susan. The only way to confront the demons in their relationship was to ask about her feelings for Ralph and what they meant for him. Spending another night at Merlin's was not appealing. His wife had become all too ordinary. She no longer captivated him.

Richard continued his walk, occasionally passing shop owners who had come outside to enjoy what the day had to offer. Dennis owned an unfinished furniture shop. He was replacing rocking chairs on the sidewalk that he removed just before the rain began. LaDonna owned a restaurant and was rewriting the specials of the day on a chalkboard. It was still wet and she struggled to keep the chalk from caking and falling away from the board. There was no one in the cell phone store. It appeared that whoever was supposed to be staffing it decided to leave for the day.

Richard was lost in his thoughts. The other shop owners said nothing to him as he passed. He had grown accustomed to being made to feel unwelcome. It was easily ignored. Every relationship he ever had seemed to be nothing more than a signpost on life's highway; a point of reference.

When he reached the northern end of Maine Street, where it intersected First Avenue, Richard crossed and began to walk back toward the store. Shop owners on this side were doing the same as their counterparts across the way, re-displaying their wares on the wet, steamy sidewalk. Sweat began to bead on his forehead.

Walking and staring upward, he watched the clouds as they cleared, revealing the familiar light-blue canvas of sky. He found himself longing for the dry air of fall that everyone had gotten a taste of days earlier. A pretty young lady walked by without him noticing. She noticed him, though.

The girl turned around and called to him as they passed one another. "Hey mister."

Her summon did not pierce his consciousness at first. After a couple of seconds he realized that someone was speaking to him. Richard stopped and turned around. "Yes, ma'am?"

"Are you the man who owns the mercantile shop across the street?" the girl asked, as she pointed in the direction of the store.

"Yes, I am."

The young lady smiled and extended her hand in friendship. "My name is Talitha Keys."

Richard took a couple steps closer and shook her hand. "I'm Richard Styles."

"Have you gotten used to living in a town this small yet?" she asked with a mischievous grin on her face. Her eyes were warm and inviting.

"To be honest Talitha, it's been a much bigger adjustment than we had planned for," Richard said.

She laughed. The smile quickly dissolved from her face. "Everyone in our community knows the kind of man you are."

Richard smiled nervously and replied, "I'm not sure what you mean by that."

"Don't worry. It's a good thing. The black folks in this town know about the kindness that you show *everyone.* It didn't take long for one and all to hear how you carried Minnie Johnson's groceries to her car for her; much less extending her credit. Treating people with respect and dignity goes a long way, even in Erstwhile."

"Well, I've always made an effort to treat people the way I would want to be treated." Richard ached knowing that his words were not completely true. When he met Susan he found what it meant to be genuine and the peace it provided. He wished for the same growth from every encounter he had. His desire did nothing to change his past and he knew it.

"That's a good policy to have, but it has a tendency to create trouble for people who don't understand how this town operates." She paused. "That's why I stopped you. I wanted to let you know the rumors some residents of Erstwhile are spreading about you and your wife." Richard did not respond. She saw the curious look on his face and continued. "The first one is that you're drug dealers bringing stuff in from your *connections* in Orlando. You're up here to push your product onto the young people of this community."

"That's insane!"

"I know. But it is a function of the kindness you show people."

"I don't understand." Richard was incredulous.

"The man you hired to do work on your beach house while you were still living in Orlando … "

"Stephen Talquin?" Richard interrupted.

"Yes. Well, he's probably the biggest drug addict this town has ever seen. His folks have plenty of money, so he doesn't have to work."

"And by being nice to him, I have placed my wife and me on a short list of undesirables?" Richard asked.

"A very short list," Talitha said. "When people don't have the capacity for understanding, the truth becomes a casualty."

He was disturbed by Talitha's comments. However, he had been too preoccupied to notice anything outside of the burden of being Richard Styles and it showed. "What should I do about it?" His willingness to acquiesce was offered up to her passionately. "How can I change?"

"Just be very cautious. Don't allow them to isolate you, because once they do, they've won the war." Talitha smiled warmly. "But even if they do succeed in branding you an outcast, you'll always be welcome on our side of the tracks." The better part of her conscience took over. "Well, it's not like all of them are talking; only those select few. Regardless, you're seen as a carpet-bagger by all."

118

Richard laughed at what he assumed was an exaggeration. "Aren't you being a bit melodramatic?"

"Not at all," she said without hesitation. "Let me tell you a story about a family, not unlike yours, that moved here last year. They came from Atlanta and had roots in this town, just like you. The wife's grandfather had been the superintendent of schools for forty years. They too wanted to simplify their lives and get back to basics and felt Erstwhile would be the best place to accomplish all of their life's goals. The only problem was that around here that is tantamount to having a basic ignorance about most everything."

"What happened?" Richard asked.

"To make a long story short, the husband and wife were out jogging one day. Since they ran at different paces, they had taken different routes. They each had the misfortune of running by the same house at different times. Each of them was viciously attacked by a rottweiler."

Richard's heart sank. "Don't tell me they were killed."

"Okay, I won't," Talitha said. "Both of them had some pretty nasty bites, but the true travesty was that the dumb-ass redneck who owned the dog tried to place the blame on them for getting his dog riled-up."

Richard laughed. "You've got to be kidding."

Talitha shook her head. "It gets even better. When the couple couldn't get this guy to take responsibility for his dog's actions, they hired an attorney."

"How did they want the man to take responsibility? I mean, was it within reason?" Richard asked, trying to remain objective.

"They wanted the guy to pay their medical bills."

"That seems pretty reasonable to me!"

"One would think!" Talitha agreed. "Anyway, the attorney they hired used stall tactics and put them off as long as he could. And why, might you ask? The attorney they hired was not only the brother-in-law of the redneck's attorney, but they served together on the Board of Directors of the Paper Maker's Union at the mill."

"So how did this couple find out about the relationship between the two attorneys?"

Talitha smiled. "Let's just say a little birdie told them, and we'll leave it at that."

"So how does this story end?" Richard asked. "Happily, I hope."

Talitha pointed to the middle of Maine Street. "Do you see those skid marks on the road?"

He looked to where she pointed. "Yes."

"The couple got smart. They fired the local attorney and hired one out of Atlanta. They got a huge settlement and bought a Porsche with some of the money. Those skid marks," she once again pointed to the middle of Maine Street, "lead all the way back to Atlanta."

"I guess they wanted to leave something behind for the citizens of Erstwhile to remember them by, huh?"

Talitha smiled. She then looked up and down Maine Street at all the storefronts. "I don't want to alarm you, and don't turn around, but every shop owner out here is staring at us."

"*Really?*"

Talitha and Richard laughed together; each a little more expressively than they may have under normal circumstances. They were simpatico.

120

She imitated the redneck dialect that most residents of Erstwhile spoke with, "It ain't no good for a white man to be talking to no black woman in public *and* be happy doin' it."

Richard laughed. "You know, I like your style."

"What is it you like the most?"

"You don't let these people get you down."

"You can't, Mr. Styles."

"Please, call me Richard." He grinned at the realization that this was the first conversation he had with a resident of Erstwhile that was of substance. He embraced the prospect of finding a new friend. "Tell me about you. Did you grow up here?"

"Would you like to go into the coffee shop and get a cup of coffee while we talk?" Talitha asked.

Richard replied, "I don't want to be rude, but no. I want to stand out here on the street with you and talk so that everyone who passes can see us."

She smiled, "I like *your* style, Richard." She continued, "Yes, I was born and raised here. I graduated at the top of my class in high school, scored a fifteen hundred on the SAT and got a full ride to Tulane University."

"Tulane! *Great* school!" It felt good to him to offer positive affirmation to someone.

"And now I'm back here."

"If you don't mind my asking, *why*? Erstwhile has nothing to offer someone of your caliber."

"Family. My family is the reason I have been so successful, and they need me right now. There will be plenty of time for my own accomplishments later."

"What kind of work do you do?"

"I work at the phone company."

Richard shook his head. "I hope you don't take this the wrong way, but that's beneath you."

"I'm not going to do that forever. If I stay here, one day I'll own every building on this street," Talitha boasted confidently as she motioned with her arms across the backdrop of Maine Street.

Richard smiled. He felt himself being drawn into this woman. Her smile was infectious. Her positive energy drew him in like a magnet. He was starved for anything that would give him the emotional boost he craved. "So, have you saved any money for a down payment on your first purchase?"

"I have a little, but it's been tough. The phone company doesn't pay that well and my grandmother has been sick. I've had to pay for her doctor bills and medications."

Richard's eyes swept the length of Maine Street. "Which building would you buy first?"

"*Yours*," Talitha said without hesitation. "The way I have it figured, my first business should be in consumer staples, something for which there will always be a demand. Then I'll venture into a more entertainment-oriented business like buying that old theatre." Talitha pointed to an old dilapidated building directly across the street from where they stood. The marquis was dented and the neon letters that once spelled the name of the theatre, *Bijou,* looked as if they had not been cared for in decades. "And, unlike others in Erstwhile, I'll pay you fair market value."

Richard was so enamored with her that he forgot about what troubled him. Her effervescent smile pushed all of the demons from his mind.

Before parting ways Talitha felt led to pass along advice that her grandmother had given her years earlier. "Richard, humans spend a lot of energy either trying to cling to their ideals or trying to escape their bonds. Those who do neither are without direction and are doomed."

Chapter Seventeen

Richard and Susan rode in silence to the restaurant. He nervously and silently rehearsed the words he wanted to say to communicate how it upset him to find her letter to Ralph. The question he hadn't been able to ask was whether their relationship was over. Experience had taught him that love triangles were complicated. Would she be able to answer him honestly, without consulting Ralph? Richard wanted *her* answer, not theirs.

Susan worried that her husband would say something that would devastate her. She never imagined he would do anything to hurt her, but the guilt she felt over her passion for Ralph and Courtney and any other failed relationship that she clung to for the nostalgia of youthful passion created a pressurized bubble whenever they were together.

After parking the truck Richard peered through the windshield and watched as kids played on the beach. Their freshly sunburned faces attested to the fact that they were tourists. Without a word to one another, they opened their doors and stepped out of the truck. He walked around the back. When he emerged on the other side he found that Susan had not waited for him. He followed, keeping distance between them.

Buster's was the name of the restaurant. The close proximity of Erstwhile to the gulf guaranteed the seafood would be fresh. This was their spot to come together. It was here that they made the decision to move from Orlando. Never had they been there with anyone else. They even had a favorite waiter, Tom.

Richard hoped to sit on the back deck and enjoy the sunset. He knew however that would be almost impossible. Tourists filled the restaurant and those tables would be in great demand.

The couple approached the hostess stand and took their place in line. Several people of varying shades of sun exposure stood ahead of them. Their colors ranged from lightly tanned to boiled-lobster-red. Richard and Susan waited patiently without a word as the hostess dutifully wrote down the name and number in each party.

Richard desperately tried to think of a way that he could gently segue into the conversation about Ralph. He had no desire to be confrontational. That would not be an easy task.

At the same time Susan juggled her emotional quandary, trying not to drop any clues to the true identity of her many faces. She struggled to put forth the woman that her husband fell in love with and avoid making reference to any cute innuendo shared with the others about whom she fantasized.

When it came time for the couple to give the hostess their name, she recognized them and reached into a large wooden pocket on the side of the hostess stand and removed two menus. "Follow me," she said, as she walked into the dining room. The restaurant was too busy for pleasantries.

Richard looked at his wife and asked, "Did you make reservations?"

She nodded.

"Great!"

The couple followed the hostess through the dining room and onto the deck, just as they had hoped. Regardless of the myriad of emotions that Richard felt about Susan, he strolled across the dining room floor on a cushion of air, proud that he was there with the most beautiful woman he had ever known.

"Did you ask for a table on the deck?"

Once again, Susan only nodded.

"Thanks," Richard said. "You know how much I enjoy the sunsets."

When she did not respond he began to worry. It was not good that his wife was unwilling or unable to talk to him. He turned his attention to the hostess. "Ma'am, is this Tom's section?"

"Yes it is."

"Thank you," Richard said.

The couple sat down in the booth on opposite sides of the table. Ever so briefly, Richard thought about asking his wife to sit on the same side, as they always had. But what he had to say and the questions he had to ask, he needed to look her squarely in the eye.

Susan nervously began to straighten the sugar tray, salt and pepper shakers, and ketchup bottle. Richard picked up a menu in one hand and searched for an entrée that fancied him as he twirled a glass jar filled with tartar sauce with his free hand. The jar had a silver lid with a plastic spoon protruding through a hole in its top. Dried sauce was caked around the rim and had turned brown.

Tom rolled up to the table in his wheelchair. "Well, hello." His words were slowed by his deep southern accent.

"Hey Tom," Richard replied.

Susan only smiled at their waiter.

Tom pointed to her. "Merlot?"

"Not tonight. I think I'll have a Tanquray and tonic, please," she said.

Tom quickly scratched his pen across the receipt book he held in his hand. He looked hesitantly at Richard. "So, are you going to have your usual, beer?"

"No thanks. I'll have a Maker's Mark and Diet Coke."

While writing down his drink order the waiter asked, "Need a minute before you order?"

"Yes, please," Richard said.

With that response, Tom placed his left hand down around his waist and cupped his hand under his large belly that had grown over years of inactivity and lifted his tummy. He wedged his receipt book between the flesh of his stomach and his left thigh, and allowed his over-sized abdomen to flop on top, securing it before propelling himself from the deck, into the dining room and out of sight.

Richard took a deep breath and began, "Do you know that ever since we met, I feel like I have done everything I could do to make you happy?" His words felt cumbersome.

Susan shrugged her shoulders and bobbed her head from side-to-side, not really committing to an answer.

"Well, at least I feel like I have, and maybe that's the problem. In my defense, I've never been one to hang out in bars. I've never been one to spend all of my weekends on a golf course, or on a boat, away from you. I've always wanted to spend as much time with you as possible. Maybe we have found ourselves in a situation where no matter what either of us do, we can't make the other happy."

Susan saw his attempt at reconciliation as a weakness. She longed for a man who would take charge. Her life had always been defined by the will of others; only she had yet to realize it.

Just as he was about to continue, Emma appeared from nowhere. She stood at the end of the table, grinning. "Hey kids," she said loudly, as if she wanted everyone in the restaurant to hear her. Richard looked around to see if anyone was looking their way. "Mind if I sit with you all?" she continued as she dropped her oversized body onto the bench next to Susan. She slid down so that she faced Richard squarely. Her big body pressed against Susan's petite frame pushing her against the inner wall of the booth.

"Whatcha' talkin' about?" the uninvited guest asked brashly.

Richard stared into Emma's eyes, not answering her. This was quickly becoming more uncomfortable for him, more so than the conversation he feared having with Susan alone. This woman was obviously a friend. He wanted his wife to ask her to leave.

Her obnoxious manner filled the void in Susan's psyche created by her upbringing. It seemed her esteem was acquiesced to those who subjugated it from her. Emma gladly filled the unwitting role of protectorate that Richard played until their move to Erstwhile. Smugly, Susan replied, "Richard was just explaining how devoted he has always been to me."

"That's funny," Emma said, looking at Susan. She then looked Richard in the eye and accusingly continued, "Because I hear that you've been spending all night away from home. So who is it that you've been with?"

Richard looked at Emma. Then he looked at his wife. From both, all he garnered were emotionless stares. He had no desire to get into anything with a woman he did not know and had no idea how she fit into their marriage. Once again, he was made to face someone with whom Susan shared details of his short-comings.

"Who are you?" Richard asked.

"We met on the beach … " Susan started.

"Years ago," Emma finished. "Imagine my surprise when we ran into each other again after all these years." She chuckled. "Which beach was it we met on?"

"It was … " Susan tried to pick up on the game she played, but Emma was simply too astute at manipulation.

Once again, she finished Susan's sentence. "Was it Captain's Bay?" Not waiting for an answer, she continued. "We were both as naked as the day God brought us into this world. Man! Was that beach hard to get to? But it was nice and secluded, and the *men there*." She finished in a breathy, ecstatic tone. "God, I can't imagine having more fun than we did the week we spent there. I can probably count the number of hours we were clothed on one hand." The woman turned to Susan, seemingly without stopping for a breath and continued. "Are your breasts just as perky as they were fifteen years ago?"

Richard looked at his wife. He raised his eyebrows as he waited for her answer.

"I suppose," was the only response she could muster.

Richard had more questions about the woman he married than when they arrived at the restaurant. Before he had too much time to think about it, Talitha appeared at the table.

"Hey Richard," she said.

Richard greeted her with a smile, which caused Emma to slide her forearm across the edge of the table, elbowing Susan's arm to alert her that there was something more here than met the eye. "Hello, Talitha. How are you tonight?"

"Good."

Richard held his hand, palm upward, toward Susan. "This is my wife, Susan."

Talitha extended her hand. "It's nice to meet you. My name is Talitha Keys."

Susan shook her hand. "Susan Styles," she said, without looking her in the eyes.

He looked at Emma. "I have no idea who this is," he said to Talitha.

Talitha smiled at the woman in such a manner that put her on-notice that she knew the kind of games she was known to play. "I know Emma," she responded smugly.

"Then it appears that everyone here has me at a disadvantage," Richard continued.

"Is there something that you're feeling guilty about?" Emma asked.

"Not at all," he said without hesitation.

Speaking to everyone at the table, Talitha said, "Would you just look around this restaurant. Ain't that a bitch? There's not a single black person in here except for the busboy." She looked at Richard, trying to communicate non-verbally the caution required when dealing with Emma. "Remember what I told you this afternoon?"

He nodded as Emma leaned toward Susan and whispered into her ear, "I'm sure it was no accident that they are both here tonight."

"Alright, well I thought I'd just stop by and say hello, but it appears that I've worn out my welcome already," Talitha said as she excused herself. She looked at Richard. "I hope to bump into you again one day soon."

"That would be nice," he said. No one said anything as the young girl walked away. Richard became frustrated with the situation. He looked at both women. "You know, the last time I felt like I had to be on the defensive was when I was in college. I sat across from two women who raked me over the coals for carrying on a relationship with both of them at the same time."

His wife's mouth dropped open. "Were their accusations true?"

"That I had dated them simultaneously?"

"Yes!"

"Yeah," Richard admitted, sheepishly.

"Richard!"

His honesty gave Emma cause to grin. Her contempt ran deep, but like a surfacing whale it needed air to survive, and craved to be seen and felt, in order to sustain life. She began to look around the deck, nonchalantly, then sat up straight and stretched her neck, looking toward the inside dining room, as if she was focusing on something or someone in particular.

"Susan, is that Joseph?" gasped Emma in a giddy tone.

Susan looked to where her friend pointed. All she could see were the tables and booths filled with families. There were people walking about, between the tables, to and from the restrooms. She was not sure whether the man she spoke of was real. "I think you're right," Susan said, knowing there was a purpose to her friend's question.

Emma leaned across the table toward Richard. "Joseph was the man she almost married about ten years ago." He said nothing, and she continued, "He's so tall. How tall was he, Susan, six-six?" Emma looked at Richard again. "He's a much larger man than you."

That was enough. "I tell you what; if he's not too big to fit in this booth, he can have my seat." Richard looked at his wife as he scooted toward the edge. "You're more than welcome to come home with me if you'd like." She sat perfectly still without saying a word. "Okay. I'll walk home; it's only a few miles. Do you have your keys to the Tahoe?"

She nodded.

"Goodnight," Richard said directly to his wife. He had nothing to say to Emma.

The women sat silently, watching him walk from the deck, into the dining room and past the hostess station, eventually disappearing through the front door.

Emma swung around onto the vacant bench without standing erect, sliding her body around the table. She reached across and held Susan's hands in her own. "Doesn't the strength you showed tonight make you feel better about yourself?"

"Yes," She replied. Her husband's perceived lack of desire to stay and fight for her gave more credibility to her friend's vitriol. For Susan, her new friend was filled with a substance that she found intoxicating.

Chapter Eighteen

Richard walked out of Buster's and into the parking lot. The gravel that crunched under his feet was a mixture of sand and crushed seashells. Without hesitation, he began to walk toward home. When he moved past the Tahoe he didn't stop or even look at it. Once he had made his way past all of the parked cars, the noise associated with the thriving business, tires rolling across the gravel, kids playing, and loud conversations, began to wane. Fewer people populated the beach below the roadside. He appreciated the crashing waves as he tried desperately to forget how alone he was.

The evening had flabbergasted him. What could he have done to warrant such treatment from, not only his wife, but also a perfect stranger? After all, he was not in love with a single woman from his past. He wasn't even sure he knew what love was before meeting Susan. For the first time, he felt no expectation that their marriage would last.

He placed one foot in front of the other and looked down the road at the long walk ahead as he recalled a similar trek he made in college. It too was a result of being confronted by two angry women. The only difference, in Richard's mind, was that those girls had a legitimate gripe; Susan didn't. At some point between the two he had satiated his uncontrollable desire to conquer women and began a search for something more fulfilling. Purely physical relationships proved hollow and without substance, and the women he was attracted to afforded little hope for him.

The shoulder of the road was never less than six feet across at any point. There were no streetlights and he had to concentrate on each stride to avoid stepping in a hole. He vividly recalled spending the night in the hospital when Susan broke a bone in her foot while walking along the side of the road in front of their house. He remembered how happy he was that he was there to help.

He estimated that it was only a few miles to the house. It would make for a brisk walk; something he had not done in a while. All the time he spent at the store did not afford many opportunities to be active. The most exercise he had gotten was when he stocked the shelves. His new sedentary lifestyle was counterbalanced by an overactive imagination. Richard thought about how the two of them should be working shoulder-to-shoulder. Instead, they stood at the brink of estrangement.

Lost in his thoughts, he did not hear the hum of truck tires on the highway as it approached him from behind. The approaching sound was masked by that of the waves crashing along the shoreline.

"Yeeeee-haw!" a voice exploded from the passenger's window as a pickup roared past him. Richard was startled. The tires on the right side of the truck ran off the road, kicking up sand and shells. Debris hit his pant's leg. Calmly, he moved farther from the road and onto the shoulder, then continued toward home.

His imagination continued to work in overdrive. *Aw Man, how can I be so stupid? Ralph is here, and tonight was all a setup to get them together.* Richard realized his paranoia was causing him to think illogically. *But I was the one who asked her to dinner.* Just as quickly, Susan's supposed rendezvous once again became rational. *That doesn't matter, my request fit perfectly in their plan. Should I confront her about it? No!*

She is going to have to come clean. If she doesn't want me around any longer, I'm not going to make it easy for her. He laughed at the pain. It was too familiar, and he was as inept at filling in the voids in Susan's life as he was his own.

Richard moved farther away from the road as he heard the hum of another set of truck tires approaching from behind. "Asshole!" the voice yelled from the open passenger's window.

Sweat soaked through his clothes. The armpits of his shirt were drenched. Occasionally, a drop would trickle down his spinal column and onto the waistband of his boxers. His brow was dotted with beads of perspiration that he wiped dry with his open hand every minute or so and then would sling it away. He unbuttoned his shirt to his waste. The cool gulf breeze on his wet skin felt refreshing.

Richard guessed he had covered about a mile. Whenever he walked along the beach, it was in the opposite direction of Buster's, so he had no landmarks to gauge his progress. He would readily accept a ride from a friend, but the only friend in town he had was Talitha, and surely she hadn't finished her dinner. He plodded forward.

Inevitably, his thoughts began to repeat themselves. There was no reason why Susan should question his devotion to her. Comparisons of his wife and women past were the only logical means to the answer of how it would all end. The chronology of those relationships illustrated growth for him, so he thought.

Richard had to smile as he remembered some of his early encounters with girls. He knew that as an adolescent he was incapable of emotional depth, but mistook the urges he felt as a worldliness known by no other. Those early memories centered on exploring the physical nature of being a man. The first time a woman touched him in a sexual manner was when he was fourteen. It happened in the Haunted House at the Miracle Strip Amusement Park, on a hot summer evening. The house had no outside windows and only one door to allow for the circulation of air. A layer of sweat was the only thing that afforded relief from the heat. A girl, who was close in age, grabbed his butt. When he turned to face her, she smiled coyly at him. He ignored the advance and nervously continued through the house, fearing it may happen again and not knowing how to react. The fact that there was an anonymous woman in Georgia, Alabama or Tennessee to thank for his first sexual experience brought a smile to his face.

In October of the same year he recalled feeling a bare breast for the first time. Richard and his family were attending the Fall Festival at their church. All of the teenagers had gathered together to spew forth their adolescent bravado. It wasn't clear to him, at the time, but a young lady had her eyes on him. When the conversation ended the boys decided to play football in the courtyard of the church and ignore the girls. Finally, the young woman felt the night and her opportunity slipping away. She saw the opportunity to get his attention; so she stole the football and ran into the vacant church offices. He pursued her and ran into the building behind her, stopping and watching as she ran into the bathroom at the end of the hallway. Richard walked slowly down the corridor and into the lavatory. She stood against the back wall holding the football tightly in her hands, and smiled at him. He smiled back and then moved slowly toward her. He took the ball from her hands, firmly but gently. She resisted only slightly. He dropped it onto the floor, then leaned into her, pinning her back against the wall, and kissed her with as much passion as he could muster. While they kissed, Richard slowly slid his hand under her shirt. He moved it along the soft skin of her tummy, and upward. When his hand came to her bra, he wiggled his fingers, desperately trying to negotiate his hand beneath it. Finally, he was able to slide his hand underneath without causing any major bruising. The memory was vivid of how soft her flesh was. He recalled being afraid to touch her nipple.

His mind then progressed to his seventeenth birthday, as always, it was the middle of summer and steamy hot. Midnight approached and the magic that surrounded the anniversary of his physical entry into the world waned. Richard swam in the pool behind his girlfriend's house. The warm summer breeze did not offer much relief from the heat, even at such a late hour. The water in the pool was cool and refreshing.

The house had been built on a hill, well above the bay that oscillated below them. There was a dock and a boathouse at the foot of the mound that extended into the water fifty feet. A thirty-two foot Pursuit fishing boat dangled from the boatlift and swayed slightly in the breeze, causing the steel cables to creek. There was a full moon without a cloud in the sky to obstruct it. Beams of light danced across the gentle water as Richard and Maria swam. Each acted as if they were the only one in the pool; ignoring the other, but both had the same desires stimulating their libidos.

When his lust for her overcame him, he stopped swimming and positioned himself in the shallow end of the pool, with his back against its side. He watched as Maria swam. Her head occasionally broke the surface of the water. Each time she looked at him, and then disappeared. He watched, patiently, as this sport went on for several minutes. She emerged at the deep end of the pool, as far away from him as she could possibly be and remain in the pool. It worried him that she hadn't moved closer. Staring directly into his eyes she reached up and grabbed the diving board by placing her hands on either side and hung there. Neither knew the words to express what they wanted or how they felt. She then pulled herself up. When her body rose out of the water, she dropped her head so that it didn't hit the board. Richard did not watch this. He focused on her breasts as they appeared from beneath the water. No longer being buoyed, they fell into the cups of her bathing suit, stretching the string around her neck to its tautest. Urges raged inside him as he drank in the sights of his girlfriend's nubile body.

Acting on impulse she let go of the diving board, plunged into the water and stayed below for several seconds. Richard looked across the surface, waiting for her to emerge. Then he saw her shadowy form in the water approaching him. It danced back-and-forth with the action of the waves. She emerged in front of him and stood, slowly sliding her body against his. He felt her breasts as they brushed along his torso. The couple embraced as they stood in the shallows. She stood on her tiptoes and reached to kiss him. He slouched to kiss her. Neither cared how uncomfortable their posture was. They were exactly where they wanted to be.

Richard fidgeted as he wondered what to do with his hands. At one point he interlaced his fingers behind her back. At yet another, he placed his hands on her hips. After a few moments he pressed his hands against her back and pulled her body into his. When he loosened the embrace she backed away and dropped beneath the water. Her head remained exposed as she affixed her eyes with his. She drifted away a few feet and stopped. He had no idea what to do next, neither did Maria. The well-developed muscles in his back caused his arms to hang away from his body. His shoulders were broad and his back plunged into his narrow waistline. Maria could not see his equally muscular legs, but her imagination created the vision of their limbs fervently intertwined.

She moved slowly back toward him and he dropped his body into the water leveling their fixated eyes. He made up his mind to make a move, but had no idea what it was he should do to please her. She was just as unsure.

They embraced a second time and kissed. Regardless of his indecision, Richard's courage could not be stopped. They continued to embrace and kiss as he slid his hands up her back to where her bathing suit top was tied. Fumbling with the multitude of strings, he could not readily discern how to release it. She remained patient with him.

He struggled desperately to maintain a quality kiss while figuring out how to untie her bikini. For an instant he wondered if she had double knotted the strings. Finally, he found which string to pull so that it fell apart.

Feeling the tension dissolve from her top piqued his anxiety to view the treasure he had uncovered. He did not want to seem too eager, so he maintained the kiss for a second longer. When he tried to back away he realized that he was pinned against the wall of the pool, and Maria's modesty caused her to secure the embrace. At first, Richard did not appreciate her moving closer, until he realized her bare breasts were pressing against his chest.

When he could stand the suspense no longer he placed a hand on each of her shoulders and pushed her away. Instinct took over and she covered her chest with her hands. Her top was still knotted behind her neck, and it floated on the surface of the water directly in Richard's line of sight. Maria lifted it over her head and threw it onto the pool deck, still covering herself with one arm. The wet fabric stuck to the concrete behind his head as she returned both arms to their original position. When Richard finally coaxed Maria, without words, to remove her hands, he was disappointed because the undulating waves distorted his perception. She then lifted her legs beneath her, treading water while removing her bathing suit bottom. His heart pounded inside his chest. He knew what to do, but not really *how* to go about doing it. She tossed the bathing suit next to her top.

Richard waited, not knowing if he should allow her to remove his bathing suit. Once again, she moved closer. He looked at the surface of the water intently, wishing for a clear vision of her nude body.

Maria approached him, then reached out and gently tugged on the waste band of his swim trunks. She wanted them off and she wanted him to do it. He obliged.

The adolescent couple held each other closely. The dark, warm water was like an amniotic fluid, protecting them, keeping them from facing complete nudity at such a tender age. Holding her naked body was the most wonderful feeling this seventeen year-old ever imagined.

Richard was so caught up in the memory of his first sexual experience that he passed his house without recognizing it. He walked to the one next door before realizing what he had done. When he stepped onto his porch he removed the keys from his pocket and opened the door. The emptiness of the house reminded him of the void in his soul that was once occupied by Susan. She had been everything to him. Ralph had stolen his lover and Emma his friend. Maria was the first woman he had ever told he loved. The irony was that he still had no idea what it was a woman needed from a man. That realization crushed his fragile soul. His breaths became shallow and quick as the desperate reality that he may never find someone so special began to take hold.

Chapter Nineteen

Susan was in no mood to eat. She could never remember a time when Richard was so willing to simply walk out on her. It never happened before, although she found herself wishing it had. If he expected her to blindly follow him he had a lot to learn. Men had always doted over her and Richard's expectation of a relationship was too much for her to give. Maybe not caring was the key to happiness.

She sat silently watching Emma devour her Captain's Platter. The grease from the fried seafood coated her friend's lips. Little pieces of batter were stuck to her chin, and had fallen onto her blouse. Susan drank from her gin-and-tonic while witnessing the annihilation. Emma grabbed a piece of Grouper with her fingers and plunged it into a small silver cup of tartar sauce. Her fingers were not spared the mess. She lifted the fish from the paste and inserted it along with her hand into her mouth. After grinding the greasy mass into a compact ball she pushed it with her tongue into her cheek. She then inserted each finger, individually, into her mouth, sucking off the excess pap.

That was enough. Susan could no longer face her friend as she ate. She slid to the inside of the booth, leaned her back against the wall and propped her feet up on the bench. She watched the activity in the restaurant as she continued to sip her drink. Servers in khaki shorts and Hawaiian-styled shirts continually negotiated the maze of tables, chairs and tourists that had been baked by the sun. Susan found herself examining the faces of all the women in the restaurant.

At the table directly across from her was a woman laughing, genuinely and hysterically as she played a game with her kids. The sound of the children laughing was refreshing. The woman had on a vibrant sundress with big yellow sunflowers covering it. Her skin was tan, which contrasted with her sun-bleached white hair. There was a boy and a girl that looked to be ten and twelve years old, Susan guessed. The daughter appeared to be instructing everyone about the rules of the game. Susan could not tell what the contest was. They were using a crayon to write on her paper place mat and she could only assume that it was tick-tack-toe, or hangman. There was also a baby girl in a high chair. Noticeably absent was the father. *He must still be out on the boat fishing with all the other men*, Susan thought to herself. The tone in her psyche was one of anger.

Her attention shifted to a couple at the table adjacent to the game-playing family. It was a couple that appeared to be in their mid-thirties. There were no children with them. The woman sat perfectly straight in her chair with her left arm lying across her stomach. Her right elbow rested on her wrist. In her hand was a glass of white wine. She held it high, next to her face. The Rolex on her right wrist hung loosely about her arm. They both were dressed in designer clothes that were neatly pressed, looking as though they had stepped from the pages of a catalogue. The man wore an equally expensive watch. It was big, chunky, and silver with a band of gold that wrapped around the middle of the bracelet. He had a solid athletic build. His forearms rested on the edge of the table and his hands were clasped. There was no conversation between them. He avoided his wife by looking around the room. She glared at him.

I wonder what this guy's done?, Susan asked herself. She noticed that the woman had her legs crossed beneath the table with her right one on top. Nervously, she swayed it back-and-forth. The motion was constant and shook her body, rhythmically, along with the wine in her glass. Her lips were pursed tightly and her eyes squinted as she stared across the table at her husband. Having been ignored long enough, the woman adjusted the swing of her leg and kicked her husband squarely on the shin. Startled, he jumped in his seat. He looked questioningly across the table at her. Had she done that on purpose? He said nothing, and neither did she.

"Asshole," Susan muttered.

"What's that?" Emma asked, briefly looking up from her plate.

Susan looked toward her friend. All that remained on her plate were some French fries and two hush puppies. Emma reached over and picked up the plastic bottle of ketchup at the end of the table next to the wall. She flipped the lid open, turned the spout downward and squeezed as hard as she could. Flatulently, ketchup poured onto the plate. She waved the bottle above her food, covering almost every fry and both hush puppies. Susan watched incredulously as she ravenously shoved ketchup soaked French fries into her mouth. She could not believe that after eating a plate full of fish, crabs, oysters and shrimp, Emma could still be that hungry. She showed no signs of slowing.

Susan's attention was drawn away from Emma as Tom approached the table.

"Can I get you another drink?" he asked her.

Susan looked at Emma and asked, "Are you planning on ordering dessert?"

"Damn right," she replied through a mouthful of fries.

She looked at Tom and tried to be overly polite in her response to make up for the lack of couth shown by her friend. "Yes, *thank you*, Tom." She shook her empty glass, listening to the sound the ice made. When there was one fry remaining, Emma picked it up and swabbed it through the last bit of ketchup. Only the hushpuppies had been spared, until she dutifully picked them up and placed them in the middle of the plate, side-by-side.

"I've got a cousin in Jacksonville that has a kid, a little boy. They went to a restaurant one night and when he was asked what he wanted to eat, he said, 'dog balls.' It took them a while to figure out he was talking about hush puppies."

Susan laughed sincerely. "That's cute."

Without any sign of jest, Emma continued as if her segue was natural. "I saw how you ran your finger along your gums this afternoon. It doesn't shock me that you're a user."

"But I'm not. I haven't done that since I was twenty-one."

"Let's not fool ourselves, Susan. Once a user, always a user."

Susan looked away trying hard to ignore the fact that she had to always consider herself an addict in order to avoid falling back into behavior that had almost taken her life. She noticed a handsome man walking across the dining room. He had a slim build and was wearing a green smock. *He is obviously a doctor*, Susan thought. She allowed her imagination to create the story of his life. *He just came from the Emergency Room at the hospital, where he had delivered twins to a poor*

*family of farmers that lived nearby. Or maybe he had
just helped the victims of some unfortunate accident.
Regardless, he had just come from doing something
worthwhile.*

Susan continued to watch as he made his way
closer to where she sat with her friend. The fantasy she
created advanced. She imagined him walking toward
her and sitting down beside her. Instead, he walked directly to the woman in the sunflower dress. Before sitting down, he gave his wife a soft, caring kiss. Susan
missed that. The two oldest children yelled, in a happy
tone and in unison, "Daddy!" The baby excitedly
slapped her hands on the tray attached to her chair.

"I think I'll have some Key Lime pie," Emma
announced as she shoved the empty plate away from
her and toward the edge of the table.

At that moment, Tom approached the table.
There was a small tray attached to the armrest of his
chair, on which Susan's drink sat. He stopped, removed
the drink and placed it in front of her. "Can I get you
ladies anything for dessert?"

"Key Lime pie," Emma said without congenial-
ity.

Tom looked at Susan. "Maybe a cup of coffee,"
she said. He wrote the ladies' order on their check and
rolled away without a word. Emma shooed him away
with her hand once his back was turned.

When she leaned across the table it shifted underneath, frightening her. She grabbed its edge to secure
it. After steadying the table, she continued, whispering,
"Girl, if you want to feel like a kid again, all you have
to do is say the word. I can get you anything you need
to lift your spirits."

She knew what a bump of cocaine could do for her and she craved that experience. Many years had passed since her last flirtation with the drug, but no matter how hard she tried to avoid it she found herself justifying the need to experience a high like that, again. Sobriety had not provided her the life that she wanted. Many friends were lost due to her addiction, as were several when she broke herself from its grip. Forbidden fantasies had always breached her consciousness. They were born of her desires and not influenced by anyone else. Modesty prevented her from acting upon them, but she thought about them frequently. The yearning was to be caressed all over by many men. It was nothing more than the desire to capture the feeling of complete ecstasy; a sensation that she had only been able to acquire through the use of drugs. So many years ago she had rationalized it as the lesser of two evils.

Tom rolled back to the table and jostled her from her fantasy world. On his tray was Emma's pie. He removed it and came just short of tossing it onto the table in front of her. The plate barely slid to a stop before Emma had a fork in her hand. She plunged it into the pie and took an oversized bite. "Shit, that's good!" She said with her mouth full, and without offering any to her friend. Her gluttony was insatiable.

Remorse came over Susan as she regretted all of the negative thoughts she had about her husband. Several times during their marriage she had been overcome with a sense of déjà vu whenever Richard swept her into his arms. The recollection was of a medieval knight who rescued a damsel in the bowels of a dark and dank castle. She remembered it being very cold. His embrace was warm and safe. Susan never told him about the feeling because she feared he would think it was silly.

An overwhelming dread rattled her soul as she became anxious at the prospect of not experiencing that feeling for another millennium. She ached to be held like that, again. It was that vision and the certainty it instilled in her that Richard would provide the strength she needed to be true to herself that was the reason she married him. She was no longer sure that he was the right man for her. Courtney, Ralph and a good many others had given Susan experiences that broadened her horizons. She could not distinguish between the carefree thrills of youth and the strength of a committed relationship, because she had never been given the opportunity to grow her self-image as a child. It was unfortunate that she was blessed with great beauty. No one ever looked past it or gave her the opportunity to display the vast intellect that was bestowed upon her. Whenever anyone engaged Susan they quickly found themselves mesmerized by the hypnotic pleasure of gazing at her. Invariably, that inducement was followed by the desire to make one's self a part of her life, no matter the consequences. Affairs with such superficial underpinnings never lasted. The result was that she found herself lost and looking for direction wherever she could find it. That left her vulnerable to the whims of others.

Chapter Twenty

Richard sat in his partially reclined chair. The soles of his feet were on the edge of the footrest, and a Hemingway novel lay in his lap. He picked up the remote control for the television, pushed the power button and mindlessly searched the channels, driven more by nerves than a desire to watch anything. It was nine forty-five and he had no idea what time he should expect Susan to come home. He knew that he could have done a much better job with his exit, but did not appreciate being placed on the defensive with so little help from his wife. And answer for what? That baffled him the most. Why did his wife feel that it was necessary to enlist the aid of a friend? He had always encouraged her to feel free to say anything she needed to him. That would be how he approached the conversation when she got home; that she was free to say anything. The only question he had of her was whether their future would be spent together or apart. Uncertainty drove him mad.

Richard recalled the night on the beach when his wife was the aggressor. The thought of it brought a smile to his face. He enjoyed feeling wanted and needed. Watching her nude body sway gently back-and-forth in the dim light of the bonfire was the most sensual expression of her need for him that she had ever displayed. It wasn't as though they had no sex life. It was wonderful and caring, gentle, yet explosive. It made him feel special. He knew that she had been with other men in her life. That night on the beach made him feel like she was telling him he was the most special person she had ever known and *wanted* to show him. Feeling as though he was third behind Ralph and Emma left him with a sense that there was no purpose to his life.

Sex with other women paled in comparison to his experience with Susan. He always attributed that to the emotional bond that resulted from having a pure lover and a true friend. When they made love it was like they were one, with a single heartbeat. His mind darted about, searching for a way to describe what they had together that would capture the expression of love between them. *Why do I need to describe it? I know what it's like.* Then it came to him, *I need to let Susan know how special I think it is.* The thoughts that came to mind were of how physically beautiful she was. He needed her to know the emotional, spiritual attachment he felt. The best he could do would be to tell her that she is the only woman he'd ever known that he knew he could not live without. That was too cliché. She was special and deserved more. Richard struggled to come up with the words and he began to resent having to do so. *She should know how I feel about her. Why do I have to tell her? My actions show her every day. I made a vow to her when we got married.* The unspoken words sounded ridiculous to him. *I have to tell her, but how?*

Hours passed while Richard sat and thought about how to communicate to his wife what she meant to him and to avoid anything else going wrong in their marriage. It frustrated him that the words did not readily come to mind. He sat staring at the television with the open book in his lap. Nervously, he looked at his watch, wondering where she could be.

He stood and walked over to the bar-cart. There were four highball glasses turned upside down on its top. He picked one up and placed it right-side-up in the exact spot from where he removed it, then picked up his favorite whiskey, opened the bottle and poured until the glass was half full. When he screwed the top back on the bottle and placed it back where it belonged he noticed a smudge on the mirrored glass top. It looked like the tip of a finger had been dragged across it. Susan had always taken a great deal of pride that their house remained spotless. He shrugged it off and went into the kitchen to fill his glass with ice and Diet Coke.

Richard returned to his chair and placed the highball glass on his right thigh. He sipped the drink occasionally, until he had completed it. When he finished the second, he fixed another, and then another. Each time he got out of his chair he checked his watch. The later it became, the more his worry turned into anger. At one point he walked across the living room, down the hall and into their bedroom. He switched on the light to see if Susan had somehow snuck past him, maybe when he had gone to the bathroom. She was not there.

Richard walked to the back of the house. He peered through the window onto the beach. Maybe she had too much to drink and decided to walk home from Buster's. It was past midnight, and he saw no one. He was blinded by the fury that raged within him, to the point of not understanding the strain that his own actions placed on their relationship. After ten minutes he walked back into the living room and stood in the middle of the floor. He lifted the highball glass to his mouth, tilted his head back and finished it. The ice was cold against his upper lip. He then moved back over to the bar-cart, placed his glass in the spot from where he had removed it earlier that night. "I'm not sleeping in the same room with that bitch," he said aloud as he walked to the guest bedroom. He still believed she would be coming home. It was best that they not see each other until they had a chance to calm down. The alcohol that Richard consumed exposed his rawest emotions. He thought about a time when he was living with a young girl who swore she was committed to him, but would stay out until all hours of the night with her *friends*. One night she came home at four-thirty in the morning. He was so angry with her that he could visualize himself choking her to death. The memory was vivid, and Richard knew he did not need to confront Susan tonight.

He opened the door to the guest bedroom, reached in and turned on the light. His legs wobbled as he walked to the end of the bed, sat down and began to remove his shoes. Richard stood and removed his clothes, tossing them onto a chair in the corner. He walked to the head of the bed and noticed something that he had never seen before; a photograph on the nightstand. He picked it up and looked at it. It was Susan. She had a smile on her face like he had not seen in a long while. His wife stood next to a man, atop a picturesque mountain. Richard turned the picture over and looked at the back. He saw where the corrugated paperboard that held the photograph firmly in the frame had been torn away. In the center of the tattered patch was a round indentation that was the same size and shape as a ring. He traced the outline of the band gently with his finger, trying to ignore the pounding in his chest.

He placed the picture back on the nightstand. His wife's feelings for other men were obviously stronger than their relationship. He lay down, crossed his hands over his chest as he stared up at the ceiling.

Death became a welcome alternative. The alarm clock on the bedside table projected the time-of-day onto the ceiling above his head. It read, *1:34 A.M.* Richard watched every minute of his life pass by that night.

Chapter Twenty-One

Susan drove the Tahoe slowly behind her friend's Volkswagen Beetle. They pulled into the driveway of her stepmother's house. Emma drove under the carport awning and parked next to the owner's car. Susan applied the brakes gently and the truck rolled to a stop just shy of the bumper of the car in front of her. The driveway was short and she feared the rear of her vehicle might be protruding into the street.

Emma opened her door. The carport was too small to allow it to fully release. The edge met the side of the Toyota Land Cruiser parked next to it. Susan watched through the windshield as her friend squeezed her large frame through the narrow opening. Her sizeable breasts flattened against the window as she wriggled loose. Once free, she looked at Susan and smiled as she grabbed her boobs and rubbed away the pain.

Susan rolled down her window. "Can you see if the back of the car is sticking into the highway?" she called out.

Without a word, Emma walked past the open window and to the rear of the truck. She examined the situation and came back to the open window. "You're fine. Come on in."

Before turning off the ignition, she rolled up the window; then removed the keys and dropped them into her purse. In one motion she pulled the door handle and pushed with her forearm. Her legs wobbled as she slid off the high seat and landed on the driveway. The alcohol she consumed at Buster's eliminated any trace of the dignity that had always defined her. She tugged on the front of her pant legs to straighten them as she reached into the truck and removed her purse. After closing the door she followed her friend up the driveway, through the carport and into the house, clutching her Dooney and Burke purse at her side.

Emma opened the door and walked in. Susan followed. The two made their way through the kitchen and onto a small porch. At one end sat Emma's stepmother, Claire. At the other was a television. The glow from the screen provided the only light in the room.

Susan followed her friend to a sofa situated against a concrete block wall that divided the porch and kitchen. The opposite wall was replete with jalousie windows, all of which were open, allowing the refreshing evening breeze to circulate throughout the house. An old episode of The Avengers on BBC America blared throughout the porch. Claire sat silently, reclined in her favorite chair, staring at the show. Behind her were bookshelves that extended from floor to ceiling. There were no knick-knacks, only volumes of classic literature. She did not bother to welcome her stepdaughter home. Susan sensed tension between the two the moment they entered the room. Neither made an effort to say a single word to the other. Emma stood and faced Susan. "I'm going to get a bottle of wine. Would you like anything to drink?"

"Wine is good."

"Red, white, or rose?"

"Whatever you're having is fine."

Emma disappeared into the kitchen. Susan sat silently, not sure whether she should introduce herself. She decided the better part of decorum dictated she do so. Looking at the elder woman, she said, "My name is Susan."

The woman sat up straight in her chair, stood and walked to her. "I'm Claire," she said as she extended her hand. The woman stood so closely that she was unable to stand to offer a proper greeting.

When Emma re-entered the room, the adversaries exchanged a glare. Claire turned and walked back to her chair. Ignoring the old woman, Emma held up a bottle of chardonnay. Susan preferred red wine, but did not object.

"You didn't offer *me* a glass of wine," Claire said, without removing her stare from the television.

Looking at Susan, with her back to her stepmother, Emma rolled her eyes. "Would you like a glass of wine, Claire?" She asked, loudly, without looking.

"Why, yes I would. And, I already have a glass." She picked it up from a small table next to her chair and held it up.

Emma stood and walked toward her stepmother. After pouring the wine, she made her way back and held up the glasses she carried by their stems. Susan took one and held it to be filled. As she poured the wine it nearly eclipsed its rim. She was no less indulgent when she poured her own. "Silly little me," Emma said daintily, just before slurping, and gulping nearly a third of the contents of her glass.

Susan attempted to open dialogue with Claire. "I see you're watching The Avengers."

Emma, still with her back to Claire, looked harshly at her friend and whispered, "Now you've done it. She'll drone on incessantly for hours."

Susan ignored Emma's warning and looked toward Claire, awaiting a response.

"I first saw the Avengers in 1965. My husband and I were in London on vacation. After J.F.K.'s assassination, we told ourselves we would not allow life to pass us by. We didn't. I went all over the world with him, Italy, Sweden, Africa."

"It sounded like you had a wonderful time together. What happened?"

"He died."

"I'm sorry to hear that," Susan said.

"It's okay. We did a lot of the things we wanted to do before he passed away, so I really don't have any regrets."

Before Susan could respond, Emma interjected, "Not like dad, huh?"

Claire ignored her stepdaughter and continued. "I think Diana Rigg is my favorite Mrs. Peel. Although I think Honor Blackman was the prettiest, and well, she *was* a Bond girl after all. I like the shows that were shot live, too. They just have a nostalgic feel to them. Of course, all the live shows were Honor Blackman shows." It was much more information than Susan wanted. She understood Emma's concern that Claire would dominate the conversation. Seemingly without taking a breath, she kept talking without transitioning between stories. "You know I had to have my middle toe removed a couple of years ago." Claire pointed to her foot. Susan could tell that her feet were bare, but there was not enough light in the room to count toes. "I remember being horrified when the doctor told me I would have to have a toe removed. I worried that I wouldn't be able to walk properly. I worried how it would look with a big gap between my toes. But you know, damned if my other toes didn't squeeze together. You can barely tell."

"That's it," Emma said as she stood. "Susan and I are going back to my room to talk."

Emma stood and grabbed the bottle of wine around the neck in the manner a drunken sailor would. Susan dutifully followed. Fixated on Claire's feet as she walked past, she could not see the missing digit. She moved slowly trying to enhance her vision in the dimly lit room by squinting. Suddenly, a daylight scene on television provided the luminosity for her to see; there on Claire's left foot, only four toes. Afraid of the message that the look on her face might convey, she quickly looked at Emma's back and continued to follow her.

When they got to her room, Emma fumbled with the handle because of the bottle of wine in her hand. It banged against the door and the frame as she struggled. Susan stepped in, and with her free hand opened the door. The room was dark. She felt the wall inside the door, searching for the light switch. It took her a few seconds, but she finally found it. The glare was almost unbearable. Everything in the room was bright pink. Susan walked in and stepped aside to allow Emma to lead the way. She did, and walked to the bed and plopped her large frame on the mattress. Susan sat gently at its foot, looking around the room in awe. There had to be hundreds of brightly colored statuettes of fairies, unicorns and other characters, some iconic, others obscure. The explosion of color hurt her eyes. There was nothing about the room that conveyed stability. The furniture was large and gave the room a bulky feel. It appeared to Susan that her friend had moved everything she ever owned into this one room.

Emma sat nodding her head so vigorously that it shook her body and the bed. "Don't you love it?"

Susan hated lying. She responded with a hesitant, "*Yeah.*"

"I knew you'd love it. I could tell that about you, that you and I are a lot alike." Emma pointed in Claire's direction. "That old bitch wouldn't let me decorate the house. So, I had to do it in here. Don't you think it's just so … *petite* and … *pretty*?"

"Those are the exact words I would use." Susan took a large sip of wine, trying to drown the lie. She could feel the gin from dinner rejecting the wine. She thought better of consuming more, but took a second sip, anyway.

Emma stood and walked over to a small compact disc player. She opened a large case that lay on the dresser, removed a CD and placed it in the player. When the music began Susan recognized the band. It was Duran-Duran.

"They're the best, don't you think?" Emma asked, as she pointed to the wall behind Susan.

She turned to see a twenty-year-old poster of the musical group whose sounds filled the bedroom. "Yeah, they're pretty good."

Emma walked back to the spot on the bed where she had been seated and plopped down, again. Susan held her glass away from her body to avoid spilling any wine as the undulating mattress shook her. Before the shaking stopped, her rotund friend stood and walked to the shelves against the wall. She reached between two rock-star bobble-heads and retrieved a Magic Eight ball that had been placed obscurely near the back.

"Are you going to inquire about my future?" Susan asked.

Her stout friend smiled. "No. This eight ball is about the here and now." Once she sat down, again, she held the globe firmly in her lap and twisted off the flat cap on its bottom. Susan worried that she would spill the blue water inside all over her bed and winced at the jerking motion she made while wrestling with it. She was surprised when she saw Emma turn it over after removing the cover. A tiny spoon fell onto the bed and then the floor. The hostess ignored it and continued to dig at the contents by inserting her chubby fingers into the hole. Finally, she held what she sought by pinching it between her digits. Slowly, she tugged until it was free. What Susan saw startled her. In her friend's hand was a tiny zip-lock baggy filled with cocaine; so much that it took the shape of a pillow. Susan's heart raced as the possibilities filled her mind. She knew that drug use had never been recreational for her, but surely she could handle it better, given her maturity.

Emma leaned over and picked the spoon up off the floor. She then held the contents of both her hands up toward her friend. Without a word Susan took them. With great anticipation she pulled apart the zipper and plunged the utensil into the baggy. Shaking it, she drew back a measured amount, which she immediately held to her right nostril and inhaled robustly. After doing the same for the left she held out the bag and spoon and shook them so that her friend would take them quickly, then she rubbed both sides of her nose as hard as she could to take away the sting. The feeling of invincibility took over. She fell back onto the bed and stared at the ceiling. A smile grew on her face as she became comfortable with herself again. All feelings of inadequacy left her consciousness. Anything that caused her angst became unworthy of thought. The only desire that remained was to maintain the indomitable person that coursed through her veins at that moment.

Chapter Twenty-Two

Six A.M. came slowly as Richard watched the clock tick away every minute of his fitful night's rest. Several customers had come to expect him to be at the store so they could do their shopping before work. There were enough patrons who preferred this routine that it was worth losing a little sleep. He knew that the relationships with his customers had to remain strong if the store was to survive. The discipline to do whatever it took in order to succeed had been instilled in him years earlier, no matter the sacrifice.

Throughout the morning a steady stream of customers, mostly ladies, approached the counter intermittently for Richard to ring-up their purchases. Not until then did he realize that there were not a lot of reasons for men to come into his store. He thought about stocking fishing supplies, or rifle cartridges in hopes of attracting male patrons. Hanging out with the guys was something he had not done since meeting Susan. The prospect of making new friends was palatable and it helped to distract him from the failure that was once a successful marriage.

When the number of people in the store dwindled, Richard took the opportunity to hurry from behind the counter to clean the store. Empty spaces on the shelves were made to look full by moving jars and bottles to the front, creating the facade of abundance. Once finished, Richard hurried behind the counter and retrieved a broom and dustpan. He frantically cleaned the mess left by the many shoppers who tracked in leaves and dirt. After a few minutes, the vigorous back-

and-forth action of the broom began to slow. Lack of sleep sapped him of his energy and he closed his eyes trying to briefly re-charge. His legs wobbled as he swayed from side to side. Slowly, he moved behind the counter and sat down heavily on his stool. The irony of how frantic his life had become since moving to Erstwhile was not lost on him. Their dream was to spend more time together. Reality dictated their time was best spent apart.

Richard placed his elbow on the counter in front of him. He formed a loose fist with his hand and propped his cheek against it. A surreal fog clouded his mind. His breathing was deep and labored and he knew he could fall asleep with ease. It became harder for him to hold his eyes open. Just as he closed them and drifted away from consciousness the bell above the door rang. He looked up to see his wife walking through the store. There was no longer a warm feeling whenever he saw her. She had become a pariah to him.

Susan did not look at her husband. She walked in wearing the same clothes she had on the night before. He watched as she made her way down the middle aisle, past one of the two remaining customers and into the back room, without a word to anyone. She came to tell her husband that she realized moving to Erstwhile had caused her to lose her advantage … her identity. An equally sleepless night had been spent by her and Emma examining Susan's feelings and their genesis. The conclusion drawn by the women was that there was no way she could make her life fit into the voids created by his past. Cocaine blinded them to any reflection upon themselves.

He wondered where she had been all night. Richard's heart began to beat dynamically, providing the much-needed life-blood to his body and mind. His synapses fired rapidly stimulating every neuron that was woven into the fabric of his psyche. The pictures that his thoughts created were tainted by every failed experience during his life. He could no longer appreciate the things about her that he loved. Before Richard could follow her into the back room, an elderly woman approached the counter. She placed her basket of goods in front of him and smiled sheepishly. "Did you find everything you need?" he asked, politely.

"Yes, but there is one thing that my husband loves that I haven't been able to find in here or at the I.G.A.," the woman said.

"What's that?" Richard asked, as he began to remove the items from her basket.

"Spanish Bar Cake." The woman held her hands forming a long rectangle, and began to explain. "It's a rectangular cake with raisins and white icing."

Richard smiled. "I know exactly what you're talking about. My grandmother always kept one around for my grandfather. I like them, too." He paused. "I'll see if I can find out who makes them and stock it just for you." The woman's groceries barely filled the canvas bag she brought with her. "Do you want me to carry that to the car for you?"

The woman grabbed the bag by its handles and lifted it off the counter. "No thank you, young man. I need the exercise." Her face wrinkled from the exertion of her sincere smile.

Richard watched her walk out of the store and onto the sidewalk. He looked for signs that she may need help. While still watching he heard what he thought was the sound of Susan's electric toothbrush coming from the storeroom. *She must have gone by the house before coming to the store. Surely, I would have noticed if she had left it in the storeroom. There was only a sink and a toilet in the back and I don't recall seeing it. She must have brought it in her purse.* He stopped and then asked himself, *why do I care?* He began to walk toward the storeroom when he heard a female voice call his name. "Richard!"

He stopped and turned to face Talitha. "Shouldn't you be at work?" he asked, nervously. Having his wife and a woman he was attracted to in the same building made him nervous.

"I don't have to be there until eight o'clock."

Richard looked at his watch. It was seven-thirty five. "Well, come sit down," he said as he once again stepped behind the counter. He removed the stool from behind the desk and placed it in front so that she had somewhere to sit. He moved behind the counter and rested his forearms along its edge, leaning toward her. She leaned toward him resting her arms in the same manner. They were face-to-face. Being so close to this beautiful, young woman caused him to immediately forget that his wife was in the next room. He admired her smooth, fresh skin that was void of imperfection.

The young girl had stopped by for the sole reason of saying hello to a friend. Richard craved something more and she embodied all that he desired. An uncomfortable silence filled the small space between them. He marveled at the youthfulness in her face. Her jaw-line was sharp, eyes were bright, and smile was just as he remembered it the first day they met. His heart did not beat faster, but harder, with more conviction than it had in a while.

"I thought about you all night, last night," Talitha said, quietly.

"Me?" Her confession surprised Richard. "*Why me?*"

Talitha broke the eye contact between the two and looked around the room, searching her mind for the right words. "I think it's because my heart goes out to you."

Richard wondered what she meant, but was afraid to ask.

Conscious of the importance of saying the right thing, she tried to clarify her statement. "I just know that you are a good person, and deserve better."

Richard didn't hear what she said. He was too busy imagining how soft her lips would feel to a kiss. They glistened in what little light the early morning sun could push through the front window of the store. He watched them as they formed the words that came from her mouth. The clarity in her eyes and their soft brown color conveyed warmth. There had been times during his life when he was alone, but having, and then losing Susan created a greater void than he had ever known. The desire to fill that chasm overpowered him.

At that moment, Susan emerged from the back room holding an empty bottle of Maker's Mark. She witnessed the energy between the couple at the front of the store. They were so wrapped up in each other that neither one saw her. She turned and walked back into the storeroom. The bell over the door rang as someone entered the shop. Richard stood straight and backed away from Talitha. When he knew that there was someone in the room with them, guilt was an uninvited guest. Talitha coolly and slowly leaned back on the stool, before sitting straight without facing whoever had entered the room.

Richard did not recognize the man who interrupted his fantasy. He wore jeans and a dark gray shirt with a name-patch sewn onto the left chest. On the opposite side was a logo from the Erstwhile Plumbing, Co. It was designed with a spigot and a drop of water falling from it. Talitha still did not turn around. She waited for the man to approach the counter. Richard smiled at him. "How are you today, sir?"

"If I were doin' any better they'd declare me a controlled substance," the man said.

Richard furrowed his brow as he looked at the man curiously, feeling a twinge of deja vu. "What can I help you with?"

The man stopped in front of the counter, placed both hands on its edge and leaned forward in order to look back toward Talitha. When he came into her periphery, she turned and looked at him. He smiled at her, exposing his rotting teeth. The expression she returned gleamed in comparison. "I didn't mean to interrupt anything," the man said, accusingly as he looked back-and-forth between she and Richard.

"You're not," Talitha said. Her cool demeanor had been developed over the years of living in an oppressive society. "I was just leaving." She turned to Richard and said, "I just wanted to let you know that your great aunt *was* a member of the D.A.R. That makes you eligible, not for the D.A.R., of course, but for the S.A.R. The nearest chapter is in Tallahassee. You'd have to drive a couple hours to go to meetings."

"I appreciate that bit of information." Richard had no idea what she was talking about, but tried to be cool about whatever message she tried to send.

Talitha stood and began to walk out of the store.

"Have a good day," Richard said, as he waved to her.

"*Have a good day?*" The man asked him, incredulously. "You've got a lot to learn." His demeanor changed instantly from confrontational to congenial. "You ever do any hunting?"

Richard was scared by the curious change in the man's tone. "No, but I used to fish a lot with my grandfather."

"Me and some of the other boys want you to come deer hunting on Saturday with us."

"I don't own a gun."

"I've got one you can use. Besides, the way things are going around here, our way of life is being threatened."

"I'm not sure what you mean," Richard said.

"Ever since the mill closed, the paper company has been selling all of the land they used to grow pine trees. It won't be long before they've sold all our hunting land right out from under us."

"That's too bad."

"I'll pick you up at your house at four o'clock in the morning on Saturday."

So much for sleeping in, Richard thought. "Do you need directions?" he asked.

"No. I know where you live."

His response made Richard even more uncomfortable. "I'll see you at four o'clock on Saturday," he said, as he looked at the man's name patch, "Gaylord."

The man looked down at his chest. "I'm sorry. I forgot to introduce myself." He extended his hand. "I'm Gaylord Alsobrook."

Richard shook the man's hand. "Richard Styles."

"Well, I gotta get outta here. I've got calls to make," the man said, as he walked out of the store.

"Have a good day," Richard gave his usual send-off. Gaylord passed by the front window and the two men exchanged emotionally measured waves.

Chapter Twenty-Three

Richard did not remember crossing the street, or even opening the door to Merlin's. Susan had left the store not long after arriving, without saying a word. He suddenly became aware that he was standing inside the door to the bar. A bit dazed he looked around and saw that there were more people there than usual. There were the regulars; Jake, Merlin and the two old guys in the booth near the back. As always, there was a woman at the end of the bar, but it wasn't Sara. There was something familiar about her, though.

After assessing the situation, he walked over and out of habit took his usual seat next to Jake. Before he sat down, Merlin made a drink and placed it in front of him without a word.

Richard ignored those around him. He desired the alcohol not the fellowship. Haphazard and illogical thoughts darted in and out of his mind. He finished his drink, placed the empty glass on the bar and pointed to it. Merlin quickly removed the tumbler from in front of him and made another. The second drink led to a third, and then a fourth. Sweat seeped from his pores as his state of inebriation deepened. He reeked of the bourbon that had soaked into his flesh over the months in Erstwhile. No one said anything to him, and he said nothing to anyone. It was almost as if he wasn't there; closed unto himself.

Richard glanced toward Jake long enough to see that he was drinking whiskey and not his usual beer. Something Jake was doing caught his attention. The condensation from his glass soaked the counter beneath it so that it hydroplaned when pressure was applied. His bar-mate decided to make a game of it. He touched the tips of his thumbs and forefingers together encircling his glass. The heels of his hands lay flat against the surface of the bar. He moved both hands in unison, in a circular motion maintaining the ring around the glass. When it touched a finger it slid effortlessly across the bar until coming into contact with another, which redirected it to yet another, and then another. Jake played with his drink, ad nauseam. The longer he did this the more it irritated Richard. He knew the depths of the anger that Jake held inside, which gave him pause to consider whether he should risk facing that rage. He chose, what he considered, a diplomatic approach. "You've found an interesting way to stir your drink."

Jake turned his head toward Richard. His face was expressionless as he said, "I'm not stirring."

Richard shifted his gaze to the woman at the end of the bar. Cigarette smoke hid her face. When it dissipated, she took another drag and blew smoke in several uniform rings, one after another. Her lips glistened and her eyes sparkled through the haze. Bravado born from passion puffed within him. "Merlin, do you sell cigarettes?"

Without a word, the bartender walked to a spot at the counter along the back wall. He opened a drawer. In it were several brands of cigarettes laid neatly in rows. "Any particular brand?" he asked.

"Do they still make Winston?" Richard knew the brand because it was the kind his father smoked.

Merlin removed a pack from the drawer. Before he could close it, Richard recalled getting sick as a boy after taking one of his father's cigarettes into the woods to smoke. "Could you make those cigarettes light?"

Merlin replaced the pack he held in his hand, and removed another. He walked over and tossed them onto the bar. Richard picked them up, removed the cellophane and then tore open the foil at the top, exposing a cluster of four cigarettes. He pinched one between the nails on his right thumb and forefinger before placing it between his lips. Realizing that he did not have a lighter, he began to look along the bar for an available implement. Jake saw what Richard was doing, leaned back, and reached into his front pocket and removed a Zippo lighter. All in one motion, he flipped open the lid, spun the flint-wheel igniting the wick and placed the flame where his friend could reach it. Richard leaned forward touching the tip to the fire. He drew the foul air into his lungs and noticed the artwork on the side of the lighter. It was an old Confederate soldier holding the Stars and Bars tightly by a wooden pole. He looked beaten, bedraggled and otherwise angry. The caption above his head read, 'Forget hell!'

Richard took a second drag from his cigarette. He tried to blow a ring, but his attempt was unsuccessful. To the others it appeared as if he had eaten something hot and was trying to blow away the pain. He saw the woman laughing at him.

For thirty minutes no one made an effort to acknowledge anyone else in the room. Richard spent that time smoking cigarette-after-cigarette. He tried to visualize shaping his mouth such that the perfect ring would be formed. Those mental images were manifested through a contorted face for all to see. He stopped when he snuffed out a butt and felt the tar on his teeth as he ran his tongue over them. Casually, he spun around on his stool and with his back against the bar he propped his elbows on its edge and looked to his right. There was a young girl seated a few stools away and a person who appeared to be her boyfriend stood dutifully behind her. *Chivalry isn't totally dead*, Richard thought to himself. The girl turned and saw him looking at her. She wore a small, tight, white t-shirt. Her breasts were large and round and the shirt she had on was stretched to its limit. The two made eye contact and they politely smiled at one another. Her face was young and fresh and as flawless as her body.

She stood and walked over to him. She sat down and extended her hand and said, "Hi, my name is Kelly."

He politely shook her hand. "Hello. I'm Richard."

Her boyfriend followed and stood behind her. He appeared to be very drunk and not in a congenial mood. Richard extended his hand to the young man. "My name is Richard." The guy glared at his gesture and nodded. His head wobbled and teetered. The look on his face was dazed and he appeared more intent on keeping the contents of his stomach down than making friends.

"He's Bob," Kelly said, apologetically.

"Is he okay?" Richard asked. "I mean … to drive home. Will you both be able to get home okay?"

"Yeah, he drinks all the time," she said as she stood and waved at someone across the room. "It was nice meeting you," she said as she bounced away. Bob stayed behind, still concentrating on stabilizing his world.

Richard did not wish to appear rude and turn his back on Bob, so he sat silently facing him, not knowing what to say. The young man stared blankly over the bar.

"Don't fuck with me," he said to the empty space behind the counter.

Richard looked to where Bob was staring. No one was there. He wasn't sure what he had done to warrant a threat, so he spun around on his bar stool and leaned against the counter as he had before, choosing to ignore the potential danger. He pulled another cigarette from the pack and took a deep drag after lighting it. Without another word the young man walked away to join his girlfriend and her male friend.

After a few minutes the front door to the bar opened and a tall, thin man stepped inside. Inexplicably, Richard was drawn to him. He held a pipe between his teeth. His hair was completely gray and he wore a hound's-tooth coat. The man was a very distinguished looking gentleman. Quickly, he snuffed out his cigarette and slid the ashtray as far away as he could without being conspicuous. Richard recognized the man. He was Dr. Grant, Richard's childhood dentist. More importantly, he was the father of three of his good friends. He walked toward Richard with a purpose and sat on the seat that Kelly left moments earlier.

In a deep, booming voice, the man said, "Hello, Richard."

"Hey, Dr. Grant. How have you been?" he replied nervously, in the same manner that a child who had been caught smoking might talk to an adult.

"Very well, thank you, and yourself?"

"Not too bad. How are John, Tom and Melissa?"

The man laughed, talking as he bit the stem of his pipe. "Melissa, she's perfect, as always. The boys I worried about until just a few years ago." He removed the pipe from his mouth and blew smoke into the air. "They seem to have hope for their lives now."

Richard was honored that Dr. Grant spoke to him so frankly, as if they were contemporaries. His mind filled with memories of playing little league baseball with the doctor's sons, and the kindness he had shown to the entire team. The distinctive smell of pipe tobacco sparked the pleasant reminiscences. "I'll never forget whenever we won a big game, you would take the entire team to McDonald's as a treat. We had several of those nights thanks to you."

The doctor appeared genuinely touched. "You remember that?"

"Of course! I remember a lot of things you did for us. I remember that, before every game you would bring a box of Trident gum to the dugout. There was enough for each player on the team to have a pack of their own."

He laughed. "Sugarless gum!" He extended his hand. "Richard, I have to get home, but it was good to see you. I am happy that I stumbled in here."

Richard stood and shook the man's hand while placing his left hand on the back of Dr. Grant's, embracing the pleasantry between the two. He knew he would never see him again, but the encounter helped to stifle the cavalcade of maddening life experiences, ever so briefly.

The doctor walked out as quickly as he had come in. Richard sat down. "Merlin, can I get another drink, please?"

The bartender went about the task of making another drink. While he waited, Richard looked over at Jake. His friend's posture conveyed the desire to be left alone. Once again, he found himself looking at the woman at the end of the bar. She was striking her lighter, over-and-over, waiting for the flame to appear. Richard examined her and realized that she had the same tattoo that Sara did. He looked more closely at her face. *Could it be?* He thought. It was Carol, the woman he dated just prior to meeting Susan. Merlin placed Richard's drink on the bar and he picked it up as he began to walk toward his ex-girlfriend.

"Hello, Carol," he said, as he closely examined the tattoo on her chest. It *was* the exact tattoo Sara had. Richard pointed to it. "You broke up with me because I got a tattoo while we were dating. So what's up with that?"

She looked down at her chest. "*That?* It's an ode to a man that I had no respect for while we dated."

"But there is obviously more than one name under that ribbon," he said.

"It's all the same, Richard. I have had men court me and I was a miserable bitch, I think, just for the sake of seeing how much of my bullshit they would put up with. Then, when my husband cheated on me, and we got divorced, I was more miserable than ever. That's when you came along. You tried very hard to please me and I treated you like crap."

"Let me get this straight; your idea of a successful relationship is to find a man that will put up with whatever you can dish out until one of you collapses under the pressure?"

Her smile was crooked and unconvincing. "That's what I grew up seeing in my parent's relationship. Why should I have known any better?" Her question was tinged with sympathy.

Richard hated the thought that Susan might be doing the same thing. He tried to chase away any correlation between the two women. "To be honest with you Carol, it's all forgotten."

She lit a cigarette and stared at him, refusing to offer an apology.

"I'm going for a piss," he said, flatly. Entering the bathroom he walked up to the urinal without looking at the wall in front of him. The song, <u>Solitary Man,</u> by Neil Diamond echoed through his head. He took a wide stance to steady himself on intoxicated legs.

When he returned from the bathroom he noticed there was another young lady seated at the end of the bar. This woman wore an orange and red sundress. Her tan skin perfectly complimented the colors of her outfit. He paused to absorb every line of her body. She leaned against the bar with her forearms on its edge. Richard saw her bosom under her outstretched and taut arm. Its size perfectly complimented the shape of her hips. Her hourglass figure called out to be held. He walked boldly to the empty seat next to her, sat down and looked straight ahead toward Merlin. Richard did not want to appear forward. The anticipation of who he would see when he looked into her eyes was too much to bear.

He took a sip of his drink. When he placed it back onto the bar he wiped the corners of his mouth with the thumb and forefinger of his right hand. Slowly he turned his head and saw the most beautiful woman he had ever known. Her face was distinguished and classically beautiful. The neckline of her dress plunged, exposing a wonderfully voluptuous cleavage. Her exposed skin was smooth and invited a gentle touch. "Hello Elizabeth Martin," he said to the woman he had known since childhood.

She turned calmly and faced him, not the least bit surprised to see her lifelong friend. "Hello, Richard."

"You are the last person I ever thought I'd see in here."

She shrugged her bare shoulders holding them up to her ears. "Here I am."

"Yeah, here you are." Richard's voice was soft as he admired her beauty. "So what have you been doing with yourself all these years?"

"I got married ten years ago and moved to Tampa. How about you?"

"I moved to Orlando, then got married. My wife and I moved back here a few months ago."

The smile on Elizabeth's face reflected melancholy. "Wife?" It made Richard feel good to know that she was sad to hear that he was married. "How's married life treating you?"

"It was great, but now I'm afraid my wife and I are growing apart."

"I'm sorry to hear that."

His bravado could not mask the hurt he felt. "Ah, it's no big deal. We've all had failed relationships, right?"

"I'll drink to that," Elizabeth said as she raised her wine glass into the air before taking a sip.

Richard found that he could not take his eyes off of her. She was as intoxicating as the bourbon that consumed him, but her effect was immediate. "You are the most beautiful woman I have ever seen," he blurted out.

She smiled. "I appreciate the compliment, but you haven't seen me since I was twenty years old. I was hardly a woman then."

"Elizabeth, I have known you since you were eight years old. I vividly remember your mother, you, and your two sisters walking down the road on your way to church every Sunday. All of you were dressed impeccably and were beautiful. The four of you were beautiful then, and *you* are now." The words felt good for him to say. It was a truth that he had held in the recesses of his mind, or maybe his heart, for many years.

"That is the nicest compliment I have ever received."

Richard suddenly felt uncomfortable. Words failed him. He wanted desperately to continue talking to his old friend, but he said everything he needed to in one breath, or so he thought. After a few moments the silence between the two became prickly. He decided to re-start the conversation by asking her a question that he really didn't care to hear the answer. "How did you and your husband meet?"

"I went on vacation with a few of my friends to Cancun. We met there, on the beach. In retrospect, I think it was all about lust," she confessed.

The word 'lust,' as it came from her mouth, pierced his heart. To ease the pain he thought about how great she must look in a bikini. The vision went further as he imagined her nude and how the tan lines on her body might frame her tender regions. "You know, Elizabeth, of all the women I have known in my life, you are the only one I ever questioned, 'what might have been?'"

"*Really*? That seems odd to me since we *never* dated."

"I know it's crazy!" Suddenly, Richard was embarrassed. "Forget I said anything."

"No," she said, sharply. "Do you mean to tell me that you were attracted to me; that you wanted to ask me out?"

He took another large sip of courage. "Yes, of course. *Everyone* wanted to date you."

"I never even knew that you were interested in me."

"The question still stands," Richard insisted, boldly.

"I'm sorry, I didn't realize there was a question to be answered. I thought you made a statement."

It was hard for him to say the things he had already said. He had to muster the nerve to be direct with a woman he admired for decades. "If I had asked you out, would you have said 'yes?'" Richard finished the drink in front of him, and raised the glass toward Merlin. He did not wait for, and was afraid of, the answer.

Elizabeth paused as she thought, signaling to him that he would hear something that would hurt. He anxiously awaited the delivery of his next drink.

Finally, she answered his question: "Yes." He let out a sigh of relief. She continued. "To be totally honest with you, Richard, I never saw myself as your type."

Her comment did not come as a shock. He had always held her in high regard and felt that there was no way he could ever make her happy.

"I'm not trying to come off as you weren't good enough for me, because I think you were. It's just that you always seemed to be attracted to women who were … "

"Loose?"

She nodded. "Well, yeah. The girls you went out with in high school were always the ones who had reputations."

Richard thought about his adolescent years. The memories were fresh. He ached to hold a woman that loved him and to feel the emotional bond between them. That was a feeling he searched for his entire adult life. "If it makes any difference, I would have waited as long as you wanted." Then he realized that Susan asked him to wait, and he had. *A lot of good that did.* Her lack of response signaled the end of the conversation. He walked away. Merlin placed his drink in front of him, which was finished in short order. He felt the anger of what his life had become rage inside him. Suddenly, there was nothing that could be lost by subjecting himself to Jake's wrath. "Why is it that you react to everything in anger?"

Jake leaned back on his stool slowly. The look on his face grew stern. Richard waited for the inevitable punch. It did not come. No one had ever asked him that question and he had never contemplated the answer. It came as a surprise that he was able to articulate his thoughts. "I was never taught, 'why.' My father would beat me mercilessly for doing something wrong, but never explain why what I had done was wrong. One time I remember being beaten because I ran into the road. I was four or five years old. His only reaction was to grab me and furiously beat me with his belt. I've been running head-long into traffic ever since."

"Have you tried to change that behavior with your children?"

Jake did not respond. He pulled a cigarette from the pack of Winstons on the bar in front of him as a solitary tear streamed down his left cheek; then he finished the whiskey in his glass.

Richard stood and wobbled into the bathroom more dejected than he ever remembered being. His mind drifted, while swaying back-and-forth in front of the urinal, until an epiphany rattled his soul. He knew that there was no way he could be the husband or father he needed to be for Susan, or their kids. The nausea that he felt began to choke him. Never had he felt so irrelevant.

He emerged into the chaos of Merlin's on legs that were as weak and unsteady as a newborn foal. His eyes burned and he was unable to fully focus on what lay ahead. Richard stumbled back to his stool and sat down. A woman that he recognized by the tattoo on the back of her neck sat next to him. Her hair was cropped, exposing an anatomical heart with a sword piercing it from its top through its bottom. "What's up, Sahara?" He referred to his sister using the stage name she employed as a stripper.

"Hey, Rich-turd," she replied, using the nickname that she and some friends used to belittle him during his prepubescent years. "All those years you pleaded with me to change my lifestyle and look who's on top now."

Richard's soul sank. "I only wanted what was best for you."

She laughed. "After all that you have been through you are still as arrogant as ever. How do you know what's best for me? You don't even know what's best for you."

"It's no wonder I ended up the way I did. Having an example like you of how to treat women doomed me for failure."

The hypocrisy of everything he stood for in his life was not lost on Richard. He always knew what to say, but lived his life as recklessly as the people he loved. There were only two alternatives. He had reached the most critical juncture in his life. If Susan was not interested in being his wife, the charade had to end.

Chapter Twenty-Four

For months Richard and Susan carried on a hollow relationship. Words between them had become mundane and rudimentary. That which once drew them together pushed them apart. No matter how much effort either put into it they only reminded each other of the challenges in their lives that were thought to have been overcome. Alcohol was the only constant in Richard's life. When he opened the bottle he knew what he wanted from it. There were no more days of running at five o'clock in the morning. The once fit body had begun to sag and spread. He had always taken pride in his appearance, but there seemed to be no need. Every time he saw his wife, or felt her presence, the blackness of his depression was exacerbated. His life with her had become inextricably wrapped into all of his failures.

Susan had gone for a walk on the beach. Richard sat in his chair in the living room with his favorite drink on the table next to his chair. The recliner was in the prone position and he held a photo album in his lap. It was one of five volumes that documented his adult life. Every page that he turned revealed empty spaces. He knew the moment he met Susan that she was the one and had no desire to ever relive his life before her. When he had thrown away old photographs that documented his life with other women, Richard had not taken the time fill in the gaps. He was astonished at how easily the memories came back to him. Those that surrounded the empty spaces told of where he was and whom he was with at the time. One of he and a costumed Roman soldier outside the Coliseum brought Angela back into his consciousness. They were on a trip the summer between their junior and senior years in college. He remembered feeling badly that he had not told Susan of his trip to Italy before their honeymoon, much less that it was with another woman. That was before he learned of Ralph. Medical school in the northeast took Angela away from him. He wondered how she was.

More pages were turned; more memories revealed themselves. There was Richard seated at a booth in the Oak Bar in the Plaza hotel in New York. Connie was a flight attendant and want-to-be actress who lived in California. He was in Los Angeles on business when they met. It was best that it flamed out quickly.

A few more pages were turned. Jill was a sweet girl. Richard still could not believe how poorly he treated her. He once went to her house and found an old boyfriend there. She told him that he was just there to pick up something that he left there before they broke up. He was skeptical of her story. There was nothing in her suitor's hand as he left the house, so Richard rationalized that he must have been encouraged by Jill to be there. He did not trust her because he did not trust himself. That was all the justification he needed to cheat on her whenever the opportunity presented itself. He was never sure about the truth, but he knew she was a sweet girl and deserved better. He laughed as he recalled receiving an email from her not long before he met Susan. There was no message, only a photo attachment of that year's Christmas card with her beautiful family on the snow-covered lawn in front of their mansion. He laughed as he realized the karma he introduced into his relationship with Jill had followed him into his marriage.

The sound of the back door opening startled Richard. He quickly closed the album. Susan walked into the room and sat on the couch behind him. She let out a big sigh and he ignored her. She slapped her hands on her knees, stood up and said, "I'm going to bed now. If you'd like to join me in our room tonight, feel free."

Feel free, Richard thought to himself. *She didn't say, 'Please do.'* He continued to dissect everything his wife said, and watched her out of the corner of his eye. She walked into their bedroom and closed the door. Was the closed door a retraction of the offer? He imagined her undressing and getting into her pajamas on the other side of the door. The vision of his wife's body and how her silk nightgown hung from her shoulders and accentuated her curves was almost too much for him to take. It had been quite a while since they had held each other closely. The image he conjured of them together, nude and embracing was palpable. He decided to accept.

Richard placed the photo album next to his empty glass as he stood and walked quickly toward the door of their bedroom. When he entered Susan was already in bed. She lay with her back toward him.

Hurriedly, Richard got undressed and into his pajamas. He went into the bathroom and brushed his teeth, but did not give them as much attention as he normally would. The fear that she would change her mind fueled his haste. He did not want to get into bed and find her asleep.

After he finished, Richard walked over to the bed and tried his best to slide in and not appear too eager. He lay on his side, facing her back. Minutes passed without movement. Doubts about whether he should say or do anything repeatedly entered and left

184

his mind until he finally decided to make an affectionate gesture. He reached over and slowly stroked her arm. She bristled at first, but settled into his touch without saying a word. Then he slid his hand up to her shoulder. At first his primal desire made him think of sliding it down her back toward her butt, but he knew that would not be well received. Instead, he began to gently, yet firmly, rub her shoulders. She appreciated the care in his touch.

Susan rolled over and faced her husband. He looked into her eyes. They were not clear and bright as he remembered. Stress emanated from them. She could not bring herself to smile. Richard did not say a word for fear of worsening an already bad situation.

"Where have you been?" Susan finally asked in a soft voice.

"On a journey to find myself."

Susan did not appreciate his metaphor. She wanted facts. If he were going to avoid the issue at hand, she would be happy to take him on an excursion. The more she thought about it the angrier she became. She deserved some respect. His glibly evasive response supported her belief that he had something to hide. Her defenses became heightened. Susan searched her mind for a verbal dagger that would pierce his heart. "Do you remember the first night you called me for our blind date?" she asked.

"How could I ever forget it?"

"When mother told me the phone was for me, I was hoping it was John."

The queue for his wife's affection grew in front of him, pushing her farther away. It seemed a certainty that his marriage was over. He had been through enough failed relationships to recognize the exact moment.

Richard got out of bed and walked toward the door, stopping at the foot of the bed as he grabbed the corner-post. "If you're trying to make me feel like less of a man, that's fine. There is a reason for that, I know. It's obvious that I can't make you happy. You're more than welcome to leave anytime."

Susan was taken aback by his offer. Maybe she had not thought through her tactics, but leaving was not one of the things she had considered. She blurted out the first thing that came to mind, "So our marriage is just like an abortion to you, huh? If it's inconvenient, surgically remove it, right?" Susan knew before the last word exited her mouth that she had taken the argument too far.

The two stared at one another. Richard shook his head. "I cannot believe you would choose something so personally distressing to me as ammunition."

Regardless, she was not willing to apologize. Susan was hurt and there was a part of her that enjoyed knowing he was in pain. They maintained a hateful eye contact.

There was only one thing left to say to his wife. "I knew a girl once who told me that if we ever had anything to say to one another that involved an old relationship, it should never be brought into the bedroom. She said our bedroom was a sanctuary unto us. I respected the wisdom of that young lady so much, I married her." He turned and walked through the bedroom door, closing it behind him.

Chapter Twenty-Five

The sun had not yet appeared above the trees, but the glow from the dawn breaking brought the woods to life. Richard stared at the neatly aligned rows of trees through the passenger window of Gaylord's truck as they slowly traversed a sandy logging road in the middle of a vast forest of pines. The emptiness between each column disappeared into a seemingly endless blackness. The sight drew Richard deeper into his depression.

The path was barely wide enough for a single vehicle to pass. Several trails were cut throughout the tract of land that formed one hundred acre parcels. Some blocks were freshly planted in young pines that appeared fuzzy and unable to withstand a stiff breeze. Bordering them were mature trees ready for harvest on one side, and an empty field that had recently been cut on the other. It was littered with branches that had been discarded and strewn among the turned up Earth, resembling the chaotic emptiness of a once proud forest.

Richard leaned against the door, looking through the open passenger window. The truck slowly passed a giant spider web, with what appeared to be a Brown Recluse clinging to its center. Dew had accumulated and glistened on it in the morning sun. Colorful prisms exploded from each droplet. Richard thought about how fragile the web looked, yet realized it must have been very strong to hold the weight of the water.

The truck hit a bump and the two rifles that rested with their muzzles into the floorboard and stocks along the edge of seat slid and hit the passenger on the thigh. He reached down and cautiously returned them to their original position. Since half-past four in the morning, the two men had been searching for fresh deer tracks. A two-hundred-twenty watt lamp was rigged to hang from each side-mirror bracket and shined onto the ground below. There were at least five other trucks traversing the roads within the woods, as far as Richard could tell from the activity on the C.B. radio. It appeared that the group found at least a dozen tracks that were worthy of pursuing.

The dogs in the cage mounted to the bed of the truck began to bay, as they had done several times throughout the morning when picking up a scent. Each time Gaylord reached through the open sliding rear window of the truck and slapped the top of the dog box. "Shuut..uup!" He drew out his words for effect. "This land has been harvested for decades to provide the raw materials the mill needed to operate. Our families have been hunting it for much longer than that," Gaylord said.

"As your families have grown did you ever fear that you might over-hunt the land?"

Gaylord snickered. "There's not a man or woman who has hunted here that doesn't fear just that. Whenever we try to convince some in our party to limit the number of deer we harvest, they spout off about a study that was done by the Florida Fish and Wildlife Commission that concluded that the deer population has never been healthier."

"You don't agree?"

He shook his head. "No, I don't. They send people out here and count the number of tracks on a road as many deer, when it was most likely one that crossed the road several times."

"What will happen to this land now that the mill is closed?"

"I suppose it will eventually be developed." He laughed. "I'm okay with it as long as they keep the names that we have given the roads."

"What names?"

"Well, there's Jacob's Dog Road, or J.D.R. for short. It got its name because that was where Jacob's father-in-law accidentally shot his dog. Then there's the Iron Gate Road, or I.G.R. Finally, there's Toot-Paula Road."

"Why Toot-Paula?"

"That's where Toot proposed to Paula while hunting one day." With a serious tone Gaylord exclaimed, "That's so damned romantic!" Then he added, "Some of the guys like to piss Toot off by referring to his road as T.P. Road." Gaylord reached atop his dashboard and retrieved a thermos that was wedged between it and the windshield. "Do you want some coffee?"

"I don't have a cup," Richard said.

Gaylord pointed to the floor between Richard's feet. "There's one right there."

Richard looked down. He saw a dirty Styrofoam cup that appeared to have been in the truck for as long as Gaylord had owned it. It lay amongst a couple of oily rags, a pipe wrench and a box of rifle cartridges.

"Thanks anyway. I had some before we left the house this morning."

Without a word, Gaylord opened the container and poured hot coffee into the cup that he had removed from its top. He closed it and placed it back on the dashboard. Reaching over to the glove compartment, he opened the door and removed a flask. Richard looked through the passenger window, but watched from the corner of his eye as Gaylord poured a goodly amount of the liquid into his coffee. Mixing guns and alcohol made him very uncomfortable. Using one hand to steer he turned the truck down H.T.R. When he made the turn, Richard saw several trucks gathered together at the end of the road.

"What does H.T.R. stand for?" Richard asked.

"Hangin' Tree Road," Gaylord replied flatly, without emotion.

Richard calmly nodded his head, recognizing the gravity of its name. Inside, however, he felt tense and uneasy. Nothing else was said between the two as Gaylord drove the truck to the end of the road to meet the other members of the hunting party. There was plenty of room on both shoulders for all of the trucks. After Gaylord parked his truck, Richard emerged from the passenger's door and noticed a lone tree. It was not a pine and appeared out of place. There was a single branch, sturdy in appearance, cantilevered away from its trunk near the top. His heart raced at the thought of what might have transpired on that spot in the past.

Of the group, the two eldest men remained seated in their trucks, which were parked across from one another. Each leaned out of their open window. All of the others had gathered in the space between them. Richard and Gaylord were the last to arrive. "This is Richard, everyone," he said.

Richard could only distinguish grunts and groans from the men, except one, who responded, "Howdy." He nodded toward everyone and smiled.

"Which track are we gonna put-out on first?" Gaylord asked the group.

"The best track to put the dogs on is one I found over on the T.S.R.," replied Tommy Owens in his deep southern drawl as he pointed in the direction of his track.

"Tommy, how come it's always your track that's the best one?" asked Phil Butler.

Visibly upset, Tommy's lip quivered as he responded. "Because I'm the one who gets here at one o'clock in the morning, tracking these woods. I'm the one who quits my job every year to make sure we've got deer meat on all of our tables. You people might as well stay in bed 'til daylight, because by the time you all get here, I've already tracked every inch of these loggin' roads."

"Calm down Tommy," Billy Owens said. "We'll put-out on your track."

Richard did not pay attention to the banter back-and-forth between the Owens brothers. He found himself transfixed by a man who stood back, away from the crowd, keeping to himself. The only thing that was unusual about him was that he wore a gun belt with two holsters, one on each hip. There was a nickel plated, pearl handled revolver in each.

One of the elder gentlemen started his truck and yelled to the rest, "You boys can stand around here playin' grab-ass with each other, but we're burnin' daylight and the track's growin' cold." He sped away in his truck in the direction that Tommy had pointed earlier, kicking up dust. The others raced through the cloud to their respective trucks out of fear of disappointing the old man. Seven trucks sped down the dirt road. The only one with a clear view was the leader. Every nerve ending in Richard's body tingled as he feared seeing the tailgate of the truck in front of them appear from the dense dust-cloud that engulfed them all. He braced himself by placing his hands firmly against the dashboard, and laughed nervously. The road was bumpy and the high rate of speed caused the truck to bounce across its un-graded surface. He felt the truck become airborne several times. Richard could hear the dogs in the back bouncing off the top of the cage and scraping their toenails on the bed as they tried to steady themselves. When the trucks reached the intersection of H.T.R. and I.G.R. three trucks turned to the right, and the others went left, almost as if their routes had been choreographed. This kind of unspoken simpatico had been developed over many years together. Each continued on a pre-determined path until all seven had the block entirely surrounded.

Gaylord stopped the truck at the corner of I.G.R. and B.D.R. He reached over and grabbed the butt of his gun and got out of the truck. Richard did the same, not really sure why. "I'll stay here and watch both ways," he said as he pointed down both roads. "You go stand in the middle of the block," pointing to a spot between his truck and the one at the other corner, "and look for any deer running toward you. A lot of times you'll see its white tail bouncing. If you see one, shoot it." Without a word, Richard began jogging to where he had been commanded to go, holding the gun across his chest like a soldier. "If you see anything, use hand signals. Don't yell!" Gaylord shouted a whisper to his protégé hoping not to startle the deer everyone hoped was deep in the block. Richard raised his hand into the air and waved acknowledgment as he ran away from the truck.

When he made it to the spot where he was directed to stand, he stopped and looked into the block. Then he peered to the left, and then to the right, gauging whether he was equidistant from each corner. Once he settled into his spot he realized that if a deer ran into the road he was in the line-of-fire of both Gaylord and the hunter at the other corner. He walked off the road and to the edge of the woods where he could duck for cover, if necessary.

The trees were mature and had been planted in perfectly straight rows. There were no limbs on the lower parts of the trees to obstruct the view of the woods. The trunks made it difficult to see to his right or left. However, when he looked straight down the row where he stood, he could see for a few hundred yards. A thick blanket of pine straw covered the ground. He stepped into the woods past the first couple of trees. The straw, dead and dry, crunched beneath his feet. With every step he took away from the road, he felt a bit safer.

After a few minutes, Richard realized that he had to pee. He looked around and thought, *why not*? He leaned his rifle against a tree, unzipped his pants and began to urinate. His body tingled. When he finished there was a large patch of straw that was wet and shiny.

Before he could zip and button his pants, Richard heard the sound of dogs baying in the distance. Quickly, he closed his pants and reached for his rifle. He could see nothing in the woods around him, but the barking grew louder.

After another minute, Richard began to question his position. He walked back out of the woods and onto the road. Gaylord's truck was still at the corner, and he was standing on top of the dog-box. He waved Richard back off the road and into the woods. Richard obliged.

Suddenly, Richard heard a twig snap. He looked down the center of the row where he stood, but saw nothing. He looked closely at the brown blanket of dead straw on the ground. There it was! A deer was running

directly toward him. It was camouflaged by the sur-
roundings. Apparently, it did not see Richard. He
slowly raised the butt of his gun against his shoulder
and held it tightly there. When the bead at the end of
the barrel lined up with the sight at the rear, and the two
together found a spot on the chest of the deer, he gently
squeezed the trigger. The thunder of the gun hurt his
ears and echoed throughout the trees, and the recoil
caused him to become disoriented, momentarily. He re-
gained his composure in time to see the deer move
sharply to his left, toward Gaylord.

Richard ran as quickly as he could onto the
road. He waved his arm vigorously toward Gaylord,
hoping that he understood the deer was heading his
way. Apparently, he did. Gaylord readied his rifle
against his shoulder and swept the barrel from side-to-
side practicing the timing he would need when the deer
crossed the road at full speed. Richard watched as his
friend became very still. He saw a burst of smoke come
from the end of the gun and then heard the shot.
Gaylord jumped down off the dog-box, got in the truck
and sped down the road, out of Richard's sight. He was
unsure whether he should abandon his position. The
truck that was at the opposite corner approached him
from behind at a high rate of speed.

"Hop on!" the driver yelled. Richard saw the
man's daughter in the passenger seat, so he knew the
man meant to get on top of the dog's cage, which he
did.

Richard held on as the man accelerated. The
metal diamond pattern on the box scraped his knees as
they all bounced along the road. The truck came to a
hard stop at the intersection Gaylord had vacated moments earlier. A cloud of dust overtook the truck just

194

before the driver made a right turn. Once the truck was back up to speed and out of the dust, Richard saw Gaylord's truck stopped about a hundred yards away. There was no sign of him.

When the truck Richard was riding on came to a stop, the dogs that had been chasing the deer emerged from the woods, crossed the road and continued into the next block. Richard jumped off the truck. The driver and his daughter got out. All three followed the dogs into the woods. They quickly lost sight of them.

"Over here!" a voice called out from a few rows over. It was Gaylord.

Without answering the three ran toward him, high-stepping in the straw. When they got to the spot where he was they saw the dogs. They were sniffing and occasionally barking at the carcass of the deer that lay motionless.

Gaylord looked at Richard. "I don't know if it was your shot or mine that got him."

Richard felt pride. Maybe he had slain the beast. The thought gave him a primal pleasure that he had never felt before.

"If you killed it, you have to clean it," the driver of the second truck said. He and Gaylord laughed as they saw a look of fear on Richard's face.

"Help me drag it out of here," Gaylord said as he grabbed a hind leg, leaving the other for Richard. He reached down and grabbed it and the two men pulled as they walked. Richard looked back and watched as the lifeless body bounced across the pine straw, its head bobbing from side-to-side and its tongue hanging from its mouth. The pride he felt moments earlier quickly left him. This was the first time he had taken a life. "I'll clean and dress the deer tonight when I get home and bring your portion by the store for you," Gaylord said in a matter-of-fact tone. "We usually split the kill amongst ourselves, if that's alright?"

"Of course," Richard said.

The two men continued until they reached the center of the road. The dogs had been following closely the entire time, sniffing, growling and biting at one another; laying claim to the prize that lie dead in front of them.

"Put the dogs up, boys. They've smelled enough of the kill," commanded one of the elders who had arrived on scene and gotten out of his truck. Everyone dutifully followed his instructions and placed the dogs in the cages in which they belonged. Some dogs jumped onto the tailgate and ran into their cages willingly; others had to be dragged by the collar. Once Gaylord and Richard had put away their dogs, they walked back to where the deer lay on the ground. Pick-up trucks and men preening surrounded it. Each man grabbed a set of legs and carried it to the truck. Standing beside it, they rocked the deer back-and-forth until there was enough momentum to sling the dead animal on top of the dog-box. The others waited silently until Richard and Gaylord came back to the inner-circle.

"Which track are we going to put-out on now?" one elder asked.

Without hesitation, Tommy spoke up. "I found one this morning … " Laughter from all the other men drowned out Tommy's sentence before he could complete it.

In a very calm and cool voice, the man who wore two guns asked Richard, "Was that your first kill?"

196

"I don't think it was me who killed the deer. I believe it was Gaylord," Richard said. "That deer was still running full-steam when he hit the road in front of Gaylord."

Two Guns ignored his protest and said. "It's your first kill. You have to wear the sign of the Erstwhile Hunter."

The others nodded in agreement. Richard became nervous, unsure of what was in store for him. The last time he had been hazed was his freshman year in high school as a member of the football team. It was not a pleasant experience.

Gaylord hopped up on his tailgate and began searching the bed of his truck. He picked up an empty can and moved toward the dead animal. Placing a knee on each side of the deer Gaylord pressed and pumped vigorously on the chest just above where the bullet had entered the body. He held the can beneath the puncture. Blood pulsed from the wound with each compression. The men waited silently until he was finished, then he jumped down from the tailgate and made his way to the group. Each man took a turn to dip his index finger into the can. One after the other walked up to Richard and ran their blood-soaked finger across his face. He could not tell if there was any rhyme or reason to this ceremony. Everyone was silent. Richard tried desperately to visualize how his face looked. He felt like there may be a 'V' on his forehead, but he wasn't sure. The gaminess of the blood reeked and made his stomach uneasy. When everyone was finished painting his face, they all stood back and clapped. There was no laughter, only serious applause.

"I damn sure wish they'd still let us hunt those two-legged animals," the elder man said.

197

"I guaran-damn-tee ya' that if we were out here huntin' them people, his bullet," Two-Guns pointed at Richard and continued, "wouldn't 'a been the one that pierced the animal's chest." Nausea boiled within him as he endured what seemed to be an eternity filled with racial epithets and threats. Just as quickly as he had become a member of the group, he was once again alone in the crowd. Would the disgust he felt show on his face? He tried to stay calm while not allowing himself to fall in with the majority. His stomach churned and bubbled. The taste of copper oozed from his throat into the back of his mouth. The acidy liquid coated his teeth. Not wanting to spit out the regurgitated fluid, Richard swallowed and tried to remove the taste from his mouth by rubbing his tongue along his teeth. He had no desire to visit H.T.R. again, ever.

Finally, the decision was made to continue the hunt. Richard hurried to the passenger's door of Gaylord's truck. When he opened the door, he caught a glimpse of his reflection in the large side-view mirror. He adjusted the door so that he could see more clearly what the men had painted on his face. It was a Confederate flag.

Chapter Twenty-Six

While Richard was hunting, Susan sat in her chair on the beach. The cool gulf breeze seemed to whisk away the torrent of her life. She sat sideways with her back against one arm and her legs dangling over the other. It was a bit cool for her taste. She and Richard had allowed the summer to pass without enjoying the benefits that came with living with the gulf just outside their back door. She wore a pair of khaki shorts, a sleeveless t-shirt and a printed blouse, unbuttoned. Her flip-flops slapped against her heels as she flexed her toes. The sun was low in the sky as it made its annual migration toward the southern hemisphere casting elongated shadows onto the sand. Susan watched the silhouette of her feet dance across the ground beneath her. A few old dance steps from an aged ballerina effortlessly graced the beach. After she had gone through all the steps she had ever learned for the third time, she leaned her head against the wide arm of the chair and closed her eyes. It was one of the loneliest times she had ever experienced. This was not her home. It was not her great aunt's store. Nothing about her life seemed to fit her circumstances. Ralph and Courtney were familiar and made her happy, but they could not satiate her needs the way cocaine could. She removed the plastic baggy that Emma had given her from her pocket. Its contents were sparse and she scraped the tiny silver spoon against the sides and bottom to fill the bowl. She inhaled, but the drug was not as effective. Unpleasant thoughts still clouded her mind. Her desire for more exceeded that which was readily available. Emma wasn't at home and she had nowhere else to turn, so she stayed on the beach and continued to search for the remedy that would make her whole again.

With her consciousness drifting to decades earlier when Susan was in fifth grade. She noticed a group of girls in one corner of the playground at school and was hurt that she had not been asked to join them. So, she boldly walked over uninvited. When she approached, she realized what they were doing. They sat in a circle. Each girl wore shorts and took turns pulling back on the legs of their pants, exposing themselves to the others. Over the years she had taken pride in the fact that she was not invited to participate because, as one of the girls told her later, she was a good girl.

When she entered puberty and began to transition into a beautiful woman, people began to treat her differently. Boys gave her more attention and her girlfriends gave her less. Lifelong friends did not want her around because they didn't appreciate how their boyfriends looked longingly at her. She couldn't even escape being outcast in her own home. Sally, her portly older sister, wanted nothing to do with her for the same reasons. While she enjoyed the benefits of being a physical beauty, Sally trained her mind so successfully that she had been awarded advanced degrees in Physics and had become a tenured professor at Cal-Tech. It never occurred to her that after graduating with a Bachelors degree in Early Childhood Education she went to work as a cocktail waitress because she saw herself as a beauty and nothing more.

She struggled to justify so much time spent at dance class when she could have been better preparing herself for life. Susan dedicated herself to the discipline, taking lessons from the age of three until she was sixteen. A slipped disk in her back dashed all of her dreams of appearing on Broadway. It was a blow that set her back emotionally, until she tried cocaine for the first time. After that, her happiest moments included being placed in the company of men. Her dance for Richard on the beach was the last time she felt fulfilled. It was not only a performance for him, but them all. She wasn't sure what that meant for their future together.

She never had a steady boyfriend, and hung out with the same group of people, usually at some secluded spot. They had things to do in which no one else could be involved. Susan worried that she may have done things while she was in an altered state that she did not remember. Most of her high school days were spent on the fringe. Why couldn't she share these things with Emma? Surely her friend thought Susan was some sort of square-peg.

The cool fall afternoon breeze and the warmth of the Florida sun offered a pleasant contrast, as the affect of each ebbed and waned, never overpowering the other. Susan closed her eyes behind her sunglasses. The steamy hot days of summer with a beach filled with people had given way to a more desolate landscape.

Susan's only other serious relationship with a man had been with Courtney. It ended when she found out that he had been cheating on her. The ring on her finger then, and the one now, meant something to her. She had taken each commitment very seriously, whether it be to dance or to partners. It became clear to her that nothing was meant to last forever.

She reached into the coin pocket of her shorts, removed the ring that Courtney had given her eighteen years earlier and slid it onto her ring finger, covering the two that Richard had given her. Why had she kept it all these years? Did she honestly hope that one day they

201

would be reunited? She had offered to give it back to him, but he insisted she keep it. Maybe he hoped they would be together again, too.

The breakup was an ugly one. A single mother, Karen, who was in the young couple's circle of friends, became pregnant. Something deep down told Susan that Courtney was the father. Maybe it was something he said. Maybe it was the manner in which he doted over Karen during her pregnancy. All she knew was that he spent a lot more time with Karen during those nine months than he did with her. *What a fool I was*. Susan recalled how she attributed all the attention Courtney gave their friend in need to his generous and caring nature. After all, he was the one who convinced Susan that she needed to place herself in rehab. He was just looking out for those in need. *Yeah, right!*

It was Richard's turn to trample her heart. Was he sleeping with Talitha? The vision of her husband sleeping with that beautiful young girl gave her visceral pains. She always appreciated the care he took when making love to her and could not stomach the same attention being given to another woman.

It was not the first time Susan felt he had neglected to care about what she was going through. Not long after they met, she knew she needed to tell him of an incident that happened during her teen years. Her date forced his intentions upon her after she politely refused his advances. Richard listened and calmly supported her and asked if there was anything he could do to help her deal with the emotional stress of that night. The fact that he supported her was not important, she was filled with anger and wanted him to be angry, too. He just did not care enough to understand how that night affected her.

"Hello," a man's voice startled her.

She opened her eyes and sat up in her chair. Standing before her was a young man, a handsome man. "Hello," she said.

He wore a baggy bathing suit and an unbuttoned white linen shirt, revealing a well-developed abdomen, and had equally muscular legs. Susan appreciated how his thighs tapered down and around his kneecaps, as did his calves to his thin, athletic ankles. The young man walked over to Richard's chair and removed the carryall that contained towels, sun block, reading material and other beach essentials. "Do you mind if I sit down?" he asked, as he sat down.

"Not at all."

"Do you live here?"

"Yes," Susan replied, avoiding pointing to the house behind them.

"My name is Charles Coleman."

"I'm Susan."

The man looked out over the gulf waters. "I just love this time of year. The beach is deserted and it's so uncluttered. It's almost as if you have it all to yourself."

Susan nodded. "Do you live here?"

"No. I'm from Birmingham. I always come to Erstwhile some time after Labor Day to take advantage of the serenity."

Susan shifted in her chair to face Charles. "Are you married?"

"No. I have too much life to live to tie myself down like that." He stared at her. "Has anyone ever told you that you look just like Susan St. James?"

She blushed. "No, but I've heard Andy McDowell, before."

Charles nodded and smiled. "Yeah, I can see that."

Susan volunteered, "I had aspirations of a career on Broadway." She was not sure why she was so quick to open herself to this man, but something about having a personal conversation felt good.

"You certainly have the looks and the physique. Why didn't you pursue it?"

"I slipped a disk in my back that ended my dance career."

"That must have been hard on you."

"It was. Without dance to occupy my time, it wasn't long before I began getting into trouble."

"What kind of trouble?"

"Oh, nothing really bad." Susan thought better about revealing her weakness to him. "You haven't asked me if I was married."

Charles shrugged his shoulders. "It doesn't really matter, does it?"

"In the grand scheme of things, I guess not," she said, giddily as she began to acknowledge her primal attraction to this man.

"Tell me, what's missing in your life?"

Susan drew a deep breath. Fear caused her to retreat from the position in which she found herself. "I can't think of anything. I've got it pretty good."

Not deterred, Charles employed a new tactic. "Well, I'm not sure how your husband feels about you, but I can tell you that I am in awe of the woman I see before me. I can tell that you have a strength about you that allows you to make your own decisions in life. I bet your husband is afraid of you, isn't he? I'd also bet that he tries to spend as much time away from you as he can because you have effectively emasculated him."

"He hasn't been around much lately," she conceded.

The door to a carnal experience opened. The two sat and talked for hours, drawing emotionally closer to one another as time passed. Although Charles was young, she thought he was wise in the ways of the world, and he knew how to communicate just what he could do for Susan. She needed to and wanted to feel like the woman she once was; the woman she was for Richard, Ralph and Courtney.

They stood and walked over the dunes to the house. Charles followed closely behind her, grinning with satisfaction at another conquest. Susan negotiated the first couple of steps leading from the beach to the deck and removed her over-shirt, exposing her shoulders and back. Charles' curiosity was piqued. He was a little nervous, because he wanted to perform well for her, but his overriding sentiment was of the conquest and experiencing someone new.

Susan reached into her pocket and removed the key to the house. She unlocked and opened the door. "Come on in," she said, playfully.

He followed her inside. She stopped briefly in the middle of the living room, unsure of whether decorum would allow her to simply walk straight into the bedroom. She turned, faced Charles, and tiptoed to reach up and kiss him. The two kissed for a few minutes, but both knew they were not fooling the other. Their embrace was meant to create a feeling of history together.

Susan pulled away, took Charles by the hand and led him into her and Richard's bedroom. Suddenly, the argument the couple had in their bedroom came to mind. She stopped, turned and led him back across the living room and into the guest room.

They entered the room and Susan turned on the light. Charles walked around to the far side of the room, removed his shirt and tossed it across the back of the chair in the corner. He picked up the picture of Susan and Courtney as he lay down on the bed. "Is this your husband?" he asked.

"No," she replied, realizing at that moment that Richard must have seen the picture. Susan had not thought about it since she placed it on the bedside table months ago.

Charles laughed. "You're my kind of woman. Just get up in his face," he held up the picture, referring to it, "and rub this in it." He laughed again as he placed the picture back down.

For the briefest of moments, Susan had doubts about Charles, but no more doubt than she had about her relationship with Richard. She went with what she knew would make her feel good.

It did not take long before the experienced couple was naked and in each other's arms. Lovemaking with Charles was enjoyable, but clinical. He stimulated her here and there, each time waiting for a reaction to assess his performance. It lacked the feeling that Susan craved when making love. When he was done on top, he rolled her over. When he was done from behind, he rolled her onto her back. The rhythm was harsh and lacked sensitivity. His touch had no feeling; he groped and grabbed her everywhere. It seemed to be more about physical accomplishment than emotional climax. The void in Susan's psyche grew.

Chapter Twenty-Seven

Richard looked around the shop. Everything appeared to be in order. The shelves were stocked, the floor swept and the paperwork had been done. It was mid-morning and there were hardly any customers this time of the day. He tried to keep his mind off the latest argument he had with Susan by searching for something to keep him occupied. Whenever she entered his mind he quickly chased away the thought. His mind had become fragile under the weight of a lifetime of failure.

He held his watch in front of his face: 10:47. Richard looked at the front door that he had propped open earlier to allow the cool fall air to flow freely. Surely there was something in the back room he could do, but what if a customer came in? The bell would not ring, alerting him to that fact. Certainly no one who shopped in his store would steal anything if they came in and found the store unattended, would they? Guilt overcame him. It was okay if he questioned the kind of man he was, but he was uncomfortable doing the same with others. Being made to feel worthless was a concept he embraced, but refused to project.

He succumbed to his guilt and decided to forgo working in the back room so that he didn't have to extend that level of trust to anyone. Richard walked up and down the aisles looking for something, anything to do. Thoughts of Susan continued to drift in and out of his mind. They were not pleasant. He was distressed and looked at his watch again. It was 10:50. Time was moving too slowly for a man in desperate need of resolution.

He looked at the front door again, and through the front window along the sidewalk. There were no signs of humanity. Forgetting his trust issues, he turned and walked into the back room.

When he entered the small space he looked at a stack of boxes against the back wall. They were positioned precariously with smaller containers providing the foundation. Richard walked over and opened the one on top, reached in and removed a bottle of Maker's Mark. There was barely any bourbon left inside. He held the bottle by the neck in front of his face and shook it, watching the sparse contents splash around. The liquor store was not open this early, and Merlin's didn't have a package license. He would just have to make the best of it.

Richard walked across the room and stopped in front of another stack of boxes. He pulled at the glue-lined top of the container until it popped opened, reached inside and removed a sleeve of plastic cups. Tearing open the covering, he removed the outermost cup and dropped the rest back into the box. He opened the bottle and poured its contents into the cup while shaking it up-and-down in an effort to consume every drop of liquor. The empty bottle went inside the open box, nestled between the sheathed cups. He took his drink and moved with purpose toward an undersized refrigerator. When he opened its door he saw that there were no mixers available. Not deterred, he opened the small freezer and removed the ice-tray. There was no ice either. A thought came to him. Richard moved into the small bathroom where he found an open can of soda on the back of the toilet. There were a couple of sugar ants making their way in and out of its opening. Without a second thought he picked them off and squashed them between his fingers before pouring the remaining soda into his cup. He swirled the mixture just before bringing the rim to his lips and drinking the contents without pause.

There was not enough alcohol to suffocate his grief, but the warmth he felt as it went down made him feel better. He drew in a deep breath and exhaled, slowly.

"Hello," a voice called from the store.

Richard jumped, nervously. He cupped his hand and held it to his mouth as he breathed into it. The odor of alcohol was negligible, but that didn't keep him from rubbing his teeth and gums vigorously with his index finger to brush away any detectable stench.

He quickly made his way from the back room into the store. When he walked through the door he could see someone standing near the front, but her back was to him and he could not tell who it was. The shelves blocked his view of everything but her head. When he made his way to the aisle where she stood, he was able to get a look at her full body. It was Talitha. "Hello, Talitha," Richard called joyfully to her.

"There you are," she replied, as she turned to face him.

"What can I do for you?" he asked, walking toward her.

"Nothing. I just came by to say, 'hi,'" she said, as she walked toward him. The two stopped as they came together mid-way down the aisle.

Richard placed his elbow and arm along the edge of the top shelf and leaned against it. "Shouldn't you be at work?"

"I've got break-time, and you're only a couple minutes away." She flashed her trademark smile that had captivated him from the moment he met her. "*And*, I would much rather be here talking to you than sitting outside with the smokers."

It felt good to Richard that someone enjoyed his company. He grinned at her without saying a word.

"Some of those people have been smoking since they were teenagers. There's one person that is thirty years old and her voice is already gravelly. It's *really* sad."

Without acknowledging her statement, Richard asked, "So what is it you want to talk about?"

"Oh, duh," she rolled her eyes in a silly fashion. "I wanted to see if you were able to pick up on my signal the other day."

"Signal? What signal?"

"When Gaylord came in here and I started talking about your aunt being in the D.A.R. I *wasn't* talking about the Daughters of the American Revolution. He's the dumb-ass redneck whose dog bit that nice couple from Atlanta."

Richard laughed. "Sorry, I didn't pick up on that. I guess you're too shifty for me."

"You know that's not true," she protested.

"In my defense, my aunt was in the D.A.R. So there really was no need for me to question anything you said."

The winning smile fell away from her beautifully smooth brown face, and was replaced by an equally powerful, and serious look. "There's something else I needed to tell you."

"Need to?" Richard laughed. The smile quickly ran away from his face as he looked into her warm, gold-flecked, tawny eyes. She projected an unmistakable look of concern.

"Yes, I *need* to tell you something and it's better that it comes from a friend and not one of these hateful people who have nothing better to do than revel in someone else's misery."

"What is it?" His heart pounded.

Talitha took a deep breath. "Some people saw a man walking with your wife into your house yesterday. Now, he could have been the cable guy, or a plumber, but they went in through the back door, from the beach."

Richard's stomach felt as though it would back-up into his throat. Talitha placed her hand on his shoulder and tried to comfort him. He took a couple of deep breaths to try and suppress the feeling of nausea. Everything he feared had been confirmed. Ralph was obviously the man Susan preferred. All he could think to do was extricate himself from the situation in the most efficient manner. "Wow!" was the only thing he could say, filtering the expletives that entered his mind. It was obvious to him that she set up the fight between them in order to send the message about her true feelings. Why did she not have the strength to tell him it was over between them? Her flirtations with Ralph were present throughout their marriage, so he wasn't totally shocked. However, it had cost him a great deal of his sanity.

"Are you going to be okay?" Talitha asked.

"Yeah."

"I debated whether or not to say anything."

"Why did you decide to tell me?" The pain Richard felt leached from his pores and clung to Talitha. He could not understand why she would want to cause such distress for him.

"I feel like it's best to be honest with everyone no matter how much it may hurt."

"Yeah, but isn't that kind of honesty reserved for a husband and wife?" He could not shake the vision of Ralph making love to his wife.

"Maybe so," Talitha said. "Maybe I shouldn't have told you."

He felt her emotionally backing away from him and he could not accept that. No longer did he have to consider anyone else in the decisions he made. Anything he wanted to do, he could do without fear of reprisal. Once again, he noticed the beautiful young girl that stood before him. He smiled at her and she returned the gesture. Her eyes were bright and they radiated into his soul and warmed it in a manner that had been absent for too long. Richard felt himself drawn to a woman other than Susan. He welcomed the feeling. The nervousness associated with discovering a new lover tingled his every extremity. It was too easy for him to remove any thought associated with his wife. The only thing he focused on was the beautiful girl in front of him and how she caused a deep-seeded desire to hold her, tightly. He wanted to feel her quiver in ecstasy as they experienced their desire for each other. Richard placed his hands on each side of her narrow waist, and pulled her close to him, then leaned toward her and touched his lips to hers. They were soft and moist, and felt divine. Then he slid his hands around her back, down to her buttocks and held them confidently. They were young and firm. Her breasts pressed against his chest.

She ran her hands along his back, holding him just as closely as she could, pressing her lips against his. His stubble rubbed against her face. Its masculinity

212

caused her to swoon. Richard moved his hands from her buttocks to her hips and then down the back of her thigh. He gripped and pulled, trying to lift her leg up to his hip.

Suddenly, Talitha moved her hands from his back to his chest and pushed him away firmly. "This isn't right!"

"What do you mean it's not right? Don't you want it to happen?" he asked, trying to maintain the kiss between them.

"Not like this," she said.

"Like what?"

Talitha turned her back to him and took a couple of steps away, then turned to face him again and continued. "There are two reasons you made a pass at me just now, and neither one of them is right."

Richard thought momentarily, "Okay, I can figure out what the first one is: my wife, right?"

"Yes. People don't make the wisest decisions based on emotion."

"Yeah, yeah." He brushed aside her concern. "What's the second?"

"I know you've been spending time with the rednecks in the woods. I think you may be trying to prove to yourself that you aren't a racist by making a pass at the little black girl."

Richard did not know how to respond. He looked deeply into Talitha's eyes, searching for a glimmer of concern for her friend. He saw none as she returned his stare.

"Tell me I'm wrong," she said, boldly.

Richard held his arms out, palms skyward. "How can I? That's like asking me to prove there is a God in Heaven. I can't. You just have to have faith that

213

it's true … or not true, in this case," Richard stammered through his confusion. "Do you know what I mean?"

"That's just not good enough," she replied, before turning and walking out of the store.

He could only watch as she walked along the sidewalk and past the window. Failure came at a much faster pace than ever before. He needed something to cling to, but it seemed that no one in his life gave him the validation he so desperately sought.

Chapter Twenty-Eight

Susan sat quietly in a chair in the only salon in town. There was nothing she could do to make the feeling of guilt go away. It did not matter that she recognized her reflection; the woman she saw disgusted her. She had overcome so much in her life, but found herself making the same mistakes she did as an adolescent. Her father was no longer there for her. She ached to see him; to talk to him. He always told her that having kids motivated him to clean up his act, but never got the chance to explain why or how. Was he as confused as she about the depth of true commitment? Did he harbor feelings for past loves? His marriage to her mother ended ugly and his life plunged into an abyss of vices that left him a mere shell of the man he once was, until it finally cost him his life. She was sure that his experiences would have been invaluable to her if he had only shared them.

There were no familiar faces in the store and Susan did not feel comfortable striking up a conversation with anyone around her, so she picked up a magazine and began to quickly turn the pages. Maybe she could find the hairstyle that reflected the woman she had become. There were seven people there, all women who carried on at least three different conversations, and each one was involved in them all. Susan flipped mindlessly through the pages of the magazine as she eavesdropped on what was being said. It was obvious that Karen owned the shop. Susan appreciated how she paid attention to each customer in the store whether they were in her chair or waiting. Karen bossed around the other hairdresser and was very loud and boisterous as she attempted to entertain everyone in the shop.

"Honey, I don't know what I'm gonna do," Karen said in her consistently loud tone, addressing everyone in the shop while waving a pair of scissors. She continued, "Tryin' to juggle two men at one time is about to kill me, honey."

The women laughed, except Susan. She stared at the shop owner in a judgmental fashion, and then recalled her own betrayal and it pained her to realize that she had allowed her emotional infidelity to become physical.

One lady replied, "I can't understand why the hell you'd want two of them. If you want three you can have mine."

Laughter erupted throughout the shop again.

"Honey, I wouldn't be able to do it if it weren't for my Prozac," Karen said. "If I took your man off your hands, Dr. Wheeler would have to double up my prescription."

Yet again, laughter filled the salon. Susan smiled nervously at the remarks, masking her pain. She looked around at the ladies and noticed one who had a tolerant smile on her face. The two made eye contact and exchanged a pleasant nod.

When Karen was finished with the lady who sat in her chair, she walked with her to the counter. The woman said, "I'll see you in two weeks, okay?" as she removed cash from her purse.

"Sweetie, you come back whenever you like," Karen said to the woman as she walked out of the shop. She turned to the woman who sat next to Susan. "Judy, you're next, hun!"

Judy stood and walked over to the empty barber chair. The lady Susan had exchanged a glance with stood and walked over to the vacant chair and sat down. She carried with her the magazine she was reading and laid it in her lap. She looked at Susan and smiled. In a soft tone she introduced herself, "Hi, I'm Cindy Stein."

"Hi, I'm Susan Styles."

"You aren't from Erstwhile are you?" Cindy asked. "I mean, I've never seen you in here before." She attempted to soften her tone.

"No. My husband and I have only been here for three months."

"Are you retired?" Cindy asked.

"No. We own the mercantile store down the street."

"Oh! That's you? I've been meaning to shop there. I'll have to make a point of it now."

"Are you retired?" Susan asked.

"Yes. My husband and I are from Kansas. We came down right before the big real estate boom at the beach. Not that we saw it coming. We were just lucky."

The small talk did not last, as the ladies were afraid their whispers would be frowned upon. They began reading their magazines again. After a few minutes, Susan sensed that there was something else that Cindy wanted to say. She looked over as Cindy leaned in to whisper. "So, what do you think of these people?"

"Oh, I don't know. They seem nice," Susan said.

"It didn't take Jerry and I, Jerry is my husband, very long to realize that we had stepped back in time," Cindy said, raising her eyebrows. She continued to whisper, "This place truly is the 'Old South.'"

"*Really*," was all she said. How could she feel secure enough in the person she was to offer criticism of others? The laughter in the shop continued at a raucous level. The conversation mostly centered on men and how they had no idea what made women happy. Although she was tempted, Susan resisted airing details of her past.

Cindy leaned toward Susan, again. "All they ever do when they come in here is talk about how horribly their spouses treat them. And, they talk about how everyone in town, except them, is getting rich. And, if I hear one more time about how that mill company screwed everyone I swear I'll puke. I mean, if your life is bad, you're the only one that can change that, am I right?" Without taking a breath she continued, "Look at their mouths, I mean, when they're not laughing. The corners of their mouths turn downward, they droop. They just *look* miserable."

"Well, they don't look happy," Susan agreed, but knew the words Cindy spoke could just as easily describe her.

"I don't know about you, but Jerry and I have been married for thirty seven years. Every morning when I wake up, I give thanks that he is in my life, and he knows it!"

"I was just thinking the same thing," Susan lied because the disdain she felt for herself was overwhelming. "Richard and I have only been married for a few years, but I *know* I'm lucky. We don't always agree but we work it out, amicably."

Cindy sensed the reticence in her friend. "I know it may be a bit uncouth, me talking like this, but I guess I saw you sitting over here and could tell you weren't from around here. Just don't let the animals get you down." The woman felt compelled to explain. "I guess I let some of these people piss me off sometimes. Jerry and I were riding bikes one day and someone's dog attacked us. The dog wasn't fenced, or leashed, and bit my foot. I had running shoes on and the thick rubber sole protected me from the bite. When Jerry went to the guy's house and asked if he'd keep his dog locked up. Do you know what he said to Jerry?"

"No," Susan said.

"That there wasn't a leash law at the beach. Can you believe that?"

"What was the man's name?"

"Gaylord something-or-other," Cindy answered. "Listen, Jerry and I have a group of friends that get together for drinks every now and then. Would you and your husband like to come some time?"

"Sure."

The women were interrupted when Karen shouted loudly, "Cindy, get over here. I'm a dollar waitin' on a dime, girl!"

Cindy stood and walked toward the empty chair. She stopped and turned toward Susan. "I'll give you a call sometime."

"That would be nice."

When Cindy sat down, Karen continued to entertain the ladies. "Ya'll know my friend Jocelyn, right?"

Several of the ladies replied in unison, "Yeah."

"Well, the other day that girl went to Panama, to the plastic surgeon, to get those Botox injections. Man, that girl has Botox in her forehead, collagen in her lips and silicon in her tits. I'm afraid if she has any other parts replaced, she'll be more like a mannequin in a dress shop than the girl I grew up with!"

The salon erupted in laughter, louder than any time before. Instead of participating in the innocent mirth, Susan wished that she could replace her soul with a synthetic substitute. No matter how difficult her life had been, she had never held such an ill opinion of herself.

Chapter Twenty-Nine

On the way home from work Richard drove past the house without slowing. He did not wish for another argument that had become all too common of an occurrence. There would be alcohol at Buster's, and that was all he desired. It had been the only constant in his life. Within moments of passing the house he stopped the Tahoe in front of the restaurant, engaged the left blinker and waited for oncoming traffic to clear. When it did, he turned the large truck into the parking lot. Gravel ground under the tires as he maneuvered into a spot near the front door. His head ached, craving the next drink that would numb his soul. He hurried out of the truck, imagining the smoky taste of the bourbon he was about to consume. Saliva formed in his mouth as he approached the entrance. When he reached the door he opened it and entered, moved past the hostess without a word and made his way to an empty seat at the bar. The stools had no backs and Richard plopped himself onto the chair by lifting his right leg over and around its seat. He stared at the bartender until he was noticed. "Maker's Mark and diet," he said.

"Comin' right up," the bartender replied as he grabbed a highball glass from a shelf above his head. "Are you going to be ordering food?" he asked while continuing to make the drink.

"That will do me fine," Richard said, as he pointed to the tumbler on the bar.

"Alright, but I'll leave a menu just in case." The bartender grabbed one from beneath the bar and placed it in front of Richard. "The specials are on the board," he continued while pointing at a lighted glass display at the end of the bar. The specials of the day had been scrawled on it with a yellow marker.

The stuffed flounder looked appetizing, but Richard was more interested in numbing the pain caused by his failed relationship. He could no longer ignore the deeds of his past. They bubbled into his consciousness and consumed any self-esteem that he might have been so bold to embrace. Dinner could wait. With a drink in his hand, he spun around on top of his chair and began to scan the crowd in the restaurant. He examined each table searching for Ralph. Anger and hatred welled up inside him at the thought of the man. It had been several years since he had seen him, and he was not sure he would recognize him. Regardless, he had always been an uninvited party in Richard's marriage.

When he finished examining the room, Richard turned and leaned against the bar. He looked to his left and then to his right, examining the faces at the bar just as he had done those in the restaurant. There were two women seated to his left. Each wore an ornate ring on the third finger of their left hand. He wondered if they were married, until he noticed that the rings were of the same design. *They must be lesbians.* His bitterness was projected onto innocent bystanders. To his right was a handsome young couple that seemed very much caught up in themselves. *The honeymoon won't last.* The thought caused him a visceral pain that swelled into his throat. He tried to drown it with a large swallow from his drink.

There were two empty chairs to his left and one to his right. Richard spent the better part of an hour getting stoned on booze. Talitha's rejection of his advance further isolated him. After his fourth drink, he began to feel the affect of the alcohol on his empty stomach. He became queasy. In order to get the bartender's attention, he held his hand in the air, index finger extended. When the man noticed him he said, "You know what?" the words felt uncomfortable exiting his bourbon soaked mouth. Richard flexed his cheek muscles and wagged his numb tongue. He tried to clearly annunciate his request. "You know what? I think I *would* like to order some dinner."

"What'll you have?" the bartender asked, responding quickly to his request as he continued making drinks for the diners.

"Stuffed flounder," he said, pointing to the menu board on the wall.

"You got it." The bartender walked quickly over to his point-of-sale system and pounded his right index finger onto the screen as he entered the order.

Richard brought the highball glass to his lips, leaned back, and tilted it upward, finishing the drink. He held the empty glass up so that the bartender could see it. When he did and nodded confirmation of another drink order, Richard placed the empty on the bar in front of him and began to slide it between both hands.

He sat playing with his empty glass when a young lady approached the bar and sat on the stool to his left. Richard looked over and the two exchanged a pleasant smile. *She's pretty*. He looked to the right and then to the left, past the young lady. There were several empty stools around the bar. That meant she had chosen to sit next to him. Richard sat up straight slowly so she wouldn't notice him removing the bow from his sagging back. His mind, numbed by alcohol, began to race with possibilities. When he felt that he had gained his composure, he turned toward the young lady. "Are you from around here?"

She smiled politely, responding only with a shake of her head.

"I have a house down the beach." He attempted, once again, to start a conversation. Then he remembered Susan. Slowly he moved his left hand under his right, pinched his wedding ring between his middle finger and thumb, and slid it off. He dropped his hand down by his side and shoved the band into his front pocket.

"That's nice," she said with a smile, like before.

Richard worried that he was being too forward and decided to back off. He squared his shoulders to the bar and continued to drink.

"I'm Paula," she said as she extended her hand.

Richard turned to the girl, took her hand in his and began to serenade her. The alcohol was responsible for the bold nature of his gesture. "Heeey, heeey, Paula. I want to marry you." Realizing from her blank stare that she was not familiar with the song, he explained. "That was a hit song many years ago, by Paul and Paula."

"Ah," she said, not overly enthused.

"You're obviously too young to be familiar with the song. I'm sorry. It seemed like an appropriate icebreaker."

She nodded and smiled. "You do have a nice voice."

"Thanks." Richard desired to continue the conversation, but did not want to come across as being pushy. He didn't have to say anything.

"You asked a minute ago, whether or not I lived here," Paula started. "The answer is, I kinda do, but I don't really." She noticed the confused look on Richard's face. "My grandmother has a house here, just a couple of blocks off the beach. Every now and then I'll come and stay with her."

"You didn't bring her with you tonight?" he asked.

"No. Sometimes we like to have our time away from each other."

Richard turned and faced Paula once again. His movement allowed him to appreciate what a beautiful girl sat before him. She wore jeans, an old white t-shirt and leather work-boots. A tweed coat looked as if it was meant to add a bit of dressiness to her outfit. She was thin, tan, and blonde, but something about her conveyed strength, both physical and emotional. Her hair did not have the steely tinge associated with bleaching by chemicals. The highlights looked natural. "So, where do you live when you aren't visiting your grandmother?"

"All over the world," she replied, in a matter-of-fact tone.

"Your business takes you around the world?"

"Yeah."

"What is your business?" he asked.

"I'm a deck hand on a cargo ship."

"Wow!" Although her answer had not fully registered with him, he was truly impressed. "How'd you get started doing that?"

"Out of high school I knew that there was much more to this world than my little hometown could offer. Hopping on a boat and earning my keep was the only way I could afford to see it."

Richard was ready to declare Paula the most interesting woman he had ever met. She was impressive and had worldliness associated with an advanced age.

He became jealous at the notion that someone so young could have it all together while his life crumbled around him. "You *never* had any emotional attachments that kept you in one place?" he asked.

Paula shook her head without saying a word.

"Where was the last place you visited?"

"I just got off a boat that traveled throughout the Pacific Rim. We went to Japan, China, New Zealand, Australia … all over that part of the world, really."

They talked for several minutes. The more conversation there was the more Richard became impressed with her. This woman was like no other he had ever known. It may have been his imagination running amuck, but Paula's voice began to sing to him. "Do I detect an accent?"

The look on her face conveyed shock. She hesitated before answering. "It's a speech impediment."

"I … I'm sorry," he said as he quickly turned away from her and faced the bar. He had no idea what to say, other than the apology he offered.

Paula finished her drink, paid her check and got down off the stool. "It was nice talking to you," she said just before walking away.

He could only nod in response and give a half-hearted wave as he recognized the impediment for what it was. Richard finished his drink and held the empty glass up for the bartender to see. When he had, Richard held it to his lips and shook a piece of ice from it into his mouth and began to chew nervously. He placed it back on the bar as he waited for his refill. An expeditor appeared in front of him with a plate of food, carrying it with a cloth dishtowel to avoid being burned. He had lost his appetite, but knew that if he planned on drinking more, he should eat something. Sitting quietly as he

226

ate, he worried that those around him may have over-heard his gaff and was too embarrassed to make eye contact with anyone, especially the bartender.

A little old man appeared behind the bar with a garbage can filled with ice. He dragged it along the floor until he reached a large steel bin that sat on the floor beneath the bar. It was obvious that the man's appearance was more aged than the chronology of his years. His skin was leathery with deep wrinkles, and his hair was perfectly white, void of any trace of color. When he bent over to lift the container and pour the ice into the bin, Richard saw a pack of filter-less Camel cigarettes in his left shirt pocket. He was so engaged in observing the actions of this old man that he did not notice a young man who had taken the empty stool to his right.

"Hey Sol," the young man said to the old bar-back.

"Hey, kiddo. What's up?"

"I'm pissed," the kid responded.

"Why? What happened?" the old man asked.

"Some asshole smashed out the window to my truck. He stole my wallet, my fishing pole and my iPod."

The old man looked confused. "*iPod*? You deserve to have it stolen."

"*What*?"

"Yeah, ain't that one of them pot-smoking devices?"

Richard laughed as he held his napkin to his mouth to keep from spewing masticated flounder across the bar. The kid laughed as he looked at Richard. "It's a device that stores music, Sol," the kid explained.

"Oh. Well, you stay away from them drugs anyway," Sol said as he walked back into the kitchen, carrying the empty garbage can behind him. It was clear to the two that the old man did not appreciate being the object of their laughter.

Richard finished his dinner and slid the plate across the bar to be cleared away. He sat, just as he had done the previous two hours, sipping from a drink and wiping the condensation from the glass with his thumb. A woman approached and sat on the stool that had been occupied earlier by Paula. Richard, still a bit gun-shy, looked over at her and offered only a smile, which was returned. "This seat isn't taken … by your wife, is it?" she asked.

Richard shook his head as he held up his left hand, wiggling his third finger showing that there was not a ring on it.

"Where are you from?" she asked, as she crawled on top of the stool.

"Here. I have a house just down the beach." Richard pointed in the direction of the house.

"Oh, how nice. I've always dreamed of owning a house on the beach." She smiled. "Maybe one day."

Her body language conveyed her desire to continue the conversation, so he turned and faced her. "My name is Richard," he said, extending his hand.

"I'm Monica," she replied, and took his hand in hers. He noticed that her grip was soft, not nearly as strong as Paula's. She wore a pair of teal clam diggers, a bright orange tube-top underneath an unbuttoned Hawaiian shirt whose panels were tied in a knot at her waist. Her makeup consisted of bright blue eye shadow, red blush and orange lipstick. It was hard for Richard to discern the true color of her hair. There were yellow, or-

ange and red highlights streaked through it in a haphazard and unnatural manner. *She does have a nice body*,
Richard thought. He looked her over and noticed that
between the open panels of her shirt that she had a
rather impressive cleavage heaving above the top that
wrapped her body. "So, Monica, are you married?" he
asked.

She hesitated, as she played with the rings on
her left hand with the thumb of the same hand. "Yeah,
but that doesn't matter tonight," she replied while smiling.

He felt as though this relationship had been
defined from the moment of its inception, and he became sure of it. His body tingled with excitement as he
became caught up in the thrill of the chase. There was
nothing about her that could deliver him from his emotional malaise, but she would fulfill his most basic of
needs. "Has anyone ever told you that you look like,"
Richard paused. He was going to say Raquel Welch, but
felt she would be too young to know Raquel. Out of the
blue, it came to him, "Christina Aguilera?" The moment
the words came from his mouth he realized that he had
never given Susan a compliment like that. Maybe it was
because she was such a beautiful woman in her own
right that her beauty didn't need to be justified by such
a comparison.

"No. That's so sweet, though," Monica said.
"Ever since I've gone red, my father calls me his little
Raquel Welch."

Richard tried not to laugh. "Yeah, I can see that.
They are both beautiful women."

"Thank you," she said. "Now let's see … who
do you look like?" She examined every inch of
Richard's face. "Yeah, that's it. I saw this actor once on

a television show. He's older, like you, I think his name is Timothy Hutton."

Richard once again chuckled to himself at the irony that Timothy Hutton's career had spanned decades and yet Monica seemed to be aware of only an obscure television show. "I know exactly who you're talking about. I'll take that as a compliment."

"It was meant to be one," Monica said.

The two sat for over an hour drinking and talking mundanely. Richard had quite a head start on Monica, and he drank water while she quickly drank four fruity, yet powerful drinks. She slid off her shoes, allowed them to drop to the floor and began to rub her feet along his shin, sensually caressing his leg. He took one last sip of ice water. "Monica," he announced, "I'm a little too old to play footsie with you. Let's cut to the chase. Would you like to take a walk on the beach with me?"

She did not respond. Instead, she slid herself from her stool, reached down and picked up her shoes and began to walk toward the door. Richard was not sure if he was supposed to follow her, but he did. The two left the restaurant, walked across the deck, and went down the stairs to the beach. Giant floodlights mounted on the roof shined onto the sand below, which made it necessary for them to walk far away in order to have the privacy they desired. They walked to the shoreline, turned and proceeded down the beach.

"I know the perfect spot," Richard said, as he pointed toward the house. The fifteen-minute trek provided them the opportunity to playfully frolic in the surf, and to embrace. Kissing Monica was odd. He was used to holding Susan. Her back was broader than his wife's. It didn't matter. He ached for a physical encounter with a woman, any woman.

When they reached the house, he almost pointed it out to her, then thought better of it. He walked over to the Adirondack chairs, where there was an oversized beach towel Susan left a couple days before, removed it and led Monica to the secluded spot in the dunes where he and Susan had made love several times. Once the towel was spread evenly on the sand, he held her hand as she lowered herself onto the makeshift bed. He knelt beside her. They kissed. Richard untied her shirttail, removed it from her shoulders and laid it gently on one corner of the towel. She pulled away from the kiss and hastily unbuttoned his shirt. She slid it off his shoulders and down his back, then tossed it aside carelessly. He laughed.

Richard found himself unsure of whether he should pull the tube-top over her head or slide it down her hips and off her legs. It didn't matter. She crossed her arms and grabbed the bottom of it and in one motion pulled it over her head, then tossed it aside in the same manner that she had done his shirt. There was no bra to remove. The cleavage that burgeoned from her top was still evident. Her breasts hadn't moved. *They're fake*, Richard thought as he reached out with his right hand and placed it on her left breast. He stroked her nipple with his thumb. No matter how gently he touched it, full stimulation did not occur.

After several minutes of wrestling each other from their remaining clothes they lay side-by-side on the towel, touching and pawing each other while vigorously kissing. He held a breast in his hand, but could not seem to concentrate on making love to this woman. Instead, he found himself thinking about how he could feel the difference between her natural flesh and the silicon pouch. He did not find this stimulating. It was more of a distraction.

Finally, he rolled Monica onto her back, and positioned himself over her. He took the time to look at her naked body. His eyes scanned every curve, slowly, all the way down to her waist. He leaned back, sitting on his heels. He looked over her legs and caressed them.

She drew in her legs and allowed them to fall open, inviting him to couple with her. He leaned forward and supported his weight by placing his hands on the towel on each side of her head. The sense of pleasure was broken when he threw his head back in ecstasy and opened his eyes. In the window of the house, swaying from side-to-side, and illuminated by the kitchen light hung the stained-glass heart that Susan's father had given her. In that instant, Richard realized that he had once again allowed himself to succumb to an experience that would not last. Yet again, a casual relationship undermined one that was meant to be eternal.

Chapter Thirty

The next morning Richard drove toward town. It was close to noon, but he did not care. He had let Susan down. Who cared about a few customers? Regardless of what Susan had supposedly done, he *knew* that he cheated on her. His dalliance with Monica burdened his mind. He wondered how he could have worked so hard to overcome his past, only to allow it to overtake him. There was no other resolution. The relationship with his wife was over. He had always known the reality of what his life would be without her. No one had given him the tools necessary to be the kind of man his wife deserved; someone who could handle adversity without crisis. For that reason, Richard knew his life was a mere trifle and each day passed without growth. He had seen the changes to his appearance each day as he looked in the mirror, and growing old without accomplishment was not appealing to him. His body was decaying without the enrichment he craved that would yield the self-esteem that had never been instilled in him.

There were so many thoughts racing through his mind that he did not notice as he drove over the railroad tracks that divided the town, jostling the truck. Just as he passed them he saw a small shopping center on the side of the road. He passed it twice daily, on the way to and from work. Quickly, he steered the truck into its parking lot and stopped in front of a liquor store that occupied the space at the end of the building. Richard remembered that he was out of bourbon. He had to stop.

After getting out of the truck he walked up the few steps to an elevated landing that ran the length of the center. When he approached the front door of the store he stopped suddenly and stood holding the door open as he shook his head in disbelief. *There's no way*, Richard thought. He walked inside and proceeded to the section of shelving against the back wall that contained several varieties of bourbon. Removing the brand he wanted, he made his way to the register and paid. He left the store and walked to the opposite end of the landing, pausing at its edge. There were no steps and the drop was nearly four feet. Richard stood and stared down the side street. The visual representation of what he had come to understand about Erstwhile was gut wrenching. In front of him was a row of shanty houses; homes that were occupied by the poorest residents of the small town. Railroad tracks divided the neighborhood and the downtown district. He leaned over so that he could see farther down the road. There was a baseball field a couple hundred yards away, directly behind the plaza. On it several children played a pick-up game; all of their faces were black.

He jumped off the sidewalk and onto the gravel shoulder next to the road. Placing the paper bag containing the bottle of bourbon on the landing against the wall, he attempted to make it as inconspicuous as possible; then began to walk, passing one shanty after another. Each one, although quite similar in design to the next, had its own personality. Richard knew that children lived in one of the homes because there were small bikes on the front porch. The thought of children and their innocence made him smile as he remembered his own youth. That was the last time he remembered believing in his dreams.

The next dwelling had two brand new rocking chairs on its deck, and Richard noticed the bottom panel of the screen door had been torn out.

After passing several homes and imagining the type of existence each occupant led, Richard saw an old lady sitting outside of her house. She sat on an old two-seater sliding rocker made of steel. It was painted white and mottled with rust. There was a green clamshell pattern on its back. He walked off the road and approached the house. When he got closer he saw that she was holding a glass of lemonade on her leg. Her thigh was so thin and boney that the bottom of the glass completely covered it with room to spare on either side. The ice had melted, leaving the heavier lemonade at the bottom of the glass and a layer of water on top. Condensation dripped along the outside. The old woman lifted it with her off-hand, freeing the one in which she had held the lemonade so that she could sling the water from her fingers, before returning it to its original position.

"Hello," Richard called to her. The closer he got the woman's frailty became more apparent.

"Hello young man," she replied, cheerfully.

"Mind if I have a seat?" He sat at the edge of the porch, conscious of not intruding, un-invited.

"Go right ahead. Would you like a glass of lemonade?" she asked as she held up her glass.

"Yes, thank you."

Reaching down by her side she lifted a pitcher of something that resembled the contents of her glass; lemonade on bottom, melted ice on top; then placed it on her unoccupied thigh. The glass she held was set atop the arm of the rocker. Then she shifted the carafe of lemonade to her dominant hand, freeing the other to retrieve a clean goblet from a tray next to her feet. Richard watched in amazement at how limber this elderly woman was. She blew into the glass to remove any debris that may have settled in it. Richard smiled. After filling the glass, she leaned forward and handed it to him.

"Thank you."

"You're welcome," she replied, as she placed the pitcher down beside the rocker and lifted her glass of lemonade from its arm. "My doctor doesn't like me to have lemonade. 'Too much sugar,' he says."

Richard took a sip. He chewed on the pulp that burst with fresh juice. "Wow! This is *the best* lemonade I've ever had."

"My grandma used to make it for me when I was a girl. There's nothing better on an Indian summer day. Don't know how many more days like this I'm gonna have, so I figure I'll get as much of it as I can stand."

"What is your name?" he asked.

"Harriett Tubman Eubanks," she responded proudly, as she stuck out her boney chest, rooster-like and smiled.

"Powerful name!" he said. "I'm Richard Styles."

"Pleased to make your acquaintance, Mr. Styles."

"Likewise, Mrs. Eubanks."

The two sat quietly sipping their lemonade. An occasional car drove past and Richard noticed that he was getting a few stares. It didn't bother him. He knew they were only concerned for Harriett.

"Mr. Styles, it might not do my reputation any good for a widow woman, such as myself, to be seen with a young man, such as yourself," she said jokingly, pointing her boney finger at him. Harriett sensed that he was uncomfortable and wished to lighten the mood.

"I can assure you, and your folks, that my intentions are honorable, Mrs. Eubanks." Richard referenced a time when parents were truly their child's guardian, having their best interest at heart.

Harriett giggled giddily.

"Have you lived here all your life?" He asked, before drinking from his lemonade.

"Oh no, I've been all over the world," the woman said. "I volunteered as a nurse during World War II. I saw duty in Italy, France and I was in London … Trafalgar Square, to be exact, when Winston Churchill declared the Allied victory." She continued, "Boy, there was some partying going on over there."

"Tell me about it. I'd love to hear your story."

She rocked in her chair and thought for a moment. "There was joy everywhere. We had all been through that horrible war together. We'd seen the worst that human beings could do to one other. And then, we celebrated together. It was a time when the pain was over and joy took its place." The expression on Harriett's face dropped. "It didn't matter whether you were an American, English, French, black or white, we all accomplished that victory together." In an attempt to lighten the mood she quipped, "Hell, I think we even had a few Russians partying with us."

Chills ran down his spine as he watched her face light up with pride. "I went to Trafalgar Square with my wife on our honeymoon." Richard paused at the thought of the failed relationship. "That was a long time ago."

"How long?"

"Three years."

She laughed as hysterically as her frail body would allow. He appreciated the great difference in his life perspective compared to Harriett's.

"Okay, I realize how silly that statement was," he conceded.

"There is a reason why you feel your honeymoon was so long ago. You got troubles?"

Her wisdom pierced his soul. "Yes."

She furrowed her brow. "I know it's none of my business, but isn't the reason you moved to Erstwhile so that you could spend more time with your wife?"

"You know about me?"

"We all do," she said, sweeping her hand over the landscape of the shanty homes.

He continued, "Getting in touch with one's past is not always a good thing."

Harriett wagged her finger at Richard. "Don't put too much pressure on yourself. People are people. We all make mistakes."

"Or, maybe I haven't tried hard enough," he countered.

"Whatever!" She took a sip of lemonade.

Her response caused him to stop and think about her words for a moment. "I've already let Susan down."

"How?"

"By forcing her to move to Erstwhile. She's obviously not happy here."

She laughed. "I hate to burst your ego, but your wife didn't do anything she didn't want to do. She came here because she loves you. I'm sure of that." She gave Richard a few seconds to respond. When he didn't, she continued, "Have I got to draw you a picture? You can't make her happy unless you're happy. Not until all of what's inside you is resolved can you even begin to hope to make her happy."

He admired her honesty, but it hurt because he was not sure he was the man Susan wanted. He was trapped in a situation where he could not be content knowing she desired someone other than him.

"Do you mind if I ask how old you are?"

"Ninety-three."

"So, you were in your thirties during the war."

"Yep."

Richard struggled for a tactful manner in which to ask his next question. "It seems that things in Europe were good for you after the war. And, since you were a mature young woman who, I am sure, could take care of herself …"

"Ask your question and stop beating around the bush," Harriett demanded as she turned her glass up, emptying it.

"Why didn't you stay?" She did not answer. Richard saw tears welling up in her eyes. He asked, "Did you fall in love over there?"

She smiled. "Several times. I fell in love with every man I took care of that had been wounded in battle."

Somewhat frustrated, he pressed, "Did you have a *true* love?"

"A lady doesn't discuss such things." She smiled, briefly.

"I'm sorry," Richard said.

"There's no need to be sorry. It's just that I haven't thought about this for a long time." She composed herself and continued, "I was in love with a Russian officer. We met at a state function in London after the war. He wanted to get married. I agreed at first, but then called it off."

"*Why?*"

"Because I grew up in the south, I wasn't good enough for a man that wasn't black, much less an officer, or so that is what I was led to believe."

"Do you regret not staying?"

"Oh no! You can't regret things in life. I had a wonderful husband. We were married for fifty years. He died ten years ago." She paused, thinking more about her answer, "All my children live in big cities; that's what I passed to them, a realization that this way of life didn't offer anything for them, and they don't owe me anything. The answer to your question is, no, I don't mind sacrificing a little of my happiness for their well-being. That's what families do. We're supposed to make it a little better for the next generation." The smile returned to her face. "Besides, I could have spent the entire Cold War living in Moscow."

Richard laughed. "Any other regrets?"

She thought for a moment. "My biggest regret is that I haven't lived up to my name. Of course, that goes against everything I've just said to you. It is a pretty big burden to place on any kid, to live up to someone else's name. Life is to live, Richard. It is filled with decisions that we all have to make. We can't regret the ones we do make. We learn from the bad ones and then move on."

"What about how … I mean these nice people, how they're treated here?"

"Are you talkin' about these racist bastards?" She pointed toward the downtown buildings.

"Yes."

"Richard, if I am not who they say I am, then they are not who they think they are."

Richard pondered Harriett's words. He felt strength in them. "I think that is the greatest single quote I've ever heard in my life. Can I cite you?"

"Ain't my words to give. They belong to James Baldwin, but I'm sure he wouldn't mind being quoted."

"I'm embarrassed that I didn't know that."

"Richard, there's no need for you to be embarrassed. I know you treat people with the same sort of respect that you expect from everyone. You live your life within the spirit of that quote." She smiled. The wrinkles around her eyes and cheeks were exaggerated by her expression. He took comfort in the wisdom they represented.

"I really need to get to work." Richard placed his empty glass on the porch. "You take care of yourself, Harriett." He walked toward his truck without looking back. As he strolled along the avenue he replayed the Baldwin quote over-and-over in his mind. Guilt over his association with Gaylord wracked his core. He could not overcome the person he had been brought up to be, and he knew it was hopeless to try. His fate had been determined decades earlier. There had been one moment of clarity for him while attending college. The only 'A' that he received in a Philosophy class was given after searching deep within his soul. Conveyance of his inability to push himself to a higher state of consciousness was contained in his only answer on a midterm exam. The test had five essay questions, but Richard only wrote one sentence across the top of his page: *Passive participation in an ill-conceived quest stifles the passion for ambition.*

When he came to the rear of the shopping center, Richard grabbed the bottle of bourbon, got in the truck and drove to the store.

Chapter Thirty-One

Richard lay asleep in the guest room. He found it impossible to face Susan after his tryst with Monica. Most of the day had been spent thinking about his conversation with Harriett. It had been difficult for him to translate her experiences into his own, enabling him to heed her counsel. Not a single customer came into the store during the day. At least, not that he saw. He had alienated everyone around him for no other reason than his inability to view them through anything less than the tainted spectacle of his own existence. The bottle of bourbon he purchased on the way to work remained sealed. His depression manifested itself physically and made him feel as though he was encased in lead, unable to move freely. An emotional anvil pressed down on his psyche and removed the inspiration for accomplishment. The alarm clock projected the numbers "3:36" onto the ceiling above him. His slumber was fitful at best. He tossed and turned all night, fluffing his pillow continuously, and throwing it against the wall on one occasion.

Suddenly, Richard sat straight up in bed. He awoke from his shallow sleep and gasped mightily, trying to fill his lungs with air. His heart beat rapidly. Never had he felt so helpless and out of control. When he was finally able to calm down and catch his breath, he tried to think about what might have caused his panic attack. He could not discern the array of thoughts that entered his mind as either fantasy or reality. Should he wake Susan, or not? Would she even care? He decided to let her sleep. Lifting himself out of bed was difficult. The burdens of his life had accumulated and made it difficult to negotiate his way, emotionally and physically. He stopped and leaned against the doorframe and tried to regain his bearing. After a few moments, he resumed his march into the living room. His breathing normalized with each step. The refreshing breaths made him feel better. He did not want to die this way; weak and without resolution. In an effort to gain control he walked in circles around the floor of the living room. The oxygen that filled his lungs felt good. When he was able to breathe normally, he sat on the sofa and turned on the television using its remote control.

Richard never had a panic attack before, and his thoughts raced, wondering what may have caused it. *My left arm isn't numb, so it can't be a heart attack, right?* Mindlessly he channel-surfed and was oblivious to the shows that quickly flashed on the screen. Without thinking, he stopped on the always-entertaining local access station. Maybe it was the sound of dogs barking that caused him to do so, but he was still more concerned with what caused his ailment than the programming.

As he gained his composure Richard seemed to recall the details of a dream that fluttered in-and-out of his consciousness. He was never one to have vivid dreams, but when he did they were spectacular, and often quite odd. The dream was vague, but he recalled being on a plane from Stockholm. Where the plane was going Richard could not quite remember, but he was sure that Susan was waiting for him at the end of his flight. *I remember getting to the airport and Susan being there, and then realizing that I had forgotten my luggage in Stockholm*, he thought to himself. *Then I got right back on the plane, by myself, to go back and get it.* He shook his head and wondered why that would have caused him to have a panic attack. It all seemed so mundane.

The constant sound of barking dogs drew his attention away from his thoughts and to the program. He watched several men and young boys who were in the woods before dawn; each had a miner's light attached to their caps. They were gathered at the base of a tree and all of them were looking up. One young boy, who appeared to be no more than twelve years old, had a hand-held light and shined it into the top of the tree. Among the men and boys were six or seven dogs, barking and howling upward as they pawed at the trunk. A voice off camera said, "We got him treed boys!" Richard recognized the voice as the same man who officiated the cast net contest. When the camera panned the crowd he recognized Gaylord and Two-Guns.

The young boy holding the light in his hand pointed to the top of the tree, and in a disturbingly excited tone yelled, "There he is. *Shoot him!*"

A grown man with a rifle stepped in front of the young man, took aim and shot into the top of the tree. It was not a powerful gunshot. Richard assumed the gun to be .22 caliber.

"Did you hit 'im?" another voice off camera asked.

"I think so," the man said, as he aimed again and fired the rifle several more times. Off camera the sounds of an agonizing squeal could be heard. Richard realized there must have been a raccoon in the top of the tree that had been hit several times.

Gleefully, the man with the rifle bragged, "Did you hear him squeal? I nailed him!" He aimed again and let loose another volley of four or five shots. They came in such a rapid succession that Richard could not count them all. Suddenly, something fell into and then out of the view of the camera from top to bottom. It entered and exited the screen too quickly for Richard to see what it was. A member of the hunting party walked over to the wounded animal. The cameraman focused on him. He picked the raccoon up by its beautifully ringed tail and held it up for all to see; well away from his body. The raccoon squirmed for its very survival. The man made every effort to keep it as far away from his body to avoid being bitten or scratched. The distressful sound of the raccoon's squeals began to fade.

Richard began to cry. It was not the death of the raccoon that caused his distress, but the vivid recollection of the dream that woke him. Tears welled in his eyes as he watched the man holding the raccoon toss it onto the ground in the middle of the dogs. They attacked it, biting and pulling. Four dogs had the animal firmly clinched in their jaws, pulling with all the force their legs could produce in different directions. The sound of the raccoon's cry rose sharply and then the animal fell silent.

Richard's heart began to race, once again, witnessing the barbarity. Was he capable of that kind of barbarous action? His dream seemed to confirm that he was. What bothered him most was that he was not sure whether or not it was only a nightmare. He could not only see; he felt the murderous action, right down to the flexing of his triceps and biceps as he shook Susan by the throat. *It can't be true, it just can't.* He was not capable of killing his wife, was he? Or, were his actions true to his soul that had been exposed by his excessive use of alcohol? *What kind of man am I to even have these thoughts?*

Richard looked at his hands. He could feel Susan's throat being crushed by his tightening fingers; her larynx falling apart under his thumbs as they squeezed, reducing the bones to mere fragments. The sense of power and control in his thoughts scared him, badly.

Without changing out of his pajamas, or taking the time to put on shoes, Richard walked through the kitchen and grabbed the keys to the Tahoe from a hook on the wall next to the back door. He could have checked the master bedroom to see whether or not Susan was there and if she was all right. The truth either did not interest him, or he was scared of what he might find. He simply couldn't face it. Whether it was real or imaginary, they were his thoughts, and he needed to make sure they never turned into deeds. Richard had not had anything to drink in over twenty-four hours, so he could blame none of this on alcohol. He walked out of the house and into the garage with a sense of determination.

Chapter Thirty-Two

Merlin's was filled with patrons when Richard walked through the door. There were so many people there that he found himself in a state of confusion. Everyone's voice echoed through his head and it hurt. The seat next to Jake was the only one empty and the two old men who always occupied the last booth against the far wall were there. Richard saw that one of them had his hand on a small stack of paper on the table in front of him. It was held together with a black Acco clip, fastened in the upper left corner. The old man drummed his fingers on the stack as he made eye contact with Richard. It confused him. Was the old man extending an invitation, or simply staring? He shook away the thought and walked to the seat he normally occupied and sat down.

Merlin saw him and began to make a drink without the two men exchanging a word. The blackness of his depression clouded his mind and made it heavy. He had no desire to talk to any of his friends. He only wanted to drink in peace and sort through the many thoughts that disturbed him. There was no way that he could concentrate. The sound of pool balls cracking as they slammed into one another on the table behind him ricocheted off the inner walls of his skull. He teetered between madness and lucidity.

Merlin placed the drink on the bar in front of Richard. He immediately picked it up and drank it in one long swallow. The bartender shook his head as his friend reached across and placed the empty on the far edge of the counter, silently requesting another.

"What are you doing here so early in the morning?" Jake asked.

"Just need a drink," Richard replied. "What about you?"

Jake laughed. "Don't you know? I live here. This place is like my living room."

Richard took the second drink that Merlin placed in front of him and drank half in a single gulp. Logic crept into his mind and he decided not to drink it too rapidly. He needed his wits about him to accomplish the task at hand. In the corner of the bar sat a beautiful dark-skinned woman. Jet-black, wavy hair hung well below her shoulders. Her eyes were light brown and bright. She appeared to be very tall, judging from how high she sat relative to the top of the bar. Richard found himself wondering how long her legs were. They exchanged smiles.

He looked around the room and noticed that Gaylord and Two-Guns were seated in the booth next to the two old men. He found it odd that Two-Guns wore his holsters, guns and all. He finished his second drink and held the glass up, signifying his desire for another. Merlin obliged. Richard looked at the woman at the end of the bar. She smiled at him, again. Pointing toward the end of the bar, he motioned to Merlin that he would take his drink there. He got up and walked the familiar path to the end of the bar and around its edge. The young lady spun around on top of her chair to face him as he approached her from behind. There wasn't a seat available next to her.

He extended his hand. "I'm Richard."

The young lady took his hand in hers and gave one exaggerated shake. "Neferet."

Richard knew this name, or at least its meaning. "Your name means beautiful woman. And I would say it is quite apropos."

"You are correct, and thank you," she said.

"Are you visiting from out of town?"

"You could say that."

He shrugged his shoulders and furrowed his brow, not understanding what other option there could be.

"Actually, I came here to see you," she admitted.

"Me?"

"You don't remember me, do you?"

"I would *never* forget a beautiful woman like you."

She smiled. "Okay, it's a little unfair of me because I've changed my name. It used to be Marianne, Marianne Massarat."

He recognized the name as that of a high school classmate. "The name you chose shows that you definitely don't lack any confidence." He thought about Sara and the affect he had on her self esteem.

"No thanks to you," Neferet said.

Richard dropped his head and shook it. He could not believe the day he was having. "And exactly how did I destroy *your* confidence?"

"You wouldn't go out with me because you couldn't understand that I wasn't black. I'm Egyptian, asshole!"

Richard drew in a deep breath and exhaled every bit of air in his lungs. He tried to remain calm. "Marianne, it sounds to me like you're the one that has a problem, because you didn't want to be thought of as black."

"I didn't care what people thought of me. You're the only one I ever gave a damn about."

"Can't it simply be explained that I was not interested in dating you, for no other reason than just *not … being … interested*?"

"Yeah, you weren't interested because you thought I was black," she insisted.

"Look Marianne, I just told you I thought you were a beautiful woman." Richard's response bordered on pleading. "I came over to talk to you, didn't I?"

"Yeah, and why did you come over here?" She didn't wait for a response. "Because you're trying to prove to yourself that you aren't a racist. I'm not a stupid little school-girl that you can toy with, Richard."

In a calm tone that masked the turmoil inside, he responded, "I came over because you smiled at me. I thought you wanted to get to know me. Instead you've done nothing but berate me. So, I'm going back over to my seat."

Richard strolled across the floor on legs numbed by alcohol. When he rounded the corner of the bar, he looked at the booths along the wall. The old man was still drumming his fingers on top of the stack of paper. They made eye contact and the elder motioned with his right hand for Richard to come over. He did. "Yes, sir?" he inquired, as he approached the booth.

The old man slid further into the booth, making room for Richard. He slapped the seat next to him, for the first time removing his left hand from the stack of paper. "Sit down." Richard sat silently, waiting for the man to speak. "Do you know who I am?" the old man asked. Richard shook his head. The man slid the stack toward him. The name on the top of the page, Wilbur, was that of his late grandfather; a man that he had loved and respected more than any other. "I always intended to write down some of what I considered important details about my life so that future generations could hopefully benefit from my experiences. I always hoped that it would be relevant enough for each person who read it to get something out of it." The man paused. "I think there are a couple of things in here you need to read. You don't have to read the entire thing. I've underlined what I think is important."

"I don't want to read what you've written," Richard said. "Aren't you saying you wish you had done a better job communicating?"

Wilbur nodded.

"Well then, let's communicate with one another."

"Okay." His grandfather pulled the stack toward him and held it with both hands. "Often during my lifetime I wished that more opportunity had been available for my father and me to spend time together; that we could have known each other better. Since his death there have been many questions about his parents, grandparents, his childhood, his youth and about the times and customs of his generation that I would like to have known about. It wasn't to be: he was always busy making a living for his family. The world economy had a lot to do with it and I was concerned and busy with things about growing up, myself."

"Did you have a poor relationship with your father?"

"Oh no!" Wilbur insisted. "I just wish I had more time to spend with him for purely selfish reasons. And I wished that I had the intestinal fortitude to ask him some very hard questions. But I didn't and the opportunity passed all too quickly." He paused, thinking of what it was he wanted to say to his grandson. "We were living on our farm in Altamonte Springs, our first home in Florida that Dad had bought, sight unseen, from a friend of his in Canada so that we could live in a warmer and less severe climate, especially for mother's sake. She could not endure the cold Canadian winters." Wilbur took a sip of tea. "Wesley Thomas, a black man, probably in his thirties, lived not far away and came regularly to help Dad with the many, and always odd jobs around the house and yard. He dropped by to see us one morning and I asked him if he wanted to be white like me. I do not know what he said, but I thought he would never quit laughing and hollering."

"What brought that on?" Richard asked.

"I'll tell you," Wilbur said. "My brother Harry, about sixteen at the time, had sang, danced and played his trumpet in a Minstrel show held at Altamonte Springs Hotel the night before – a town-sponsored affair in which Harry played the part of End-Man for which they had blackened his face, neck and hands. I was not taken to the show, but watched Harry out in the back yard near the tool house upon his return, with soap and water, remove the burnt cork or whatever from his face and hands. I guess I thought that if the black could be washed away from my brother, that we could make Wesley white too."

Richard could not help but laugh at the story. "How did that affect you?"

"It hurt my feelings that Wesley laughed at me, but later on I realized what a good thing it was that he had such a good humor about my ignorance."

"I have never thought of you as an ignorant man," Richard stated, flatly.

"And I have Wesley to thank for that. I respected him so much that the ignorance I displayed in front of him hurt me deeply. From that moment forward I promised myself that I would never be ignorant of anything. If I ever encountered someone or something that I did not understand, or had a base of knowledge, I would educate myself."

Richard smiled. "I feel like I have benefited from your determination. Thank you."

Wilbur continued with another story, "I know you have heard many times how Sue and I met and how I picked her out from the very start to be my wife and your grandmother."

Richard smiled. "I do love that story. Wasn't it on a trip to Daytona Beach put together by your college fraternity?"

Wilbur smiled at the timeless memory. "Yes!"

Richard finished the story he had heard and admired numerous times. "And at the end of the evening you kissed through a plate glass window."

The smile on Wilbur's face grew wider. "I was so lucky to find your grandmother at such an early age. But no matter how long it takes, you will always know when you have found the right one."

"Did you and Sue ever have any rough times?" Richard and his cousins always called their grandmother by her first name. It was her wish.

"Oh boy, did we," Wilbur said. "Another thing I wish I had done a better job of was teaching your mother and her siblings that arguing is a part of marriage, and important because if you're arguing, you're communicating. The challenge is to learn from each other."

Richard seemed indifferent to his grandfather's advice. He saw that Wilbur's mood suddenly became very melancholy. "What's the matter?"

"There is one more thing that I have to share with you. It was the worst time of my life." Wilbur took a sip of tea, and felt obligated to start by saying, "But if I can overcome it, you can overcome any obstacle you encounter. I had something horrible happen to me as a boy that my family *never* talked about, which had a profound affect on me and was the reason I never felt comfortable discussing painful topics."

"What was it?"

Wilbur hesitated briefly as he took a deep breath. "At Scout meetings and other places, Allen Cahoon, James Godfrey and I talked about and planned a canoe trip from Wekiva Springs down to Lake Monroe and down the St. John's River to Jacksonville. I wasn't sure we could surmount the many difficulties bound to be connected with such an undertaking. Apparently, the others didn't feel this way as much as I did. With the help of troop leaders, especially Oscar Bernard and others, we obtained drawings and specifications for building canoes. James' parents allowed us to use the whole bottom floor of their two car garage apartment for the actual building. We were given most of the material needed – lumber from the McCormick Lumber Co., dad gave us the special canvas needed and someone else the green paint. Oscar Bernard was employed by the lumber co., which was a big help … brass screws, putty, hand picked cedar slating for the ribs and oak streamers for the framework came easily, so construction began and continued erratically. Working on our project was very irregular. Sometimes only one or two of us would be available in the mornings or afternoons. It took

254

probably eight weeks to complete the two canoes. I believe this was in the spring of 1923. James, Allen and I were fifteen."

"That was quite an undertaking. I admire your determination."

Wilbur continued without acknowledging his grandson's compliment. "Plans for the trip to Jacksonville began to take shape. The three of us, all Eagle Scouts, and one other, probably 'Red' Caruthers, were to make the trip. We checked with our parents for details and permission. They all reluctantly agreed with the stipulation that no guns were to be taken. Making the trip a reality progressed slowly as summer wore on. James could not make it. He was registered in Camp Idlewild with his brother, Frederick in New Hampshire on Lake Winnipesauke. Allen could not go because he was working in a machine shop, so it looked as though the trip was off until later when it would be more feasible and possible. Dad's business had been profitable to the extent that he organized a move from his East Pine Street store to a much larger and better location on the corner of Orange Avenue and Washington Street. His specialty was in imported fabrics for whom he had established a large clientele among the wealthy women of Central Florida. The need for a dressmaker developed and as a result Mrs. Gilstrap, I believe she was from Alabama, was employed. She moved to Orlando with her daughter, Ruth, a beautiful girl, probably eighteen years old and her son Mark about my age, fifteen or sixteen. He was good looking too and very personable, but chancy, always wanting to do this or that and be on the go. Somehow the canoe trip gathered interest again and was beginning to bear fruit. Red Caruthers, Mark and I were to take one of the canoes. Being ten feet long and with a wide center beam and storage compartments in both the bow and stern the three of us could travel comfortably with light gear; food, bedding, clothes and all the other necessities. The date was set. We were to push off at Wekiva Springs early one Wednesday morning. I'm not sure, but I believe Harold hauled us with the canoe and our gear to the springs in his truck. Anyway, we got started down the Wekiva River enjoying the scenery and occasionally stopping along the banks to fish. I was completely absorbed in the excitement of such an adventure. Was it real? Were we really going to Jacksonville by canoe? Yes, we were! For lunch we had sandwiches prepared for this, our first meal without stopping. As the afternoon wore on we began to look for ideal places to spend our first night under the stars. At about four in the afternoon we saw a bridge ahead. 'Maybe this would be the place,' and it was. The river here was flowing slowly east from west. To our right was a sandy beach and an opening among the background of trees and bushes. It could have been a boat landing. The bridge crossed the river going north and south. Checking our map we determined where we were. Sanford was three to five miles to the south. After landing and exploring the area we went up a steep bank to the road. There was only one house about a hundred yards north of the bridge on the right hand side. I assumed that the people living there were farmers."

Richard was enthralled, hanging on every word as the story in his mind began to take shape.

"The three of us went back to the landing, took what gear we needed from the canoe which we had pulled up on land, to fix a place to cook and pitch our tent. With this done, we proceeded to set out our trotline across the river, which I guess was about fifty yards wide at this point. Our trotline, which we had put together before leaving home with hooks, weights and all, was seventy-five yards long. Tying one end to a large myrtle tree at the shoreline down river a ways, we took the canoe and strung out the line to the other side. After adjusting the tension, we baited the hooks with bacon rind and part of a catfish we had caught on the way. Talking among ourselves while cooking supper we discussed what we would do with so many fish we were going to catch on the trotline. Of course, there were a lot of interesting stories told around the campfire; some true, I guess. Coming down the river before reaching our campsite Mark pulled from his luggage up front a pistol and asked if he might shoot at a turtle sunning on a log. I was shocked. Somehow, we had failed to impress upon him that no guns were to be brought along. I think he shot at the turtle once before we were out of range. The question came up about bullets. He had brought only those in the cylinder of the pistol. We agreed that as long as we had the gun and we might need it further along, one of us should catch a ride into Sanford to get more shells or bullets. We all slept well that night and were awakened by the rising sun. We each had a hand in cooking breakfast. When we finished a coin was flipped to see who would go into Sanford for the bullets. It turned out that Red was to go, so after cleaning up camp we got in the canoe to check the trotline. I can't remember what we had on the line. We had pulled ourselves across the river by checking the line as we went. Mark was in the bow of the canoe holding on to branches at the shoreline and suddenly he said, 'There's a snake!' I looked where he had pointed and saw the slim green snake on a bush about ten feet

257

away. He took his pistol and fired at it twice, but the snake was still there. I must have said something like, 'Mark, you couldn't hit the broad side of a barn. Let me have that gun.' As he passed it back to me the gun suddenly went off. The canoe rolled over as his weight shifted quickly to the left. I was frantic; Mark had been shot. I know I must have said, 'God help us!' Before I knew it we were both in the river. I was trying to keep his head above water and yelling for help at the same time. The water was so deep where we were that I could not touch bottom. I was yelling constantly for help while treading water. As I began to feel myself tiring, something told me to take Mark across to the other side. I put my arm across his chest with his head up above the water and swam to the other side where we had camped. I remember pulling him up on the shore, but nothing else after that until Harold came to me and said, 'We must go home.' I must have been in shock. As Harold helped me up to take me home, I realized that there were a lot of people there, where we had camped. I learned later that the farmers across the road had heard me yell for help. They were there with the sheriff and others; I would say maybe thirty in all. I asked Harold where Mark was. He replied that he had been taken to the hospital. On our way back home we stopped at the hospital in Sanford. Harold told me to stay in the car while he went in to check on Mark's condition. It was not long before he came out, started the car and was driving down the street when he told me that Mark was dead."

A chill ran down Richard's spine, and judging by the look on Wilbur's face, he was experiencing the same pain he had many years earlier.

"As time went on, I was to become a different person; for better or worse I do not know. I do know, however, that for me things were different, much different. I felt guilt, not knowing exactly how it happened. I was unsure whether or not it was my fault, or why it even happened. I had never been afraid to talk before a class or group even before the school assembly on Wednesday mornings but after this happened it was different. I avoided talking whenever I could and when it became necessary and demanding like talking before the Athletic Association meetings when I was president, it was a chore and I hated it. Harry Hughes, one of my classmates, stopped me on the sidewalk of Orange Avenue near the Angebuilt Hotel downtown to ask me how Mark was killed. I flushed up inside, so much so that I could hardly talk. It lasted only a short while, probably only a few minutes until I was able to answer him and other raw questions he posed. At first, I began to hate Harry Hughes who I had liked and thought a lot of. I didn't hate him long and later on, was glad that he had confronted me. It opened up a small passage in my psyche to let some of what I had been storing up inside come out. However, not much came out until years later."

"I've never heard that story," Richard said, overcome with sympathy for this man he had known his whole life, and a man that he wished to model his life after.

"Regarding the accident that took Mark's life; it was, and still is, strange to me that neither dad, mother or other members of the family mentioned it to me or asked questions. I know that everyone grieved immensely, but I guess they could not bring themselves to the point of discussing it and did not want to further hurt me. After Harold had brought me home that day and I was in my bedroom, mother came in, sat on the edge of the bed with me and hugged me. I felt comforted and relieved, but I do not remember our saying a word to each other that day. One day when I was visiting my sisters, Norah and Phyllis, I asked Norah how mother had taken the accident. She told me that at one point she had become hysterical and that it had been very difficult for her to endure. At the time, I guess I was thankful for not having to discuss it, pushing the thoughts far away into the recesses of my mind. Now I know differently. It would have been much better for all of us if it had been openly discussed."

Richard realized then how poignant it was that he insisted on his grandfather telling the story versus reading it.

"You see son, I'm afraid that I have failed your mother and you by not encouraging any of our family to be more open about our feelings. I did a horrible thing and kept it inside all those years, telling no one other than your grandmother, who I swore to secrecy."

"So what lesson am I supposed to take away from this?" Richard's inquiry bordered on sarcasm.

"There was not a day that went by that I did not give thanks for having your grandmother in my life. She knew every sordid detail of the man I was, and she loved me regardless. Richard, you cannot be the best person you want to be if you allow yourself to be ignorant; you cannot allow the ones you love to be ignorant of the man you are. No matter how ugly, how painful it might be, if you want someone to love you without question, they have to know you and be free of uncertainty."

The only person to ever fill that void in Richard's life had been Susan, and he was not sure she would be there to listen to the things he had to say. He looked across the table at the second old man. "You look familiar to me," Richard said. The man flashed a familiar smile. Then it dawned on him. "You're my other grandfather, aren't you? You died when I was five years old."

Without a word, the man nodded.

"What life lessons do you have for me?" Richard asked.

The man shrugged.

"It figures, from you!" Richard stood. He picked up the manuscript from in front of Wilbur. "I appreciate all the effort you put into this." He held it up. "But I'm sure it's too late for me." With that, he tossed the text back onto the table, walked back over to the bar and sat next to Jake. He placed his empty glass on the bar. Merlin picked it up and began making another drink.

Hours passed and the drinks flowed freely. Richard's pores oozed the alcohol that he consumed. He wiped the sweat from his brow and looked down at his shiny hand. Every breath was deliberate as he labored to draw in life-giving oxygen and expel the waste. His body was numb and he could not feel the stool beneath him. Merlin placed a fresh drink in front of him. It became difficult for him to focus on anything. Faces seemed familiar but were not immediately recognizable. The thoughts that entered his mind were dark and had been held well below his consciousness, until he asked. "Jake, have you ever killed anyone?"

Jake looked at Richard, astonished at the question. "I paid for an abortion for your sister, Sahara."

He took another large sip from his drink, ignoring Jake's response. "I have."

"Don't take this the wrong way my friend, but I'm not sure I believe you."

"It's true." He drank. "It was a kid that I killed. I *was* a kid. People that young should not be allowed to make a decision involving the life of a fetus. If only I could be sure that child has forgiven me, I might be able to live with myself."

Jake listened, intently.

"It's a trait that obviously runs in the family." At that moment Richard was more hurt to have learned that the man he loved and respected more than any other had been responsible for taking a boy's life. It could have easily been his grandfather that was killed that day. If that had been the case, Richard would not have to deal with the pain he felt.

"You've got murderers in your family?"

"Yep, and it's always some poor kid who won't get the opportunity to live out his life." He held his glass up in sarcastic salute.

Jake was not sure how to respond to his friend's glibness. Richard swayed involuntarily on his stool. Before the discussion could continue, there was a raucous commotion behind the two men. Jake spun around on his stool as did Richard, but more slowly. He came to rest facing the pool table and looked over to the booth where his grandfathers sat. They were no longer there. He shifted his gaze to the booth where Gaylord and Two-Guns were seated when he entered the bar and strained to focus on them through his blood-shot, burning eyes.

Standing on top of the pool table was a young man wearing battered jeans and sandals. He had a ponytail that was neatly braided and hung to the middle of his back. He began to yell, "You fucking rednecks have got to be the most ignorant lot of people that I have ever come across in my life!"

No one said a word. Everyone sat quietly, listening, which seemed to frustrate and incite the young man further. He picked up a ball from the table and threw it through the plate glass window at the front of the building. Looking around the room, it seemed surreal to the young man that no one was trying to stop him. *Maybe I'm getting through to them*, he thought. "You display this Confederate flag with pride! It's a symbol of hatred and oppression! Don't you dumb-fucks know that?" He stomped his feet all over the flag that adorned the felt on top of the table where he stood.

Still, no one responded so the young man jumped from atop the table to an empty one in a booth against the wall where the flag hung. He took a lighter from his pocket and lit the banner, then jumped back across to the pool table and admired the flames as they engulfed the flag. Miraculously, the wall was unscarred. Everyone watched silently as it burned until nothing but ashes remained, scattered across the tables and floor. The kid looked around the room. When there was no response he dejectedly hopped off the pool table and walked through the front door and onto the street.

Richard turned to Jake. "I admire that kid. He has the passion to speak his mind. I'd be a lot better off if I could do that."

"He walked out! He certainly didn't have too much conviction for his principles, did he?"

Richard ignored Jake and looked over at the booth where Gaylord and Two-Guns had been sitting, wondering if they had any reaction to the young man's speech. They were gone. He thought it was odd, because the only person he saw leave the bar was the kid, so he looked from side-to-side. The bar seemed a lot emptier than when he got there. "I'm going for a piss," Richard said to Jake as he stood from his stool and walked toward the end of the bar. He walked into the bathroom and became disoriented as he looked around. It was not the bathroom that he had known at Merlin's. Instead, Richard found himself in the back room of the store. He rubbed his lower right eye-lid as it began to twitch, nervously. Knowing exactly what he was looking for, he walked to the cabinet that hung on the wall above the toilet. Every experience he ever had swirled through his mind like a vortex. He could not make sense of anything any longer and all he wanted was peace. When he and Susan first came to Erstwhile, Richard worried that the decision to move was his and that she would not be happy. He realized that he had lived his life oblivious to how his actions affected those around him. Never once had he considered himself a selfish person, but it was apparent to him that he was, and that ate away at the very foundation of his being. No longer did he believe in himself. How could he have let down so many people in his life, and done so consistently. He opened the cabinet. Inside, on the top shelf, was a nine-millimeter gun. He removed it and held it in his open hand, steadying it by placing his middle finger through the trigger-guard. His hand was remarkably steady, but his eye continued to twitch. He pushed the cartridge release button. The sleeve fell into his open hand and he could tell that there were at least two bullets in the magazine. He placed the cartridge on the back of the toilet, and then with his free hand he pulled back on the slide to see if there was a bullet in the chamber. There was not. He replaced the magazine and repeated the motion on the slide, chambering one. With his thumb, Richard flipped the safety into the 'hot' position. He pointed the barrel of the gun toward his forehead, but held it away to look at the rifling. Making what he realized was his final decision; he pressed the gun hard against his forehead and pulled back the hammer with his index finger. His eyes were closed.

"What the *fuck* do you think you're doing?" a voice with a soft southern accent came from in front of him.

Richard opened his eyes to see his cousin, Taylor Watts. "The same fucking thing you did, only I'm going to do it with a gun." His cousin committed suicide after a bad motorcycle accident left him physically unable to lead a normal life. The once vibrant and impressive young man became dependent on a cane. He suffered a trauma to his head that left his vision severely diminished. It was the young, strong Taylor that stood before Richard.

"Just because I did it, you think that's the answer?"

"Oh no, there are a million reasons why, and not one why not," Richard said as he dropped the gun away from his head and onto his lap. He gently released the hammer against the firing pin.

"I can think of *one* reason why not that will far outweigh a trillion reasons why," Taylor said.

"What's that?"

"Susan."

He laughed. "Haven't you been paying attention?" Richard placed the gun against his head, again.

This time he rested it on his temple so that he could look his cousin in the eyes.

"Richard, you don't want to do that," Taylor said in a calm voice.

He closed his eyes, pulled back on the hammer and then heard another voice say, "Richard, you need to live with your mistakes, not die from them."

He opened his eyes and looked beyond Taylor. Standing there was Freddy Wilson. Freddy had been Richard's best friend in high school. The two lost touch when they attended different colleges. One weekend during Richard's senior year, he had gotten a call from Freddy asking if they could get together. He declined the invitation because he had a date that he didn't want to break. The next weekend Richard got a different kind of call. Freddy's brother told him that he had committed suicide. He always blamed himself for his friend's death; for not being there. Friendships after that were difficult.

Richard was surprised to see the two of them together. Taylor had grown up in and embraced the tradition of the Old South. The last time the three of them were together, Taylor and Freddy had gotten into a huge fist-fight over the racial epithets that seemed to roll endlessly from Taylor's tongue. "I'm surprised to see you here, Freddy," he said.

"I could say the same about you," his friend responded. "Haven't you learned anything from the two of us?"

"That you're both leaders and visionaries," Richard said, sarcastically.

"Don't be curt with us, Richard," Taylor chimed-in.

"Why are you here?" he pleaded as he looked at the two of them. "This would be a lot easier without having to deal with you both."

"In that case, we aren't leaving," Freddy said.

Richard stood and walked from the bathroom into the storage room. Freddy and Taylor followed. He placed the gun on the sill of a high window that opened onto a back-alley, and stared through it. "Haven't you guys been paying attention to everything that has gone on? I've never been a good friend to anyone." He turned and looked at Freddy. "You should know that."

"You can't blame yourself for what I did."

Richard continued as if he had not heard his friend. "I cheated on the best woman I've ever known; and she's only the latest in a long line of people I've let down. I have killed someone, a human being. That is how selfish I am. There is not a single person that I have ever known that is better off having known me."

"I am better off having known you." A voice that was neither Freddy nor Taylor came from behind Richard. He turned to see David Archer standing in the doorway to the bathroom. The legacy that David's family bestowed upon him was that of addiction. He found it extraordinarily difficult to avoid drugs and alcohol, and Richard's greatest regret was that he had been David's enabler for many years. The two men's relationship became strained later in life because he had seen the destructive side of his friend's dependency. Richard confronted him one day and apologized for the role he played in making his life more of a challenge than it needed to be. They had not spoken in over ten years and Richard missed the friendship terribly.

"I tried very hard to be a good friend to you, after losing these two." He pointed at Freddy and

Taylor. "For the longest time I thought that meant getting high with you, and chasing women." His tone became melancholy. "Finally, I realized what my lifestyle was doing to me, and I knew that it was doing the same to you. I'll never forget the last time we spoke on the phone. Do you remember what you asked me?"

David shook his head and said nothing.

"You said, 'All of my friends are telling me that I have to stop using drugs, and I know that I can count on you to be my savior. You know I have this under control, don't you?' That statement pierced my soul. I thought that you and I were very close, but when it came down to brass tacks, all of your friends wanted you to quit using drugs, but good old Richard would be there to get high with you. Do you even recall what I said next?"

"You pleaded with me to stop using drugs."

"And what did you do next?"

"I hung up on you."

"Were you ever aware that I came to your father's restaurant several times to try and patch up our relationship? Twice I remember seeing you through the window, but when I got inside the hostess told me that you weren't there."

He nodded.

Richard's eyes dropped to the floor at his feet. "I've lost three people that I have considered *best* friends. But, that was all right because I thought I had found the best of mates when I met Susan. She played me the fool just like you did, David. I'm not sure why. All you wanted was someone to get high with. There is nothing that I can give her that she couldn't get somewhere else." He thought about her infidelity and his heart ached. "And she's already started to seek it out."

268

Richard thought about the circumstances that surrounded the deaths of Freddy and Taylor. They were both young when they decided to take their own lives and he was not sure that either would have committed such a heinous act if they had the wisdom associated with age. They were young, emotional, and impetuous. He was sure that neither of them completely thought through their last day. Had they thought about all of the people they left behind? Richard missed having conversations with both of them about the challenges he had faced at the different stages in his life.

A sudden change of heart caused Richard to question whether he would have even been friends with David if he had been made to expect more from himself; to hold himself to a higher standard. But then he realized that he would have missed out on the love that he still felt for him.

Chapter Thirty-Three

The porch of their home was awash with the sounds of waves crashing onto the shore and of seagulls squawking. Susan was inside and Richard sat on the lanai in a bamboo chair; his legs resting on a matching ottoman. The cushions of both were adorned with large, colorful flowers. The elements had taken their toll on the fabric, but the chair fit Richard's frame perfectly and was comfortable.

He sat with one of his many Hemingway novels resting in his lap. It had been several minutes since he had turned a page. Too many thoughts occupied his mind to allow him to concentrate on the story. The gun that was once loaded and aimed at his head was unloaded and buried under six feet of sand near the wavebreak. Richard knew that in no time the sand and salt water would render it useless and it would never harm anyone.

It was late in the afternoon. He had gotten home early that morning, before Susan arose and quickly buried the gun. The peace that he finally felt allowed him to sleep soundly throughout the day. The winds whipped around the gulf waters, driving the surf onto the shore. He occasionally looked up from his book and watched the seagulls as they congregated on the sand and the pelicans as they plunged into the surf looking for an evening meal. He was so engrossed in it all that he did not hear his wife ask a question.

"Would you like to go for a walk on the beach?" Susan asked.

Only after a couple of seconds had passed did he realize his wife's voice was present in the background of his mind. He turned his head to see her standing in the doorway between the house and the porch. She closed the French door behind her as she moved into the room.

"Would you like to go for a walk on the beach?" she repeated, but with the same enthusiastic inflection in her tone as if she asked for the first time.

"Sure." He stood, placing the book on the chair behind him.

The couple made their way to the door that opened onto the beach. Richard opened it for his wife. She walked through, down four wooden steps and onto the sandy dunes behind their house. He followed.

The sand was thick and soft and with every step it poured into their shoes. They made their way down the calf-path worn through the sea oats and over the dunes. The delicate oats swayed tumultuously in the stiff afternoon breeze. Susan led the way. Richard, attempting to be a gentleman, deferred to his lady.

When they reached the water's edge they both removed their shoes, dumping the sand that had collected in them back onto the beach. They then turned and walked parallel to the breaking waves. The pile of rubble that was once the paper mill could be seen, on a point, in the distance. Giant barges were anchored at the old mill dock waiting to haul away the remnants of what was once a proud structure.

Several sandpipers foraged for food in the moist sand of the wave-break. Richard watched as they plunged their long, narrow beaks into the sand. More times than not the birds would immediately repeat the task, having come up empty.

The couple strolled casually, silently down the beach as the surf washed over their bare feet, and then ebbed back into the gulf. Both carried their shoes in their outside hand.

Susan had allowed circumstances to influence her into becoming someone that she was not happy with, as had Richard. Although it was apparent in her mind that there was something happening between her husband and Talitha, the only thing she was sure of was that she was guilty of infidelity. She had no idea how to tell him, but knew that she had to be honest, or the secret may destroy her, slowly eroding the fabric of her being from the depths of her soul. How to approach a conversation like that was not easy. So, she took what she felt was a reticent, benign leap into the conversation that needed to happen. "I've been thinking about everything that has happened since we've been here."

"And?" Richard's response was direct. Knowing what he knew, he also wished to leap headlong into the conversation.

"Ever since we arrived in town I've felt like we were cast as outsiders. It's almost as if these people are struggling against convention to maintain an outdated way of life." She chickened out, not facing her issues but deflecting them onto the people of Erstwhile.

"You know, you could be right. I hadn't thought about that," Richard said, acquiescing to his wife. He was equally afraid to address the real issues that had haunted their marriage since their honeymoon. After all, he had been unfaithful to the one woman who made his life make sense.

She was too nervous to think about the depths to which their relationship had sunk. Until their move she had never felt more loved by anyone. It was her fault that Ralph was allowed to intrude into their relationship and left the door open for others. Susan could only find the strength to steer the conversation where it *needed* to go by pushing a direct question onto her husband. "What have *you* been thinking about?"

"My past. Who I am and the kind of man I want to be," he blurted out without hesitation.

That was not the answer she expected, but Susan knew that as much time as he had spent thinking during their time in town, and as logical as his mind was, he had a very good reason for replying the way he did. "Can you help the girl," she said, "understand why you are thinking about your past?"

Richard struggled desperately to organize his thoughts so that he could effectively communicate, but the forefront of his mind was filled with so many things, realizations about his life experiences and the challenges he had faced. Regardless of the outcome of their relationship each one would continue to face obstacles for the rest of their lives. He rubbed his twitching eye vigorously trying to get it to stop. "It would be very easy for me to focus your attention onto factors other than the truth. The genesis of everything that has gone on since we came to town goes back decades." Richard searched his mind for the best manner in which to continue. "Have you ever had a conversation where you felt like you spoke very profoundly, but the people you were talking to didn't hear what you said?" Susan nodded and allowed him to continue. "When Jeff Cunningham wrecked his car into the telephone pole on Maine Street I had a conversation with Clyde Wilson about how Jeff didn't let this town down, he let himself down. I don't think I realized until early this morning that I was just as guilty as Clyde. Up until that point I blamed you for causing me to question our relationship."

Susan was stunned. She still had no idea what she could have done to cause her husband to withdraw from her and carry on a torrid affair with a local. He looked at his wife, hoping for a glimmer of understanding in her eyes. It just wasn't that easy. The couple walked silently as he searched his mind for what to say next. He felt as though he knew what needed to be said, but he knew there was a big difference between knowing and effectively communicating.

They walked as crabs began to emerge from their holes in the sand to search for food. The cool breeze off the gulf blowing against the side of their faces and the sun's warmth on their backs offered a refreshing contrast.

Susan knew that she needed to allow Richard to think about what he was going to say, but she asked the question. "Tell me about your past and the kind of man you want to be."

"I'm trying to find the right way to say what it is that I have to say," he confessed.

"Perfectionist." Her accusation was tinged in jest.

Richard smiled. "If I were such a damned perfectionist would we need to have this conversation?" His mood turned somber as he continued. "You and I have had many discussions about our pasts. There is no need to re-hash it all. What I did not realize until this morning is that every challenge I've ever faced still defines me to a great extent."

Susan listened as he paused. When he said nothing, she replied, "I think we both may have come to the same realization."

Richard watched the sandpipers as they ran away from breaking waves, and when the waves re-

274

ceded, the birds would run back toward the waterline and nervously plunge their beaks into the sand. He leaned over and picked up a shell, stood and threw it as far as he could into the gulf. He watched and waited until it splashed into the water. Then he stepped on a ledge of sand created by the high tide from the night before. The sand was soft and collapsed when he placed his weight on it. He stumbled, but did not fall, then continued to walk, thinking about how to say what it was he *had* to say, buying time with his purposeful stunt. Still not feeling comfortable with what he had to say, Richard picked up another shell and heaved it into the gulf.

Susan jogged a couple steps ahead, turned back and looked into his eyes. "*Please*. I can see that there is something else bothering you. Tell me what it is."

Richard reached toward her with his left hand and she reached with her right. They clasped hands by interlocking fingers. Richard thought to himself how nicely their hands fit together; how natural the gesture felt. It had been a long time since they had walked anywhere hand-in-hand.

They continued in silence, each concerned with how they would overcome their indiscretions and move forward; together or separately. They walked past a beautiful young, tan girl walking in the opposite direction. She wore an orange bikini that contrasted nicely with her dark skin. Her figure was one to die for and one that he found pleasing to watch. Her breasts were sufficiently large to strain the strings that held her bikini top. They bounced with every stride and shimmied with each step. Richard resisted the urge to turn and take a final look as she passed.

Moments later they came upon a small yet wide stream of water flowing from under a bridge at the highway into the gulf. Susan looked up stream, toward the highway, and allowed her eyes to follow the brown water down and into the gulf. She could not help but wonder to herself if the decades of mill operations was still having an effect on the quality of the water. Her eyes came to rest at the surf line where the merging of the two discolored the natural blue-green gulf.

Richard asked, "Do you think we can make it across without getting our feet wet?"

"I'm sure we can."

With that they retreated two steps. Still hand-in-hand they took a running start and leapt across the dingy stream. Richard's left heel barely touched the water. Susan's entire left foot plunged into it; up to her calf. "Gross!" she exclaimed.

Richard laughed. She let go of his hand and walked briskly to the water's edge and did a quick dance in the surf, washing the gunk from her feet. She looked at him. "Whew! That was a close call. I may have disintegrated before your very eyes if I hadn't washed that crud off my feet."

Richard did not respond. He merely smiled and held out his hand so that she could take it once again and continue their walk.

The silence lasted longer than it had before. Both of them were remembering things about their past that they had tucked away long ago; incidents that went a long way to shaping who they were. Susan had something on her mind that she desperately wanted to share with her husband, but she knew he had a lot to bring into the open, so she remained silent, allowing him all the time he needed to think, and to speak.

Richard stopped and played around with some shells on the ground with his feet. He then bent over and picked up a couple for no other reason than to pass time. Susan dropped her hand away from his and walked ahead of him. After a handful of steps she stopped and looked back. He needed the distance, however small, to act as a buffer between them and the truth that scared him. He looked at his beautiful wife and smiled. They came together, held hands again, and walked silently allowing the millions of thoughts racing through their minds to subside.

The couple released their clasped hands and Susan exclaimed. "My God! Do you realize how far we have walked?"

Richard stopped and took note of their sur-roundings. They appeared strange to him. He had never seen the beach from this vantage point. Then he noticed a restaurant on the highway where he and Susan once dined. Pointing to the restaurant, he said, "That restaur-ant has to be five miles from the house." Looking back down the beach toward their house he proclaimed, "It'll be dark before we get back home."

"Then we'd better start walking now," she said.

Susan changed direction and began to walk, quickly. Her husband followed. Richard knew they needed to resolve all of their issues before they got home. He wanted their home to be the sanctuary that his wife described when they first met; everything that was not completely about them had to be left on the beach.

A lump formed in his throat to the point that he was unable to swallow. Only once had he ever admitted to a woman that he had been unfaithful, and that ended badly. If he could turn back the clock and spare her feelings he would, gladly accepting whatever other fate was deemed necessary. This relationship would succeed or fail on its own merit. "During our marriage we've talked a lot about the challenges that each of us have faced," he reiterated. "Not until recently did I realize that my way of dealing with adversity was to accept defeat and move on. I faced a great conflict knowing that I had no desire to move past my relationship with you." That was the closest he would get to telling Susan about his near suicide.

Her thoughts moved away from her own infidelity as she began to picture her husband with Talitha. It angered her, yet again.

He continued. "When I drove to the store the first day we were open, I found a letter that you had written to Ralph in the glove-compartment of your car."

Suddenly, Susan's anger turned to disbelief. "I had forgotten all about that." She closed her eyes and shook her head as she spoke. "I never intended to mail it. I wrote it for the therapeutic value it possessed."

"When I found it, I understood that there was no way that I could ever be the love of your life."

"I know. I'm sorry." She acknowledged her understanding with a nod.

"Then I found a picture of you and another man on the nightstand in our guest bedroom. It became apparent to me that you keep all of your old relationships close to your heart. When we met I knew that we were meant to be together forever. I knew that somehow our souls were connected and for the first time in my life I was sure that there would be an eternity, and that I would spend it with you. When I lost that, I had no desire to be around you."

"Who were you with?"

278

"No one. I spent most of my days and a few evenings trying to drown the pain associated with the realization that I will never be important to anyone. The irony is that you were the only woman that I ever wanted to need me. When I lost you, I almost lost it all."

"Do you mean to tell me the nights you spent away you were at the store?" Susan's heart sank. She felt even more horribly, knowing what she had done.

Richard was afraid that if he did not continue, he'd never be able to confess. "Out of nowhere you seemed to develop this in-your-face attitude. You became a woman that I didn't know. That only exacerbated my fear about our future together."

"Richard, I … "

"I need to keep going, or I may not be able to do this." He paused, briefly. "When I thought I had lost you, I did what I would have always done, in the past. I ran away from you so there would be no way to be hurt by you."

"And?"

"And I found comfort in the arms of another woman."

Susan vigorously nodded her head. She quickly forgave her own infidelity, as anger beamed from her eyes and her pursed lips. "It's that Talitha, right?"

"No," Richard said.

But she was sure of it! *Why would he lie now, after confessing an extra-martial affair? To protect Talitha, that's why,* she thought.

"I met a woman at the bar at Buster's. We hit it off and ended up making love on the beach."

"Making love? So it's love? What's her name?"

"Love? No love. I don't even remember her name," he said. "I just thought that characterization was better than saying we fucked on the beach, which was all it was."

"You don't even know her name! That's *rich*." Susan was clearly hurt by his admission.

Richard paused. He wanted her to calm down a bit before he finished. "Susan, given everything that has gone on between us, I know that our love can be *unconditional and eternal*, and can be that *one true love forever*."

Susan did not respond. Her only reaction was to increase the distance between the two as they walked down the beach toward home. They took parallel paths home, but did not speak another word to each other that night. The addiction, which gripped her, instilled an inflated sense of self, and objectivity was its casualty. It was up to Richard to break its hold on his wife and show her the path that would lead her away from her physical dependencies.

Chapter Thirty-Four

The store was empty. The door was locked. A red sign with the letters C-L-O-S-E-D in white hung on the door facing the outside atrium, and was visible to anyone who approached. Richard looked around and appreciated the work that he and Susan had put in, together, to make the store what it was. A mere shell remained. Occasionally a customer stopped at the door, saw Richard inside and tapped on the glass. The first couple of people who appeared were greeted by him yelling at them through the locked door that the store was closed. When he got tired of that approach he just brushed aside their inquiries with a polite wave of his hand and a smile. The overwhelming sense that he was letting them down caused him to feel as though he should crawl into a dark hole and away from anyone who knew the seediness that resided deep within his soul. These were wonderful people who had supported his desire to be a shopkeeper. He knew that there was no way he could prosper in Erstwhile. There were too many things that haunted him. He needed everything to be perfect and wanted Susan to be a part of his quest for unconditional happiness.

They had not spoken since his confession, something to which he had grown accustomed. Regardless, he was able to sleep without interruption. Everything that he learned about himself provided an insight that he had never enjoyed. Although she had yet to confirm her infidelity, he knew that he could forgive her with every ounce of his being. Somehow they had to find a way to exist together.

Richard rubbed his twitching eye as he walked into the back room. Once inside he stopped and looked around for a box. His eyes came to rest on the windowsill where there was an empty bottle of Maker's Mark. He shook his head in disbelief and continued to look around. He smiled when he saw the quilt that he and Susan used to share an afternoon of passion, neatly folded and placed on a shelf. Lovemaking with her had never been boring or become stale. It was his selfishness that drove them apart. *Why should she not be allowed to give the same pleasure to others*? Richard laughed at the thought. That was one place he had never allowed his mind to go, but he realized that all humans could share a physical experience. Not every couple held the sacred bond that he felt for his wife.

He removed the empty bottle from the ledge with his right hand as he grabbed an empty box from a stack next to the window with his left. He dropped it into the container and began to make his way into the front room of the store. When he walked through the door he heard a vigorous rapping on the front window. At first he did not look up, choosing to ignore whomever it was. The knocking continued. Finally, he made his way to the back of the aisle that aligned with the spot where the person stood. It was Talitha. He smiled at her, and she at him. With the box still in his hand, he walked to the front door, unlocked it, and let her in.

"What are you doing?" she asked.

"I was about to start packing everything. I hope that I can get credit from my vendors," Richard said, refusing to look her in the eye.

"Why?"

"You're right. I guess I could give it to people in need."

"No ... why are you leaving?"

"Because I have finally realized that it is impossible to overcome one's past. I knew that it was a mistake to come here, but I did it because it was a familiar setting.

"Stay here and help me irritate the hell out of these rednecks," Talitha said.

"I *really* do like you." He laughed. "Don't worry! I won't grope you again." He felt obligated to reassure her. "I think you and I are a lot alike. We have faced a lot of the same challenges. The only difference is that you've found the inner peace that I am still searching for."

Talitha was not sure how to respond. "Is there anything I can do to help?"

"Don't you have to be at work?"

"I can take a day off. I *never* miss work so I probably have two months of personal days available."

Richard handed her the empty box he had in his hand. "I would appreciate your help. Just make sure that anything that you take off the shelf goes into the box that it came in. That way I can return it for credit."

Talitha took the box from him and pulled the flaps away and saw the empty bottle of whiskey. She grabbed it, held it up and asked, "What's this?"

Richard's initial thought was to lie and say that he found it in the back room. He hesitated as he gave more consideration to being a person to be respected. "That ... is my albatross."

Talitha did not respond to his characterization, other than to say, "Top-shelf whiskey. You've got expensive taste."

"You don't know how expensive," he muttered. Attempting to end the conversation, Richard searched for another box for himself, so he walked back into the storeroom. Talitha searched the shelves for the product's logo that matched the one on the container she held. When she found it, she knelt down and began to orderly remove the bottles, gingerly placing them in the container.

Richard emerged from the back room. He could not see his friend but heard the clink of bottles as she packed them away. "Talitha," he called to her over the top of the shelves.

"What?"

"I'm really not a racist." He felt the statement was obligatory. Her accusation stung and he needed her respect.

"I know that," she called back. "I'm sorry that I leveled that accusation at you. I'm not sure why I did it."

"It was probably just a defense mechanism." He could have gone without saying what he said next, but something made him feel as though he needed to give credence to his statement. "My best friend in high school was black."

Talitha impulsively replied, "*High school*? Why isn't he your best friend now?"

Richard paused before replying. "He committed suicide."

After a noticeable silence, she said, "I'm sorry."

"Actually, I now understand why my best friendships have been with African-Americans."

"Why do you think that is?"

"Because those have been the only relationships I have had where there were no pretenses, or facades to

284

get in the way. The people I've known have always been real." He paused as he thought of Freddy. "I miss him terribly. Do you know what it's like to not have a confidant?"

"I can't say that I do," she said.

"Sometimes I feel like without someone who knows me and accepts me unconditionally it is impossible for me to continue along life's journey."

Talitha digested the gravity of what he said. "I wish there was something I could do to help."

"I'm sure that there will be a day when you will make me proud to have been your friend."

Chapter Thirty-Five

It was late afternoon and Richard sat on the porch, gazing out over the waters of the Gulf of Mexico. Just as the storeroom had become his hell, this had become his sanctuary. He was in the same spot as twenty-four hours earlier, except that he had an emotional clarity like never before. Susan moved around the house and he watched her whenever she entered his sight. He looked at her in a manner that he had not done in years. The clarity he enjoyed made everything around him seem more beautiful. Her beauty was perpetual and he had found the key to maintaining this vision of his wife. External forces, no matter how troubling, had become insignificant.

Susan did not share the same freedom from the burdens of her life, past and present. Clothes had to be packed, as did the silverware and dishes. Richard told her that they were not in a hurry to leave. They had nowhere to go, nor a deadline to meet. Nervous energy kept her going, but more importantly it kept her from having to face her husband. He had done everything he could. It was up to her. He may not have been sure what the future held, whether he and Susan would be together, but he was sure that she needed to come to terms with everything that had gone wrong in their lives.

Susan made her way into the guest bedroom. The picture of her and Courtney was still on the nightstand. She walked over and picked it up. There was nothing special about it. Her indifference may have been a result of knowing that she hurt her husband by keeping such mementos. She moved over to the dresser against the wall and stood between it and the foot of the bed and opened the top drawer; reached in below some holiday table cloths and removed the ring that at one time had been taped to the back of the picture. Was her physical indiscretion a worse sin against her marriage or the harboring of feelings for someone she once loved? Maybe that question should be put to Richard.

She placed the ring on the back of the picture and pulled the tape that dangled from the cardboard, back over, securing it in place, then leaned over toward the edge of the dresser and dropped them both into a trashcan on the floor. Susan walked over and sat on the edge of the bed, fell backward and stared at the numbers projected onto the ceiling by the alarm clock. The last time she lay on this bed there was a strange man on top of her. *It was only sex*, she thought; justifying her actions. If it was only sex, she couldn't hold Richard's indiscretion against him. Why was it so easy for her to dismiss allowing a man other than her husband to perform carnal acts on her, yet it drove her out of her mind to know that another woman had done the same with her husband? There was something that her father told her long ago, when she was a young girl entering puberty. He said, 'Susan, sex can be the ugliest act between human beings, or it can be the most beautiful, passionate expression of one's love.' Maybe it was time for her to understand what he meant. Her affair lacked passion. She knew that, and never expected it. Sex with Richard was always passionate. It may have become repetitive at times, but whenever they were together their souls became one.

Susan lay on the bed watching the numbers change, but not really measuring time. She understood that she had used sex as a weapon. Richard upset her. He was the one who had withdrawn from the relationship. He deserved everything that happened. Her irrational thoughts were caused by the lack of resolution. She desired clarity, but realized that such juvenile actions would not provide it.

If she forgave him, how could she be sure that he wouldn't do it again someday? *I guess he can ask the same question of me. Only he doesn't know that I cheated on him.* The merry-go-round of thoughts that entered and exited her mind lead nowhere. Then it dawned on her. Richard had come clean to her the day before. His mind was at ease. He was willing to take the consequences and she should be too.

Susan sat up on the edge of the bed, stood, walked out of the guest bedroom and into the living room, where she saw her husband through the French door sitting on the patio. Her heart started to pound at the thought of having the conversation with him she realized would free her of the burdens she felt. Quickly, she changed directions and walked into their bedroom. Several times she allowed the thought, *what Richard doesn't know won't hurt him*, to creep into her mind. She chased it away each time, as quickly as it entered. It would do neither of them any good.

Boldly, Susan walked out of their bedroom, through the living room and onto the porch where he sat, looking out over the water. It was eerie how calm he appeared. There was a peace about him that somehow helped her feel at ease. Somehow she sensed that she could be brutally honest with him and it wouldn't change how he felt about her in the least possible way. "Can we talk?" she asked.

"Always," he said.

Susan pulled the ottoman that Richard had his feet propped up on away so that she could sit down. He drew his feet in toward his body and then placed them softly on the floor in front of the chair. She sat down and leaned toward her husband placing her forearms on her knees. He leaned in toward her. Each had the full attention of the other.

Richard noticed that his wife's eyes were bloodshot and tears were gathering on her lower eye-lid. It was confirmation of what he suspected. He had this conversation with women before, yet this time he was unusually calm and supportive. For the first time in his life his heart was totally devoted to someone, he knew it and it felt good. Richard rubbed his twitching eye and allowed his wife to begin when she was ready.

"I've been thinking a lot about what you said yesterday. It wasn't so much what you said but the point you made about being free of any burdens, and I need to un-bridal myself of some things that I have been carrying around for years."

"Okay," Richard said calmly. *Years*, he worried.

She took a deep breath and blurted it out as quickly as her mouth would allow. "I cheated on you, too." At first she looked him in the eye, but the pain of the confession was too much, so she closed her eyes, dropped her head and began shaking.

Richard placed his hand, gently on her shoulder. "It's alright … really."

The tears began to flow freely. She was very conciliatory and sad. The person she had become was unlike any other time in her life. No matter what similarities there were to her past, Susan was unable to grasp a vision of the woman she wanted to become. Richard waited patiently as she gathered her wits about her. "I was so angry with you. I thought you were having an affair with Talitha and picturing you with anyone, other than me, drove me out of my head."

"I know how you feel," he said. "Would you like to share with me how it happened?"

Susan looked at him through her tear filled eyes. "Do you really want to know?"

"If you don't want to tell me, no; but if you think it will help me understand I'll be happy to listen."

There wasn't anything significant that Richard needed to know about, but she knew that if she didn't come totally clean she risked the complete resolution she sought. "This young man approached me on the beach and one thing led to another. Before I knew it, we were up here in bed together."

Richard bristled at the thought of another man in his house making love to his wife. It was hard to contain the burning feeling in his gut, but he had to for the sake of his relationship. This was a test of his new outlook on life. He had to shake it off and show Susan that he supported her, and that their relationship was bigger than any obstacle that presented itself.

"You seem very calm. Doesn't it bother you that I cheated on you?"

"What do you want me to do, yell and scream? I can tell you from experience that doesn't work." He paused. "To answer your questions, yes, it does bother me, but what's worse is that we both allowed our relationship to get to that point before we decided to communicate with one another." Richard issued the obligatory warning against future flings. "I'm just happy that nothing serious happened to you."

Susan was taken aback. The thought never crossed her mind. Her anger totally clouded her judgment and she had not realized just how much danger could have befallen her. She was reminded of another time when her cognitive abilities lapsed that she had yet to discuss with Richard. "I have something else I need to share with you."

"Okay."

"After I graduated from high school I began to work. I put off going to college for several years. As I had always done, I allowed others to influence me, and started using cocaine. It was the eighties and the thing to do if you were young and upwardly mobile, which I fooled myself into thinking I was. I worked very hard and made pretty good money. I was living at home so my expenses were minimal." Susan went overboard with her explanation. She saw him beaming so brightly that it caused her to ask, "Why are you smiling like that?"

"You are the only woman I have known, that I have truly *known*." A tear rolled down his cheek. "I could not be more proud of, more impressed with, or more in love with, anyone."

The couple fell into each other's arms. The embrace lasted for several minutes. She whispered, "You love me warts and all?"

"I love all of you."

Susan leaned back, out of the embrace, and asked, once again, "Are you sure none of this bothers you?"

"Of course it bothers me, but you and I being together forever is much more important than anything or anyone that tries to come between us. We all make bad decisions in life and to have them held against us is wrong, and I would never do that to you." As he spoke, Richard reflected on the thoughts that clouded his mind for so long. "I've never had a healthy appreciation for the women in my life, and it showed. I want to make sure you know how much I appreciate you."

Susan knew of no better way to express her feelings than to launch herself, once again, into his arms. They embraced for several more minutes until he decided to slide his hands down her back and gently caress her bottom. Richard gripped firmly with his left hand and slid his right up, settling it in the middle of her back. Slowly he pulled her into him. The two engaged in a long, slow, deep kiss.

He leaned back and looked into her eyes. "I want to show you how much I appreciate you."

She smiled. "How?"

Richard stood, took Susan by the hand and led her through the living room and into their bedroom. It was a room that, for so long, had been filled with anxiety bordering on hostility. The ethereal energy between them gave it more of the feeling of a sanctuary, a place where they could shield themselves from the distractions that could cause a man or woman to forget the other. He wanted to cleanse the impurities that prevented them from having the strongest emotional bond possible. The only way to accomplish this would be to bring their emotional and physical senses to convergence, forsaking all other selfish desires.

Susan sat on the foot of the bed, with Richard's guidance. He stood over her. They looked longingly into each other's eyes without uttering a word. Everything that had to be communicated was done in the most effective manner possible, from the heart. The atmosphere was one in which they learned every curve of the other's body; how it felt to gently slide one's hand across its surface. Their fingertips tingled as if they were reaching into the other's soul. They were both nervous, as if it were their first time.

Richard leaned over and gently kissed his wife like he had not done in a long while. While their lips touched, he slowly began to unbutton her sleeveless Polo shirt, eventually pulling back from the kiss as he moved down to the final few buttons. He exposed her beautiful frame by sliding the opened shirt over her shoulders. Her white bra contrasted nicely against her tan skin. He leaned in for another kiss. Unsure of whether he should remove her shorts first or her bra, Richard hesitated before realizing that the bra would come off more quickly. The hook came undone easily and he held the male and female parts of the clasp in his hands. He opened the back of the bra widely and once again pulled away from the kiss. Susan held her arms out straight so that it could be readily removed. It was discarded onto the floor without a thought.

He paused as he admired his wife's beautiful body. Not a work of art had he ever beheld made him shiver with excitement like when he saw his wife in the state nature intended. A moment of doubt flashed quickly through his mind as he wondered whether she deserved better. He chased away that thought, choosing to focus on how to make this experience the most wonderful she had ever known.

The tan-lines of her bathing suit plunged from her neck and opened around her nipple, framing her perfect breasts. Richard knelt on the floor, resting his butt on his heels as he admired every curve. Susan felt this admiration and gladly sat motionless. She was a willing model for the artwork of his soul.

He gently took both of her hands in his own and offered the support she needed to stand. Richard then unbuttoned and unzipped her shorts, slowly. With a great deal of patience, he slid them gradually over her hips. Once they hit the floor, she stepped out and kicked them to the side. Carefully, he removed her panties in the same manner.

Susan dare not move as she watched him admire every inch of her body. She had never felt so wanted. Her desire became overwhelming. She leaned over and gently took his hands in hers and helped him to stand. Without appearing too hasty, she unbuttoned his shirt. Once the last button had been opened, she stretched up and on her toes, grabbed the open collar of the shirt and tossed it over his shoulders. Richard wiggled his arms to allow it to fall away from his body and onto the floor. It was her turn to admire the man she loved more than life itself. His shoulders were strong and well defined. She slid her hands along his arms that were firm, choosing a more tactile method of admiration. Susan did not stop with his arms. She caressed his pectorals and abdomen gently for several minutes before moving her hands to his shorts. After she unbuttoned and unzipped them, she slid her hands inside the waste-band of his boxers. With one motion she removed both his shorts and underwear as she moved her hands across his full, athletic rear end. When his clothes hit the floor he kicked them to the side.

She sat on the bed and leaned back, resting her weight on her hands that were propped onto the mattress. The man she saw in front of her was like no other she had known. She saw in his physique an original Olympian.

Richard became self-conscious standing at attention, so he leaned forward and slowly forced her to lie backward onto the bed. She slid her body toward the

294

headboard and he crawled over her, never touching her, just hovering and looking into her eyes and moving in unison with her.

When they stopped, he moved to one side and lay on the bed next to her. He reached over and removed a scarf that she had tied to the bedpost at some point.

"What are you doing?" she asked.

Richard chose his words carefully. "Do you remember that night on the beach when you performed a strip-tease for me?"

She grinned, acknowledging that night.

"You knew that watching you would heighten every sense that I have, and it did. All I want to do is the same for you."

"And how are you going to do that?"

"I want to blindfold you."

"Oh no!" she responded. Her desire to always be in control would not allow her to submit to his wishes.

"Hear me out, please." Susan did not respond, so he continued, "I know that you, as a woman, are not as visual as I am. All I want to do is to remove your sense of sight so that your other senses are heightened."

The explanation of his intent made her senses tingle with anticipation. "Okay," she said, somewhat reluctantly.

Gently, but firmly, Richard secured the scarf around her head and over her eyes. For several minutes Susan felt nothing, no touching, no kissing; nothing. Suddenly there was a cool gulf breeze blowing across her body; over and around her thighs, across her stomach and chest, neck and face. It tingled her nipples to the point of stimulation. She wasn't quite sure, but she thought that Richard had opened the double French doors near the foot of their bed. They opened onto a deck that overlooked the beach.

Finally, she felt the strong touch of her husband. His hands firmly, but gently massaged her feet. Then he moved his undulating fingers to her calves. By the time he got to her hips Susan had totally given herself over to the experience. Richard massaged her hips so deeply that the sensation ran down her leg and into her toes. He moved his hands from her hips and onto her stomach and lifted them so that the only contact was between her skin and his fingertips. Goosebumps covered every inch of her body. He smiled.

After focusing all of the attention he could to the front of her body, he rolled her over and began massaging her back. Every bit of stress and tension that had manifested itself in her body was gone. For what seemed like an hour, Richard magically massaged her back and buttocks, the backs of her thighs and her heels. She was so relaxed that she felt she would melt onto the sheets.

Gently, Richard rolled her onto her back. He did not want to disturb her heightened state of relaxation. When she came to rest on her back Susan reached up to remove the blindfold. He stopped her by gently holding her hand. She dropped her hands to her side. Richard admired her beautiful body once again. He appreciated how, when she laid down, her body took a different shape: a supple, hourglass.

In all the time that he spent caressing his wife, not once did he touch one of her erogenous areas. Yet as he looked over her body he could tell that she craved making love.

Love was what they made. For three days they did not leave their bedroom or bother to clothe themselves. They knew that this would be their last opportunity to express their love for each other in such a purely physical manner. Their time together gave them the opportunity to talk like they never had before. Not until then did Susan confess to her husband what the stained glass heart given to her by her father represented. It was offered to her on her fifteenth birthday as an appeasement for letting her down. That is when he confessed to her an extramarital affair resulting in his divorce from her mother. They found that they had struggled to overcome similar pasts. Their lives had been awkwardly parallel. The danger was that neither was certain how to guide the other toward a future that offered promise. Until that day neither had experienced the emotional bliss they craved. Making it last eternally remained their greatest challenge.

Chapter Thirty-Six

Richard sat, gazing out over white sandy beach, as he had done many times before. Watching the gentle action of the gulf soothed the turmoil of his life that he could not escape. The memory of how his father would whistle for him to come to dinner, like one would a dog, was an ache that he was unable to resolve. He had never been able to establish an identity and he still struggled with what his purpose in life was. He chuckled away the pain. The self-respect had been beaten out of him by his father and older brother to the point that the only time he felt a sense of value was by controlling everything around him through the anger he inherited. During his lifetime he had absorbed so much of that rage he despised himself each time he displayed the emotion. Whenever he held it in, he only took on more. He had no desire to subject anyone, especially Susan, to the ordeal that had been his life. The hatred he felt for the man he had become seethed inside him. Richard ached to find a remedy. His eye twitched as it had done ever since his epiphany that morning in the storeroom. He tried to vigorously rub it away, but it continued un-controllably.

There was an attorney who wanted to buy the house from him after his aunt's estate closed probate. He tried to convince Richard the property was only worth the assessed value on the tax rolls. He knew better. The original offer was never dignified with a response. It was time for him and Susan to get all of their affairs in order. Richard called and told him the house was for sale. The man willingly accepted, knowing there was no reason to haggle. The land included four lots and could be developed into something more than a single house. That was where he would make his money. He asked Richard to stay at the house until a runner could drop off a contract on the property. He agreed.

There were many people that he remembered being happy to have known. They had all, in their own individual manner, contributed something to Richard that he had carried with him throughout his life. It was obvious to him that he was not meant to be one of the contributors. He understood that he had become a taker and was not altogether sure he could change that. The reality of what awaited him and Susan once they left town began to overwhelm him. His life had never been better than at that moment in time, and there was no way to freeze the clock. He knew that life would continue to be a struggle, not with Susan, but with the forces that it was necessary to do battle with in order to survive. It would be a war made more difficult because he had to overcome his past in order to envision any sort of future for him and his wife.

Chapter Thirty-Seven

A void in esteem can only be filled by a sense of self. Susan was led to believe that those who knew best were her family. They molded her into the person that fit their vision without regard for her well-being. She was never able to gain satisfaction from a job well done without seeking someone else's approval. The appreciation she did receive centered on her physical beauty, which left a hollow emptiness that she desperately tried to fill. When she was a teenager it was accomplished with drug use. During her young adult life she searched for the man who could make her feel fulfilled in who she was. Facing life as an aging beauty scared her. Since there were no secrets that remained between she and Richard there was nothing left to taint the relationship. Their devotion was circular, feeding on itself and taking on a life of its own. They had shaken away the external influences and the energy that swirled around them was palpable and bound them together.

Without a word, Susan stood and moved from the porch where she sat with her husband, across the living room and into their bedroom. She put on a pair of sandals. Lying next to her purse on the kitchen counter were her keys, which she picked up on the way out the door. There was an easiness in her aura, but something hovered over her, which required Emma's counsel. She drove down the two-lane highway to her destination and thought about the woman she had allowed herself to become. It was not someone she was proud of, but it was all she knew. She reached out to Charles longing for a tangible re-creation of what she and Richard once had.

Susan sat in the Tahoe, stopped in front of the house and waited patiently for the oncoming traffic to clear; when it had she made the left turn into the driveway. The truck came to a stop, Susan shifted the transmission into Park and turned off the engine. She inhaled so deeply that her ribs ached as her lungs expanded. Without any further hesitation, she got out of the vehicle, walked to the front door and rang the bell.

After a few seconds, she saw through the opaque, etched glass, a figure moving toward her. Susan took another deep breath. The door opened. In front of her stood Emma.

"Hey Sugar." Her friend accentuated her southern accent for affect.

"Hello, Emma. Can I come in?" Susan's tone was one without emotion, flat and businesslike. She needed strength to ask for one last favor.

"Sure, baby," Emma replied as she stepped back away from the open door, allowing clear passage into the house.

She walked through the house and onto the back porch. There she saw Claire who sat in the same chair she had always seen her occupy. "Hello, Claire."

"Well Hello, Susan. It's so good to see you!" the old woman said.

Susan walked over to the sofa and sat down. Emma followed closely behind and sat down next to her.

"Honey," Emma's tone was filled with condescension, "you've got to tell me about that day on the beach."

A chill ran down Susan's spine. "What day on the beach?"

Emma shook her head slowly. "Girlfriend, *everybody* knows about it. That day you took that boy up to the house and had your way with him."

Oh, my God, Susan thought. *Everyone knows.*

Emma did not wait for a response. "Chalk one up for women all over the world." Her friend's laughter reverberated through her body and into her soul.

The time she and Richard spent in bed allowed them both to absolve the responsibilities associated with their pasts. Suddenly, all of that effort seemed for naught. Charles was too freshly in her soul and about her body. She needed to be cleansed of that burden. That necessity metastasized quickly as a result of years of repeated behavior and she found herself craving the remedy that would repair her soul. She leaned toward her friend and whispered. "Can we talk privately?"

Emma announced loudly, "Let's go back to my room."

When the women were securely behind the closed door of Emma's room, Susan made her request known, "Have you got any more cocaine?" as she pulled a wadded bundle of twenty dollar bills from her pocket, some of which fell onto the floor.

A smug expression grew on Emma's face. She knew that she had wrested away control of Susan's life, and this pleased her. Without saying a word she stood and walked to the shelf that contained the Magic Eight Ball. After removing it, she tossed it onto the bed next to Susan, who quickly picked it up and began to nervously dig at the plug on the bottom. When she was unable to remove it, she sheepishly handed the toy to her friend, who looked upon her with pity. Her false be-nevolence comforted them both.

After removing the drug, she tossed a baggy onto Susan's lap who took it and hastily pulled apart the seam. In no time she filled her soul with the confidence she lacked. It proved necessary for her to carry on with the future that she and Richard had laid out for themselves. The greatest tragedy of her life was that she was dependent on those who feigned sincerity while seeking to exert influence onto her; avoiding the acknowledgment of their own bittersweet existence. People who fed on her soul and the fact that she so readily offered it had long ago sealed Susan's fate.

Chapter Thirty-Eight

The runner had come with the contract. Richard signed it and the boy eagerly left to take it back to his boss. Richard was a bit melancholy as he realized that this property would no longer be in his family. It had been owned by several generations and because of him, that time had ended. There were still several things to do before he and Susan could end their time in Erstwhile. It was a thought that scared them as well as excited them to learn what lay ahead.

He took Susan's car to the store for the final preparations. It was odd not having any responsibility during a day in the middle of the week. He drove down the two-lane highway and passed several new homes being built on lots that had sat vacant since being platted during reconstruction. Carpenters worked hard, busying about each house. It was a time of prosperity for Erstwhile. Knowing that there were certain people in town who would do everything in their power to keep others from benefiting from that wealth was something that Richard had no desire to participate in nor did he know how to stop their erstwhile ways. When this thought crossed his mind, he felt like a quitter, but he knew there had to be something he could do. A smile slowly engulfed his face. He knew exactly what that was.

He continued to drive along the coastal highway, only his destination was not the store. Two city blocks east of Maine Street was Hale Street. It housed the professional offices; the doctors, lawyers and accountants. Richard turned down the road and began looking at all the signs searching for the office of a lawyer he knew by reputation only. When he found it, he drove into the parking lot and brought the car to a stop.

Richard walked inside and introduced himself to the secretary. She asked him to have a seat in the waiting room and said that the attorney would be with him momentarily. Before sitting down he asked, "Do you have any stationary and an envelope that I could have?"

"I think so. Let me look," the secretary said. She looked around behind the counter. The only thing she found that looked suitable had the attorney's name on it. She handed it to him. "You're not going to do anything illegal with this are you?"

Richard smiled. "No ma'am. I just want to write a note to a friend and I'll be sure to sign my name." He walked over and sat in a chair. Leaning forward, he laid the piece of paper on a stout magazine on the coffee table and lifted them both as he sat back. He placed them in his lap and began to pen a note.

Talitha,

>*Please forgive me for not speaking to you before I made a unilateral decision forcing you into a life that you may not wish to lead. However, there is something inside me that is sure you will make the most of this opportunity. I'm sorry that I have to leave without saying anything to you, but Susan and I have chosen our path together, and given your and my history together I don't wish to give you another chance to say 'no' to me.*

>*As I have had the occasion to think about the life I have led, and to take stock in it, I realize that an existence void of people to emulate does not a life make. If there is one piece of*

advice I can offer, look for the people who instill hope in you; they are truly the unselfish ones.

I know there will come a time when you and I will have the opportunity to meet again. At that time I hope that you will feel happy to have known me. I know that I am happy to have known you.

Sincerely,

Richard

When Richard finished, he folded it neatly and placed it in the matching envelope. Another twenty minutes passed as he thumbed through the pages of a Bass Master magazine. Finally, he realized there was no reason to wait on someone who was making him do so simply to feed his ego. He stood and walked toward the secretary.

Richard handed the envelope to her. On the outside he had written Talitha's name. "Would you have another piece of paper?" he asked.

Without a word, she handed him another sheet of stationary. On it he wrote Talitha's name and the address of the store.

Richard held the paper up so that the secretary could read it. He pointed to each individual item on the paper and gave his instructions to her. "I want Mr. Brown to draw up a deed for this store, conveying ownership from me to this young lady. When he has done so call me and I will come and do whatever is necessary. Please make sure that Miss Keys gets that envelope along with the deed." The secretary said nothing, so Richard asked, "Do you think you've got it?"

She smiled. "Yes, sir."

Richard exited the office, free of the final burden that had been placed upon him by his family.

Chapter Thirty-Nine

When all the loose ends had been secured it came time for Richard and Susan to begin their journey. They tried to put it off, but could do so no longer. The house had cleared escrow and no longer belonged to them. The car was packed with just the necessities. Richard drove and Susan sat in the passenger seat. She signed over the title to her car to Harriett's granddaughter. The past few days had been spent packing everything in the house into boxes. Once they had everything packed, a moving company came to the house and moved everything into a warehouse, indefinitely. Richard spent about thirty minutes at the attorney's office signing papers. He had no idea what the buyer's plans were for the property, only that it entailed demolishing the old house.

He drove to the end of the driveway, and then looked both ways for oncoming traffic. When he looked east he noticed a large yellow bulldozer bouncing on its massive tires over the bumps in the highway. He knew it would stop at the house where he and Susan had spent the most perilous days of their lives. Quickly, he drove onto the highway and watched his rear-view mirror as the dozer came to a stop. Tears began to build on his lower eye-lid. He quickly diverted his attention from the rear-view mirror and affixed it onto the road ahead. Regardless of the issues they faced early in their marriage, neither Richard nor Susan ever imagined that retreating into a simpler lifestyle would have such an adverse impact on them. Getting back to basics was supposed to provide the necessary escape from the complications of urban life. Instead it exposed a com-

plicated fabric of conflicting values that left them
without a true sense of who they were. Questions remained unresolved and left them without a true sense of
how to proceed with their lives.

When the truck rolled across the first expansion
joint of the Talquin Bridge Richard released the pressure on the accelerator and the vehicle began to stall as
it slowly crawled up the increasing gradient. There was
great trepidation within him. He summoned the courage
to continue and held his foot firmly against the pedal.
Their hearts raced as the vehicle's speed increased and
approached the apex of the bridge where Erstwhile Bay
met a man made canal one hundred feet below. Richard
released the pressure on the accelerator when the truck
eclipsed the top of the bridge and began its descent under the energy provided by the incline. Once the tires
clapped across the final joint and onto the highway,
Richard maintained a normal speed as they approached
town. Their destination was on the other side.

The truck jostled as it crossed the railroad tracks
that had come to mean so much to him. He looked
down the street with hope of catching a glimpse of Harriett, but her house was too far away for him to make
out any distinguishable figure. He dropped his eyes
down, away from his gaze on the road ahead as he sadly
realized that he would never see her or Talitha again.
They meant more to him than many people who he had
known for much longer.

Boldly Richard maneuvered the car down the
deserted road that lead from the highway into the old
mill's parking lot. It was empty and the railroad ties that
defined the front of each spot could barely be seen
through the overgrown brush. He followed the path toward the mill and beyond. He stopped at the seawall

where ships once loaded the factory's finished product, turned sharply to the left until the rear of the truck faced the bay and drove backward until it came to rest at the edge of the wall. They stepped out of the truck and walked around it until they met at its rear door. They looked into each other's eyes and smiled. Richard reached down and pulled the lever that released the lock on the tailgate and lifted until it rested in the open position above their heads. Without a word to each other they crawled in and sat, facing the setting sun, and rested their backs against the rear seats. In simpatico fashion they reached out to one another and held hands. Susan gently laid her head on her husband's shoulder.

They sat silently watching the sun until its bottom edge gently kissed the horizon. Richard's heart pounded as he removed a box-cutter from his front pocket. Gently, he slid the lever on the side, exposing a shiny, brand new blade. His thumb quivered nervously as he ran it across the underside of Susan's wrist, pressing it to expose the largest vein. When he decided on where to make the incision, he quickly, yet as gently as he could ran the tip of the blade into her skin and pulled down toward her elbow, sharply. She winced. He reached across his wife's body and proceeded to repeat the deed on her other wrist. Richard's heart pounded and his blood ran cold as he looked into her eyes knowing it would be the last time they would do so. He then settled into the last position that his earthly body would take before joining his wife along the course that they had chosen for their lives together.

Blood ran freely about their bodies. It poured warmly across their palms and onto their pants. When it soaked through it became eerily cold. One quarter of the sun had disappeared. Any sense of nervousness they felt left them both. They held each other closely. It was a natural feeling of calm.

Susan gasped for breath as she became weak. She felt drowsy and nuzzled closer to her husband. There would be no more allowing people to influence her into being someone she was not comfortable with. The strength to be her own person had never been instilled in her and she feared that she faced a lifetime of repeating the same behavior. That was something she had no desire to do.

Richard held on tightly to his wife. Never once during his life had he felt that he was letting anyone down. His self-examination revealed to him a person that he could not live with, and he had no idea how to change. He lifted his head one last time to see the sun disappear beyond the horizon, and then it dropped next to that of his beautiful wife, lifeless.

For Susan, her life had always revolved around her physical being; whether it was drug use or the desire to be wanted, she craved an existence that was more spiritual. Richard simply wanted the pain to be gone. Denying who he was and from where he came left him without direction and careening toward his death. These emotions brought them to a common course. Neither was sure, but they hoped there would be a greater existence beyond the one they despised. The last days of their lives were filled with a great euphoria derived from the newfound ability to forgive the other for their indiscretions. Regardless, their demise was a direct result of the fact they had no idea how to forgive themselves for the mistakes they made throughout their lives. Without that exoneration, their souls were doomed to ache and that pain manifested itself physically. Things might have turned out differently if they only had someone in their lives that was truly special; someone that gave them hope. Neither of them had benefitted from a relationship that instilled self-esteem so that their past became irrelevant to a future that held promise. Unscrupulous actions that they had undertaken could not be erased. The couple did not realize that the morality of enlightenment was seeded in the soil of regret.

3677000

Made in the USA